Let It Shine

ALSO BY

JOSEPHINE COX

QUEENIE'S STORY

Her Father's Sins
Let Loose the Tigers

THE EMMA GRADY TRILOGY

Outcast
Alley Urchin
Vagabonds

Angels Cry Sometimes
Take This Woman
Whistledown Woman
Don't Cry Alone
Jessica's Girl
Nobody's Darling
Born to Serve
More than Riches
A Little Badness
Living a Lie
The Devil You Know
A Time for Us
Cradle of Thorns
Miss You Forever
Love Me or Leave Me
Tomorrow the World
The Gilded Cage
Somewhere, Someday
Rainbow Days
Looking Back

JOSEPHINE COX

Let It Shine

BCA

LONDON NEW YORK SYDNEY TORONTO

This edition published 2001
By BCA
By arrangement with Headline Book Publishing
A division of Hodder headline

CN 19348

First reprint 2001

Typeset by Palimpsest Book Production Limited,
Polmont, Stirlingshire
Printed and bound in Germany by
GGP Media, Pössneck

DEDICATION

For Ivan and Barbara.
Thank you for all your support and kind comments.
You're two very special people.
Stay well. Be good (well, at least try!).
See ya, kiddos!

———➤•◉•◀———

Not forgetting our Madge
who has been through a bad time
but keeps plodding on
– like the good 'un she is.

CONTENTS

PART ONE

DECEMBER 1932
THE HOUSE IN
BUNCER LANE

Chapter One

A DA WILLIAMS WAS not a wicked woman.
In her time, she had gone through six men, amassed a fortune on the way, and lived every day to the full.

Like other lonely souls, she had made mistakes – and paid for them. She had laughed and cried, and known love of the kind that comes only once in a lifetime. Then, through a flaw in her character, her foolishness, she lost him – and in so doing, she lost her world.

It was a harsh lesson, and one that cut her to the quick. After that, Ada hardened her heart and vowed never to be hurt again.

Now, with the closing of evening, she lay back against the pillow and for a time was lost in her memories until the single, urgent tap on the bedroom door brought her back to the present.

Disappointed, she sat up, waiting for him to open the door, ready for the charm and the smile, *and the lies he told*.

Slowly, the door opened and through the lamplight she watched him cross the room to her bed; her son. Strongly built and handsome, Peter Williams belonged amidst all the finery that surrounded her. Here was a man who appreciated money and all it could buy.

'I didn't wake you, did I?' His dark, devious eyes smiled down on her. 'I'm sorry. I got talking to Ruth and she made me forget the time.'

'Talking to Ruth, you say?' Ada's voice carried a note of suspicion. 'About what?'

'Nothing for you to worry about, dear.' He set the tray down beside her. When he looked up again, he had turned a guilty shade of pink. 'I'm afraid she had to be chastised. Lately she seems to be neglecting her duties.'

Ada pushed the tray aside. 'Then it should be *me* chastising her, not you!'

Raising a finger he wagged it from side to side. 'No, no. Leave her to me. She'll be all right now she knows I'm onto her.'

Sitting on the bed, he stretched out his hand, intending to take hold of hers. When she jerked it out of his reach, he was careful to show no reaction, secretly thinking, If only the old bitch knew how much I loathe her!

'You haven't yet told me what it was about.' Anger marbled her voice. What right did Peter have, to go over her head like that? Dammit! Ruth was *her* business, not his.

'I told you, Mother – I've dealt with it.' His voice hardened. 'Now will you please stop making a fuss.'

'I can't imagine Ruth failing in her duties,' Ada fretted. 'She's always been such a help.'

Four years ago, when her health began to fail at the age of sixty-five, Ada had taken Ruth on after choosing her from eight good candidates. So far, she had not regretted her decision.

Ruth had been the perfect companion, housekeeper and friend and now, quite rightly, Ada resented Peter taking it on himself to reprimand her.

He shrugged impatiently. 'Like I said, it's nothing for you to concern yourself about. It was just . . . little things.'

'What kind of things?'

'Well . . .' he faltered, wary of being caught out.

'Go on!'

'Like I said, little things . . . forgetting to clear away the table directly I'm finished eating – oh, and of course, she's never there when I need her.' He tutted. 'And that's another thing. Having to speak with her just now made me late with your nightcap.'

He smiled, such a handsome smile, but it didn't fool Ada. 'I know what you're going to say,' he teased, 'and I'm fully aware it's one of Ruth's jobs. But I do enjoy it, Mother. Bringing up your supper tray is one of the few things I can do to show my affection for you.'

Ada was disgusted by all his gushing and lies. 'You'd best go,' she said tiredly. 'I'm sure you have things to do.' God forgive her, but just having him near her was nauseating.

'Everything's fine, so don't worry your head about it.' As he bent to kiss her on the forehead, she involuntarily stiffened. He sensed it but, as always, made no comment. 'Now that's settled, I'll leave you to enjoy your supper.' His brown eyes enveloped her. 'Leave the tray by the bed as usual, and I'll get Daisy to collect it later.'

'Oh, so Daisy isn't in your bad books then?'

'I have no qualms about that young girl. Daisy Morgan is an absolute gem.'

'Good.' In turn, Ada offered him her sweetest smile. Over the years, she had learned to do that without betraying her repugnance of him. 'I'm tired now,' she said. 'Ask Daisy to collect the tray in the morning.'

'If that's what you want.'

'It is.'

'You *will* eat your supper though, won't you?'

Ada nodded. Would he never go? 'Goodnight, Peter.'

'Goodnight, Mother. Sleep well.'

'I'm sure I will.'

She visibly relaxed as he left the room. 'The devil in disguise!' she muttered. 'You don't fool me.'

———⯈•◆•⯇———

B ENT OVER THE sink, arms deep in soap suds, Ruth didn't hear him come into the kitchen. When, with cat-like stealth he tiptoed across the floor to grab her by the waist, she screamed out. 'Shut up, you silly bitch!' Putting one hand over her mouth and the other round her waist, he drew her to him. '*She'll* hear you!'

Laughing in his face, Ruth danced to the other side of the room, where she undid her blouse to reveal the deep, soft cleavage beneath. 'Want me, do yer?' Licking her lips, she teased dangerously.

He feigned indifference. 'I can take you or leave you.'

'No, you can't.' Smiling into his eyes, she slipped the blouse off, and dropped the straps of her underslip. With her breasts uncovered, she reached down to unfasten her skirt. '*Now* d'yer want me?' Fully aware of her power over him, she stepped out of her clothes, stark-naked, daring him to take her.

Returning her smile, he came forward, arms outstretched, eyes glittering. 'Little baggage! I ought to send you packing.'

'But you won't, will you?'

Smothering her to him, he pushed her to the ground where, for a moment he looked her over. 'If you ever breathe a word to *her* . . .' he flicked a glance to the ceiling, 'I'll have to punish you.' There was no doubting his meaning.

'What makes you think I'd tell her?' Ruth said cheekily.

'Because sometimes you forget your place.'

There followed a brief span of silence, when she looked at him and was afraid. 'Don't worry,' she assured him. 'I ain't stupid. I know which side my bread's buttered.'

He gave a long, satisfied sigh. 'Good girl!'

While she stripped away his clothes, his avaricious eyes feasted on her nakedness. Perfectly shaped in every way, with a large, full mouth and tormenting green eyes to go with her glorious head of red hair, Ruth Clegg had everything he wanted from a woman. She was not too bright, nor too demanding, and she knew who was boss. Much like a dog, he thought with a rush of wicked humour.

She saw the glint in his eyes and was pleased. 'Penny for 'em?' Undoing the last button she leaned forward, nibbling him on the ear.

Running his hands through her long, fiery hair, he bent her head back and snatched her to him. 'I was just thinking what a common little tart you are,' he laughed.

Pulling away, she stared at him, her mouth set in a hard line. 'Is that what you really think?'

He kissed her, angered when she didn't respond. 'Don't refuse me,' he warned. 'Not now!' His hands encircled her waist. 'You know how upset I get.'

'D'yer really think I'm common?' Now, she was more curious than offended.

'Yes. It's what I like about you the most.'

'Bastard!'

His smile was enchanting. 'The worst.'

At that she laughed, and all was forgiven.

❧

IN HER BEDROOM, Ada heard them laughing, and her illusions about Ruth went for ever.

'A pair o' bad buggers together!' she sighed, wondering how she could have been so naive about the young woman she had genuinely liked. 'You pulled the wool over my eyes for a while,' she murmured, 'but now, Ruth, you've helped me make up my mind. What's more, I'll have no reason to feel guilty about it, not now I find that you and he have been taking me for an old fool.'

For a long time now, she had searched her heart, longing to right the wrong she had done. To her mind there seemed only one way, and even now, after hearing the goings-on downstairs, she found it a hard decision to make. After all, in spite of his failings, Peter was her own flesh and blood. 'But he's no longer a child,' she reminded herself. 'He's a grown man.'

She reconsidered this, and gave an ironic laugh. 'No, he isn't. My son is not even a man. He's a useless, lazy article – and I wish to God he'd never been born.'

Cradling her face in the palms of her hands, she remembered how it once was. She recalled herself as a young woman, tall and straight, with a ruthless streak that would serve her well in the years that lay ahead. 'A real beauty,' everyone said, 'but with ideas above her station.'

'They all wanted me to fail, but I showed 'em,' she said proudly. She had clawed and fought her way to the top. 'They couldn't keep Ada Williams down, however hard they tried!'

Feeling lonely, she reached out to the bedside cabinet and turned on the wireless. The voices were uplifted in a carol she knew well. Leaning back in bed, she let the song wash over her and suddenly, almost without realising it, she began to sing along with them. *'Hark! the herald-angels sing, Glory to the newborn king . . .'*

When the voices died away, Ada snapped off the wireless, thinking bitterly how useless and empty her life had been. She had never married again after losing her one true love, not from choice but because she was always the 'bit on the side' – the one who gave all and got little in return except for the sparkling trinkets and generous settlements; all well-earned, all squirrelled away. After all, a girl had to look out for herself.

Older now, and far wiser, she had only two regrets. One was her wayward son. It saddened her to see how cruel Peter had grown. He had no friends, not even a sensible woman to tame him. Wise men avoided him, and any unfortunate woman who caught his eye was first callously used and then discarded.

Ada's other, deeper regret was something that had happened years ago. It was a terrible thing she had done and, since then, her every waking moment was haunted by it. Even now, after all this time, when she let the memories carry her back, tears ran unheeded down her face.

Taking a deep sigh, she eventually calmed herself. 'It's no good crying,' she said shakily. 'That won't put matters right.' The tiniest of smiles lifted the corners of her mouth. 'To think it took me all these years to track them down, only to discover they live just half an hour away.'

She had been sorely tempted to go and see that family, to make herself known, and become part of their lives. But it was too late for that now. If they found out what she had done, they would drive her from the door. Bertie especially. She knew he would never forgive her – but that was no more than she could expect. 'No, it's better they don't know of my existence,' she muttered sadly. 'One day they may have to, but then it won't matter any more.' All that remained now was to make amends, and make amends she would, *by whatever means*.

'All those years!' she grieved. 'But now that you've found them,' she told herself, 'you know what you must do.'

Chapter Two

THE SOUND OF their merriment echoed down Buncer Lane. 'It's no good!' Helpless with laughter, Sylvia Bolton fell against the wall. 'The blessed thing won't go through the door.'

'I knew that already!' Betsy was the bigger of Sylvia's twelve-year-old twin daughters. 'I told you both when we were on the market. "We need to get a smaller tree," that's what I said, but nobody listened and now look!' A plump girl with hazel eyes and wispy brown hair, she spread out her two hands and gave an almighty sigh, followed by a giggle. 'We'll never get it through the door, Mam.'

'Yes, we will.' Ellie was the other twin, older by fifteen minutes. Smaller and tougher, she was as pretty as a sunny day; with her dark blue eyes and wild mop of fair hair, she was a force to be reckoned with. 'We'll just have to keep pushing till it goes through.' With that she bent her shoulders to the task.

Still grumbling under her breath, Betsy put her shoulders to the tree trunk and together the two girls heaved and pushed and shoved and grunted, yet the tree refused to budge. Wedged in the frame of the door it would go neither forwards nor backwards.

Betsy gave up. 'Oh, no! It's nearly Christmas and we'll be the only family down Buncer Lane without a tree!' With that she plonked herself down on the ice-cold step and melodramatically dropped her face into her hands.

Smiling at her daughters' antics, Sylvia stood on the pavement, breathless and defeated. 'We'll have to wait till your dad comes home. He'll know what to do.' A pretty woman in her forties, she looked ten years younger. With her bright green eyes and long fair hair, she had a zest for life that had shown itself in young Ellie.

'He'll be ages yet!' Betsy groaned.

Ellie came to stand beside her mam. 'We could ask Mick.' Pointing to the house across the street, she observed, 'He must be home, 'cause there's a light on. Look.'

So it was settled. While Betsy and her mam tried once more to get the tree inside, Ellie ran for Mick who, in no time at all, was crunching through the snow and ready to help. 'I'm not surprised you can't get it through the door,' he chuckled. 'You should have turned it trunk first, then when you pushed, the branches would fold in. *This* way, they're being forced out . . . like an umbrella, if you know what I mean. So the harder you push, the tighter it gets stuck in the doorway.'

Sylvia saw the twinkle in his eye and felt like a fool. 'All right, you! No lectures. I'm too tired and too cold,' she told him. 'Let's turn it round and get it inside before we all freeze to death.'

Shaking his head he told her, 'I'm sorry, Mrs Bolton, but you'll have to do it yourself. I'm off to get ready for my date.' When a mischievous grin broke over his features, Sylvia knew he was teasing again.

'You young devil!' Playfully punching him, she said, 'I really thought you meant to leave me struggling.'

Feigning amazement, he tutted. 'Shame on you! Would I do a thing like that?'

'I should hope not.'

Sylvia and her family had known Mick Fellowes these past five years, ever since he was a lad of seventeen. Tall and gangly, Mick was a law unto himself. He fancied the young women, and more often than not they fancied him back – which wasn't surprising. With his cheeky manner, laughing brown eyes and collar-length dark hair he was daring and different.

He had a question. 'If I get the tree inside, will it be worth a mug o' tea an' one of your home-made barmcakes?'

'Only if you set the tree in the bucket as well.'

'Oh, go on then. I've got time enough.'

'And will you make sure to put it where the girls say?'

'You drive a hard bargain.'

'I could make it *two* barmcakes?'

He laughed out loud; they both did. 'What can I say? You've twisted my arm.'

'Thanks, Mick. You'll find the bucket and logs standing by the fireside where Jim left them this morning.'

'Are you sure you don't want me to dress it an' all?' he said sarkily.

Thinking he really meant it, the twins voiced a protest. 'No! Mam promised *we* could do that!'

'Only joking,' Mick reassured them. 'I wouldn't have the first idea how to dress a Christmas tree.' Rolling up his sleeves, he said briskly, 'Right, you two. Let's be at it then.'

With Mick in charge, it took only a few minutes to swing the tree round and send it through the door feet first. 'What did I tell you?' He stood back to admire his achievement. 'Nothing to it.' Carrying the tree into the parlour, he demanded his reward. 'By the time you fetch my tea and barmcakes, I'll have the tree in the bucket, sound and secure.'

'You're a good lad,' Sylvia told him. 'I'm grateful, really I am. It means my Jim won't need to bother with the tree when he gets in from work.' Anticipating the question, Sylvia gave the answer. 'Our Larry would have done it, but he's working the late shift at the factory.'

'What – again?'

'He needs the money. Says he means to set himself up with a delivery wagon.'

'He will an' all, you see if he don't.' Sylvia's son Larry had big ambitions. 'If Larry says he'll do it, you know he will . . . even if it takes years.'

While Sylvia went to the scullery for the tea and barmcakes, Mick set to with the tree. 'Right, girls!' With the bucket in one hand and a scuttle of logs in the other, he glanced round the parlour. It was a cosy enough little room, with two soft, squashy armchairs, a small, deep sofa, and a solid sideboard polished till you could see your face in it. Around the walls were pictures of family, a ticking mantelpiece clock surrounded by bric-à-brac and, enfolding all that, a warm, cheery fire crackling up the chimney. 'Where d'you want me to set this tree?'

Ellie wanted it by the window; Betsy wanted it beside the fire. Mick solved the problem by tactfully suggesting he should place it midway. 'Then we won't have to move your dad's armchair from the fireside, and we won't be blocking the light from the window. What d'you say?' He gave a sigh of relief when the girls agreed. 'I'd best be quick then,' he joked, 'before you change your minds!'

With the twins giving instructions: 'Go left . . . Go right. It's crooked,' he wedged the tree in with the logs, driving one in here . . . filling a gap there, until the tree was upright, and secure in the bucket. 'There you are. Now you can put your trimmings on.'

While the twins busied themselves dressing the tree, Sylvia chatted to Mick, amazed by the speed with which he demolished the barmcakes. 'Good God! Anybody would think you hadn't eaten for days.'

'They'd be right an' all.'

Sylvia was shocked. 'You mean you haven't eaten for days?'

''Fraid not.' He wiped his mouth on the sleeve of his shirt. 'When you're on your own, you tend not to look after yourself properly.'

Mick's downcast face touched her deeply. 'You really miss your mam, don't you?' she said gently.

It took a moment for him to gather his emotions before answering. 'I'll always miss her,' he said quietly. 'It's been ten years since the pneumonia took her, and if I close my eyes, it seems like only yesterday.'

'Have you heard from your dad?'

Mick shook his head. 'No, and I don't want to.' His voice hardened with bitterness. 'He made his choice. Oh, I know he desperately missed our mam, but then so did I – and I was only a kid, still at school, when she died. It was hard for both of us, but he seemed to go right off the rails, out every night of the week, boozing and womanising.' He paused, remembering with shame. 'We had the worst row of our lives, but he still wouldn't see sense. I never thought he'd leave. Not with that little slag anyway. She was out to spend every last penny of his savings. I told him, "When the good times stop, she'll dump you like a sack o' bloody coal." But would he listen? Would he hell as like! He went off with her all the same. So good luck to him, and if she breaks his heart all over again, it's only what he deserves!'

'If he came knocking at your door, would you turn him away?' Sylvia knew all about it, and it saddened her.

Mick was adamant. 'Without a second thought. Like they say, he's made his bed. Besides, he's not likely to come knocking. Since I took over the tenancy, I've seen neither hide nor hair of him, and nor do I want to!'

'I'm sure he can't be that far away.'

'He can be at the other side of the world for all I care.'

'He hurt you bad, didn't he, love?'

'Bad enough.'

'And now you're not looking after yourself properly?'

'I get by.'

'I'm sorry, Mick, I had no idea. From now on, I want you to come over here every night and sit down with the rest of us. I keep a good table and there's more than enough to share with a friend.'

'I can't let you do that, Mrs Bolton.' He felt embarrassed. 'I wish I'd kept my big mouth shut now.'

'It's the least I can do. I should have realised . . . you're like a beanpole up and down, and no wonder. Not eating proper – shame on you. And shame on *me*!' She wouldn't take no for an answer. 'I mean what I say, Mick. I want you over here every night at seven o'clock, or I'll come looking for you, mark my words.'

The arrangement was made and Mick knew better than to argue. In fact, deep down he was delighted. A hot meal, regular every night, was something to look forward to. 'But not tonight,' he said. 'I've got two meat and 'tater pies in the oven. In fact, if I don't get off, they'll be burned to a crisp.'

Sylvia thanked him again for helping with the tree. 'Like

you say, you'd best be off. But you're not to forget our arrangement.'

'I won't.' In two strides he was at the door. 'I'll leave you to it. Tell Larry I'll be ready about eight o'clock.' With that he was gone, leaving Sylvia blaming herself for having neglected him.

For a while she helped the twins to trim the tree. When the mantel-clock chimed five times, she left them to it. 'Put the heavy baubles on the bottom, and the trimmings from the top,' she told them and, while they got on with it, she hurried to the scullery to organise the evening meal.

She peeled the potatoes and onions, then wiped a small measure of lard over the bottom of a big brown dish; that done, she sliced the potatoes and onions evenly into the dish and covered them with water from the kettle. On top of that she piled a generous layer of minced beef and, on top of that, yet another layer of potatoes, then a second layer of meat and onions, and to finish, a thicker layer of sliced potatoes. Next came a drop of cornflour gravy, then an offering of salt and pepper, and beaten egg for browning.

She carried the dish through to the parlour, where she put it in the oven; the range had been lit all day and was fired up nicely. Glancing at the tree, she saw how the girls were making a wonderful job of it. 'My! Your dad will be pleased,' she said, and went away, quietly smiling.

Once back in the scullery, she tore the washed cauliflower into natural chunks and dropped them into a deep earthenware dish. She sprinkled them with salt, covered them with water, replaced the lid and took it to the range, sliding it carefully onto the lower shelf, where it would cook slower than the casserole. Returning to the scullery, she prepared the rice pudding.

When all was done, she gathered the peelings and scraps

into a folded newspaper. Taking it down the back steps and into the yard, she dropped it in the midden. As she turned away, she heard a scuffling noise, then another, softer sound – a cry of pain, or so she imagined.

Thinking it might be a child, or someone hurt, she hurried across the yard, cursing when she slid in the snow and almost fell over the clothes prop, which was lying on the ground. Picking it up, she stood it against the lavvy wall. That done, she wrenched open the back-yard gate and peered along the alley – and there, out of the corner of her eye, she saw the shadow of a man . . . or it could have been a woman. Limping badly, the figure rounded the corner and disappeared. 'Who's that?' Sylvia's voice echoed eerily through the night air. There was no answer; she didn't really expect one.

It was when she turned to close the back gate that she saw the half-brick protruding through the snow. Stooping to pick it up, she realised it must have come from the top of their wall. 'That's strange,' she muttered. 'Jim's only just repaired that wall.' Feeling threatened and vulnerable in the half-light, she quickly closed and bolted the gate, before making her way across the yard and into the scullery.

Safely inside, she leaned for a moment against the door, her nerves jangling and her heart beating fifteen to the dozen. Had the shadowy figure been looking into their yard? But why would anyone want to do that? It wasn't as if they'd got anything worth stealing. All the same . . . it was odd.

Deciding a brew of tea would calm her down, she went to the sink. When she reached out to turn on the tap, she was horrified to see her hand all smeared in blood. Good God! How had it happened? She couldn't recall cutting herself. Feverishly washing her hand under the tap, she looked for a cut, a wound of some sort, but there was none. 'That's strange!' She tried to rationalise her thoughts and, for some inexplicable reason, they flew to the alley, and the shadowy figure.

Unable to rest, she lit the tilly lamp and returned to the yard. Raising the lamp, she examined the wall. Nothing amiss there, she thought. The brick was in place and tomorrow, Jim would have to cement it safely back; she didn't want it falling on the children.

Wait a minute! A thought occurred to her. She looked on the other side of the brick, and there was her answer; the surface was stained with blood. 'Not mine,' she murmured. And if it wasn't hers, then whose was it?

Lowering the lamp, she looked down to the spot where she had found the brick. Now, in the pool of light, she saw something else – a small, dark patch of blood staining the snow. 'I was right!' She glanced about, but there was no one in sight. 'Whoever it was *had* been looking into our yard!'

She worked it out in her imagination. He or she had climbed up the wall to see over; the brick slipped, they lost their grip and fell to the ground. The brick must have sliced into them when it came crashing down – splitting open an ankle, maybe? That would explain why the intruder was limping.

Afraid of her own shadow by this time, she went at a run into the scullery, where she secured herself and the children inside. Having time enough before the men arrived home from work, Sylvia washed her hands again and made herself a brew. Afterwards, she sat by the fire; the heat washed over her face, warm and soothing, making her sleepy.

But her mind wouldn't let her rest; she was too disturbed by what had happened. Somebody had been spying on them. What were they doing, looking into the Boltons' yard? What were they after? The incident had deeply unnerved her.

Suddenly, laughing and screeching, the twins were dragging her out of the chair. 'Come and see, Mam!' they cried and, for a while, she had to suppress her fears.

The tree was delightful. Flowing with paper streamers and dressed with silver-foil baubles made last year, the tree had brought Christmas into their little parlour. 'Oh, you've done a wonderful job!' Sylvia gave them each a well-deserved hug. 'Wait till Dad and Larry see it. They won't believe their eyes.'

'Can we bring the presents down?'

'No.' Sylvia was adamant. 'You know the presents don't go under the tree until Christmas Eve.' The girls didn't argue; not even when told to wash their hands and face. 'Dinner will be on the table in ten minutes.'

By the time they'd washed and put the plates out for their mammy, Larry walked through the door and, looking at him now, Sylvia's heart swelled with pride. Not only was Larry a good son, he was a friend. He was also a fine-looking young man. Tall and slim, with thick, wayward brown hair and serious green eyes, he was a catch for any woman. Besides which, at twenty-four years of age, he was mature and responsible.

'Hiya, Mam.' Having shaken his coat and flat cap at the front door, he now hung them on the nail behind the parlour door. 'It's started snowing again.' Clapping his hands together he strolled to the fireplace, where he rubbed the warmth back into his fists.

'Hello, son.' As always, Sylvia raised her face for a kiss, which was cheerfully given. 'Your dinner won't be long.'

'Whatever it is, it smells good.' The air was now heavy with the aroma of meat gravy and onions. 'Where's the kids?'

Glancing over to the tree, Sylvia could see them crouching

down, hiding; Ellie had her finger to her lips, urging her mam not to tell.

Sylvia didn't give them away. Instead she answered, 'Hmh. That's funny, they were here a minute ago.' And before she could say any more, the two of them sprang out from behind the tree, taking Larry by surprise. 'COME AND SEE THE TREE!' Catching hold of his hands, they gave him little choice.

'It's the best tree in Lancashire,' he said, and one by one, he swung them into his arms and hugged them till they squealed.

'Bet you can't guess who put the streamers on and who put the baubles on,' they challenged.

'Let me see . . .' He sat on the floor and they knelt beside him. When he pretended not to know that Ellie always put the streamers on and Betsy the baubles, they leaped on him, and he screamed in mock terror.

When the fun was over, Larry brought down his 'going-out' clothes from upstairs. While his mother dished up a piping hot meal, he stripped off his shirt and washed at the scullery sink.

With the day's grime washed away, Larry entered the parlour. His wayward brown hair shone like chestnuts, and he seemed suddenly taller and younger. 'Up to the table you two,' he growled at the twins. 'You'd best be quick! I've a lion's appetite tonight. I bet I could eat your dinner as well as my own.'

Before he'd finished speaking, they were seated at the table. 'You wouldn't!' Betsy believed him, but Ellie knew different. 'He were only joking,' she said, and laughed out loud when he made a dive at her.

Sylvia smiled to see their antics. Larry loved the girls and they loved him, but there had always been something extra special between him and Ellie. Open and honest, the older twin would confide her childish dreams and fears to Larry, while Betsy kept her own counsel, often choosing to sulk rather than get things off her chest and out into the open.

'Mick came round earlier.' Scooping up a ladleful of meat and potatoes, Sylvia dropped it skilfully onto his plate.

'What did he have to say?' Jabbing his fork into a potato, Larry popped it into his mouth, gasping for air when it proved to be hotter than he'd anticipated.

'He'll be ready for you at eight o'clock.' Next came the cauliflower, and a rap on the knuckles for starting before she'd finished serving him. 'Burned your mouth, did it? Well, it serves you right. You might wait till I'm finished dishing up in future. Your father will be in at any moment and we don't want to start without him.'

'Sorry, Mam. Trouble is, it's too good to resist.' He winked at the girls, who sniggered and tried to wink back, but they hadn't yet got the knack. When Ellie ended up cross-eyed, Betsy couldn't stop laughing – until Sylvia gave her a look that said, 'That's enough.'

'Is that all he said – that he'd be ready for eight?'

'That's all. Except he helped put up the tree, and finished off two of my barmcakes and a mug o' tea – though I'm glad of that, 'cause it turns out he's not eating properly.'

'Huh! You should see him polish off a pie and pint at the pub.' But Larry knew what she meant. 'You're right, though. He's never got any food in the house.'

'You should have told me.'

'I never thought.'

'Well, he'll be coming here for his dinner from now on, and no argument!'

Larry approved, and told her so with a compliment. 'When you produce grub like this, it's a wonder the whole *street* doesn't turn up for dinner.'

'There's far better cooks than me down this street,' she answered stoutly, putting her own share of dinner on her plate, and it was left at that.

She had just finished dishing up when they heard Jim's key turn in the lock. 'Your dad's home,' she told the girls, and they raced down the passage to greet him.

Knowing his routine like it was her own, Sylvia knew it would be a moment or two before Jim showed his face in the parlour. He would close the door, give it another push to make sure it was properly shut. Then he would take off his cap and fold it carefully with the neb tucked inside. Next, he would squeeze the cap into his overcoat pocket. Then he would hang up his coat, afterwards folding the pockets and arms neatly in. That done, he would run both his hands through his hair, which was wispy and brown, like Betsy's, and present himself to Sylvia with a broad grin and the fond question: 'How's my girl then?' His routine never varied.

So now, when Jim came into the room, the girls on either side of him, and all three struggling with a Christmas tree, Sylvia was taken by surprise. 'I found this on the doorstep,' he told her.

'It's mine,' Larry explained. 'I bought it from the market this dinner-time. I meant to put it up later on, only you'd already got one.'

'Oh, that was thoughtful of you, son.' Sylvia groaned. 'I wish you'd said, though. Me and the girls wouldn't have struggled home with that great thing.'

Betsy chipped in with, 'You won't change it, will you, Mam?'

'No, not now you and Ellie have put all the trimmings on.'

'Good! Anyway, our tree's *bigger*!'

'No matter, son. I'm sure there's somebody along the street who'll be glad of a Christmas tree.' Seeing how the tree was dripping snow onto the lino, she urged, 'Look, Jim, you'd best put it back outside for now.' Gesturing to the girls, she told them, 'You two, come and sit down afore your dinner gets cold.'

'Aye.' Jim went away to put the tree out. 'Afore *all* our dinners get cold.'

As soon as the girls had finished their meal, they asked to leave the table, and were soon engrossed in deciding what else they could do to the tree.

Keeping her voice low so they couldn't hear, Sylvia told the two men about the intruder. 'He must have been looking into our yard.' She described the brick and the blood, and how the runaway figure was limping.

Jim was up in arms. 'What? I'll mek the bugger limp if I get hold of him!'

Larry wondered if they ought to mention it to the police. 'You happened to scare him off, Mam, but somebody else might not be so lucky.'

They were still deciding what to do, when a knock came on the door. 'That'll be Mick,' Larry said. 'He's early.' The mantel-clock showed ten minutes to eight.

Flinging open the front door, he was surprised to see his grandfather standing on the step. Sylvia's father, Bertie Hill, was a big fellow, turned seventy, with a mop of grey hair and baby-blue eyes, which at the minute were weeping from the cold. 'Hello, Grandad.' Larry urged him inside out of the weather. 'I didn't know you were coming over today.'

Taking off his long-coat, the older man handed it to Larry, who hung it next to his own. 'I hadn't planned to come over,' Bertie confessed, 'but I were at a loose end so I thought I'd pop round and see how you all are.' He glanced backwards. 'What's been going on out there?'

'What do you mean?' Larry asked.

'Well, if *you* don't know, how d'you expect *me* to?' Making his way along the passage, the old fella chatted on: 'When I turned the corner into Buncer Lane, some o' the neighbours were standing about in little groups – all agitated, like. By the time I got along the street, they'd all gone back inside. Mind you, I can't blame 'em. It's enough to freeze the balls off a pawnshop sign out there.'

Shivering, he came into the parlour, his ready smile encompassing them all. 'How do!' Rubbing his hands he made a beeline for the fireplace. 'Brr! It's wicked cold out there.'

'Hello, Dad.' Getting out of her chair, Sylvia kissed him soundly on the lips. 'What's brought you here?'

'Shanks's pony then the tram – what d'you think?' A mischievous grin at the girls brought them running for a hug.

Sylvia was used to his sense of humour. 'Come on, Dad, you know what I mean. When you went home on Friday, you said you wouldn't be seeing us again till Christmas morning.'

'Aye, well, it gets a bit lonely on your own.' Sitting in the armchair, he stretched out his legs and made himself at home. 'A cuppa tea wouldn't go amiss, lass . . . an' a barmcake if there's one going.' Glancing over at his son-in-law, who was finishing his meal, he asked, 'All right, are you, Jim lad?'

'Right as rain, Dad.' Jim had to smile. Sylvia's father had always called him 'lad', and here he was with a son of twenty-four, and two lasses aged twelve.

From the scullery, Sylvia chided, 'How many times have

I said you've no need to be on your own? Jim and me would be only too glad for you to stay with us.' Coming into the room, she handed him the tea and barmcakes on a small tray. 'I for one wouldn't mind another man in the house,' she said. 'Not when there's a strange fella been peeking over our yard wall.'

Concerned, Bertie Hill sat up. 'When were this?' Taking the tray, he placed it on his lap and held it there.

'Tonight,' Jim answered quietly. 'Larry's all for telling the police.'

Just then there was another knock on the door. 'That'll be Mick,' Larry announced, clambering up. And this time, it was.

Well-scrubbed and smart in his green shirt and corduroy trousers, Mick breezed in. 'Did you hear the rumpus out there?'

'See?' The old fella wagged a finger at Larry. 'I said there were summat going on!'

Mick went on to explain, 'It seems they've caught a Peeping Tom.'

Realising the girls were listening, Jim told them, 'If you go in the front room, you might find a bag o' goodies for the tree.' When they went off in search of it, he turned to Mick. 'Right, lad. What happened exactly?'

'Madge next door saw him loitering about in the alley. First he went into her back yard, then into mine. I must have been in the bedroom getting ready, 'cause I never saw him.' He clenched his fist. 'If I *had* seen him, he'd have gone down that street with his tail on fire an' no mistake! Anyway, she grabbed Archie Benton and he caught the fellow red-handed. He held onto him, while his lad fetched the police. He denied he'd been peeping, but went quiet all the same.'

'That's it then. They've got the bugger.' Walking across to Sylvia, Jim put his arm round her. 'You can rest easy now, lass.'

'Do you think it was the same man?'

'Who else could it have been? Madge's house is only three down from us. I'd bet my life it were the same bloke!' With his information imparted, Mick nudged Larry in the ribs. 'It's time we were down the road,' he suggested with a sly wink.

'Give me five minutes.' Having left his good jacket in the bedroom, Larry went up the stairs two at a time. 'Hope you've got enough money,' he called out. 'And don't forget you owe me two bob already!'

To which Mick replied that he owed him nothing, because, 'I bought the fish and chips last week, remember?'

In no time at all, Larry had collected his jacket and was eager to be gone. 'Right, Mam. We'd best be off.' They had lingered too long already.

'What have you two fine fellas got planned for tonight then, eh?' Jim asked. 'Got some pretty girls lined up, have you?'

Mick started to answer. 'Well . . .'

But before he could finish, Larry hustled him out along the passage, with the parting words, 'We're in training for the darts match tomorrow night, Dad. See youse later.' And they were off down the street without a backward glance.

'Why didn't you let me tell them about the girls?' Mick was puzzled.

'Because each time they know I'm seeing a lass, our mam gets all serious. First she's talking engaged, then it's wedding bells and down the aisle. Before I know it, she'll have me with six kids and a house on Park Street.'

'There's nowt wrong with Park Street. All the big nobs live there.'

'Yes, and they have servants and carriages . . . motor cars even! Not to mention factories and bank loans. By! The thought of having all that responsibility frightens the pants off me. All I want is a wife and two kids, and my own delivery wagon.' He chuckled. 'First though, I wouldn't mind a good time, and a lass I'd be proud to walk down the street with.'

'You never know,' Mick teased him. 'Tonight could be the night!'

'We'll see. I've not met her yet – don't even know what she looks like,' Larry groaned. 'If she's ten yards wide with a face like a navvy, I'll have *you* to thank for it.'

'Not me!' Mick chuckled. 'It were the landlord who set us up for tonight. "Pretty as a pair o' pictures", that's what he said. Anyway, you're not the only one that's worried. What if mine's uglier than yourn?'

'In that case, there'll only be one thing for it.'

'What's that?'

'Run like the clappers!'

The two young men quickened their steps, the street echoing with their laughter.

'BETSY! ELLIE! COME on now. Into the scullery with you.' When they showed their faces at the parlour door, Sylvia beckoned them in. 'Make sure you wash behind your ears and clean your teeth,' she instructed. 'Then it's upstairs and ready for bed.'

As usual, the girls protested, but Sylvia was impervious. 'You've had a long day, and so have I,' she said. 'So I'll thank you not to give me an argument. And don't forget to say goodnight to your grandad.'

Jim and Bertie were still quietly talking about the intruder. 'I hope they put the bugger away for a long time!' Jim declared, and Bertie wholeheartedly agreed.

While the girls washed at the big pot sink, Sylvia worked round them. She made two mugs of cocoa, one for her dad, one for Jim. The girls straggled behind her into the parlour, all shining and clean, still protesting.

'Mam won't let us stay up,' Betsy sulked to her grandad.

'Mams allus know best,' he said, and kissed them goodnight.

Ellie hung onto him for a moment longer. 'I love you, Grandad,' she said, and he knew she meant it. It was his duty to love both the twins, and he did, but somehow Ellie had found her way deeper into his heart.

When Sylvia and the girls were on their way upstairs, Jim voiced his concern. 'They're growing up fast,' he said. 'Thirteen next birthday – it don't bear thinking about.' He gave a great sigh. 'Before we know it, they'll be young women, with lads at their heels.'

'Aye well, there is a long ways to go afore that happens.'

With one fearing the future, and the other fearing the past, the two men sipped their cocoa and lapsed into silence.

When Sylvia returned, Jim was still harping on about 'that bloody Peeping Tom'. 'By,' he said. 'If I'd been here, I swear I'd have torn the bugger limb from limb!'

'Then it's just as well you weren't here,' Sylvia remarked as she came through the door, 'or they might have carted *you* off instead!'

'Peeping through folks's windows, the bastard! If there's any justice they'll lock him away for a good long stretch.'

Sylvia made no comment, just went through to the scullery and heated herself a cup of cocoa, afterwards coming to sit with the two men by the fireside.

The talk soon came round to Christmas. 'I can't believe it's the day after tomorrow,' Sylvia said. She was nowhere near ready for the big day. 'I've a mountain of baking to do, and I still haven't bought the twins their presents. Ellie's never any trouble – she's always happy with whatever she gets. But Betsy is so difficult to please. Still, I'd better get them the same thing, or there'll be ructions.'

They chatted on about this and that, a family together, content in each other's company.

When the clock struck ten, Jim began to doze. 'I'm sorry.' He gave a long, weary yawn, 'I'm that tired I can't keep my eyes open.' Addressing Bertie, he asked, 'I hope you'll not be offended if I get meself off to bed?'

'Not a bit of it, lad. If I'm to catch that last tram, I'll have to be going meself in a few minutes.'

While Jim went away to his bed, Sylvia took the empty cups into the scullery. On her way back into the parlour, she noticed how her father was sat forward in his seat, his gaze fixed on the dying embers. He had one hand clamped over his mouth – an old, familiar habit that betrayed his unease.

Concerned, Sylvia crossed the room to him. 'Are you all right, Dad?'

At first he appeared not to have heard. Leaning down, she touched him on the arm. 'Dad?'

Startled, Bertie sat up, his forehead creased in a frown. 'Yes, lass?'

'Are you all right?'

He nodded. 'Aye, why shouldn't I be?'

'You were miles away.' She sensed that something was troubling him. When he seemed to drift off in his thoughts again, she stooped closer. 'Is there something on your mind?

Is that why you came over tonight . . . because you needed to see me, for some reason?'

Looking up at her, he took a moment to study her face. Such a pretty face, he thought sadly. So like her mam when she were younger.

'What's wrong, Dad?' He had never looked at her like that before – as though she was someone else.

He blinked, then looked away, redirecting his attention to the glowing coals. 'You're so like your mam.' He spoke softly, his voice trembling. 'She were a real beauty in her day.'

Sylvia was shocked. All these years, whenever she had asked him about her mother, he would clam up, refusing even to discuss her. Now, all of a sudden here he was, talking about her as if it was the normal thing.

Instinct told her not to ask any questions, at least for the time being. If she kept quiet, he might go on talking, and at long last she might learn something of the mother she had never known.

Her instinct served her right, because as though he was the only one in the room, he continued to murmur, 'Aye, she was a beauty all right. No wonder the men craved after 'er.' His voice hardened. 'I've tried forgiving her, but I can't. *I never will!*'

Suddenly, to Sylvia's astonishment, he began to cry – heart-wrenching sobs that tore her apart. When she laid her arm round his shoulders, he seemed only then to realise she had been there all along. Wide-eyed and shaking, he looked into her eyes. 'I'm sorry, lass.' He mopped his face and blew his nose, then gave a long, shuddering sigh. 'I'd best go.'

Sylvia was loath to leave it there. 'Why don't you tell me about her?' she pleaded. 'All you've ever told me is that she died when I were a babby. Aunt Margaret and you raised me, and you never married again. That's all I know.'

'That's all there is to tell.' Standing up, he prepared to leave.

'Don't go, Dad. Not yet.' Desperate, she caught hold of his arm and hung on. 'You have to tell me more! I can't ask Aunt Margaret because she's long gone. Besides, she always cried when I talked about Mam. So now I'm asking *you*.'

The anger melted and her voice softened like that of a child. 'Please, Dad. After all this time, I still think of her. I can't help wondering what were she like . . . inside, I mean. Was she a good person? Was she kind? Did she really look as pretty as you said just now? And the most important question of all: *Did she love me?*'

'For God's sake, lass! O' course she loved you! She were yer mam, weren't she?' The old man's voice broke again.

Sylvia was deeply moved, and tears rolled down her face. 'Do you realise that's the first time you've admitted that to me? Oh, Dad! There's so much I want you to tell me.'

Bertie glanced up at the mantel-clock. 'Look, it's late. I'd best go.' Shrugging her off, he made for the door.

When she called out, he paused, not daring to look back, but listening to what she had to say. He had deliberately not mentioned her mother all these years. He had hoped Sylvia had forgotten, but of course she couldn't forget. He should have known. He heard her pleas now, and his heart went out to her. But he couldn't tell. He knew from experience that if he raked up the past, it would only bring heartache. *It always did!*

Not knowing the truth, Sylvia was persistent. 'Why aren't there any pictures of her? Where is she buried? Tell me, Dad. TELL ME!'

Swinging round, he took hold of her, his fists hard against her shoulders, his eyes swimming with tears. 'You have to accept it, lass! The past is gone and good shuts to it,' he said hoarsely. 'One churchyard is as good as another, and when you're gone, you're gone. You want to know what she were like? She were a woman like any other. And now she's gone!' He bowed his head. 'And there's nothing more to say.'

Now, when he looked up, there was so much pain in his old eyes that Sylvia counted her own pain as nothing. 'I'm sorry, Dad.' She clung to him. He was glad of that.

After a while he held her at arm's length. 'It's a bad thing to torment yourself with what's gone,' he murmured. 'We can none of us change the past. All you need to know is that me and your Aunt Margaret raised you with all the love in the world. To all intents and purpose, *she* were your mam. Not that shadowy woman who gave birth to you.'

Something in his voice, in what he said, startled Sylvia. 'Tell me just one thing?' she asked hopefully.

'If I can.'

'Did you love her?'

He took a moment to reflect on what she had said. Then he smiled, the most wonderful smile. 'I adored her.'

'Then why can't you share her with me?'

His features stiffened. 'Because she's not mine to share!'

Sylvia had no answer to that.

He turned on his heel for the last time. 'Goodnight, lass.'

'Goodnight, Dad.' She knew from old, it was no use questioning him further.

At the door, he asked her, 'Will you be all right?'

'Right as rain. Now get off with you.' She looked up at the darker skies. 'It looks like we've more snow to come yet.'

'A white Christmas,' he chuckled. 'That'll please the girls.'

'Go on, Dad,' she urged, 'before the heavens open.'

'Aye. The old dog'll be wondering where I've gone. Poor old bugger, he's past his best, like me. He frets like a bairn when I'm not there.'

'Remember what me and Jim told you.' Sylvia knew how much her dad loved that old mongrel. 'If he needs the vet, we'll find the money.'

'He don't need no vet.' The old man was ever proud. 'And like I've told you afore, lass . . . he's *my* responsibility, not yourn, though o' course I'm grateful for the consideration.' Stepping down onto the pavement, he reminded her in a sombre voice, 'Mek sure this door's pushed up proper after I've gone, now we know there's bad 'uns hanging about.'

'Don't worry, Dad.' Perhaps that was the reason he'd been deep in thought? 'The Peeping Tom won't come back now,' she said confidently.

'All the same, you do as I say.'

'I will.'

She watched him go down the street, a wave of sadness washing over her. Not too long ago, her father had been a broad, strong figure of a man, with straight shoulders and a smart step. Now, almost without her noticing, his shoulders had begun to stoop, and his step wasn't quite so sprightly. 'Goodnight, Dad,' she murmured. 'God bless.'

After driving the bolt home on the front door, she hurried down the passage to the parlour. Momentarily pausing at the foot of the stairs, she cocked an ear, listening for any sound that would tell her if the girls were still awake. 'Sleeping like angels,' she whispered. 'Just as well.'

She turned to enter the parlour, but was stopped in her tracks for a while, her gaze roaming that familiar little room, with its cheery fire and pretty curtains, and the deep-pile rug nestling before the fire-range. 'You're a lucky woman, Sylvia Bolton,' she chided herself. 'You've three fine children, a cosy home, and the love of a good man.' A fleeting regret darkened her eyes. 'You mustn't crave over what you can't have.'

Quickly now, she went from the parlour to the scullery, where she satisfied herself that the back door was securely bolted. She then checked all the windows and placed the fireguard round the fire. That done, she departed from the room, her thoughts going back to her mother. 'Oh, Mam! I wish I'd known you,' she murmured. It was as though a great void had been left in her life . . . a place no one else could ever fill.

As she closed the door, she glanced again at the parlour and its familiar things, and her heart eased. 'He won't talk about you, and I can't make him,' she whispered. 'But I know you must have been a kind, gentle woman, or he would never have given you the time of day.'

In that moment, her father's words echoed in her mind: ''Course she loved you. She were yer mam, weren't she?'

Sylvia nodded, almost as though he was there, and she was acknowledging him. When she closed the door, she was smiling, a quiet, contented smile. *Her mother had loved her.* When it came right down to it, that was all she really needed to know.

Chapter Three

ADA WATCHED THE dawn break; a bright wintry dawn that lit the room and dazzled her old eyes. 'Another cold day.' Shivering, she glanced towards the hearth, to the spill of cold embers and blackened surround. 'I must get Daisy to make up the fire.'

Sighing wearily, she leaned back into the pillows. With so much playing on her mind, she found sleep impossible. These past few hours had told her many things, one of which was that she was not loved for herself, but for what she had accrued over the years. It was a painful realisation, but she should have seen it many years ago.

Suddenly, after a lull of silence no doubt while they slept, she could hear their laughter. Interspersed with delighted squeals and lewd suggestions, it left nothing to the imagination. Picturing her son and his eager mistress in the next room was a torment.

'They've no shame!' she muttered. 'No shame!' And drawing the blankets over her head, Ada buried herself deep down between the sheets. Peeking out at the bedside clock, she saw that it was almost 4 a.m. Weariness crept up on her. When her eyelids became heavy, she let the tiredness wash through her and soon she had drifted into a light, uneasy sleep.

A short time later she woke in a fright. 'Who's there? What do you want?' Scrambling up, she clutched the sheets about herself. With the sleep still on her, she couldn't seem to get her senses together. 'Who is it?'

'It's only me, ma'am . . . come to get your tray.'

When she saw the small, homely face, with its pretty blue eyes peeping through the open door, Ada gave a sigh of relief. 'Oh, it's you, Daisy.' She relaxed. 'I'm sorry, I thought—' The shame choked in her throat. 'Oh, come in, Daisy. Come in!'

As always, the girl quickly did as she was bid. 'I've brought your warm water, ma'am.' Carrying a big, rose-patterned jug, she went straight to the wash-stand in the corner and set the jug down on the floor. She tipped the used water from the wash-bowl into the other jug standing beside it, wiped the bowl round with the clean towel she had over her shoulder, and placed the newly filled jug beside the bowl. 'There! All nice and warm and ready when you are, ma'am.'

Carrying the old jug across the room, she placed it outside the door before coming back into the room and flinging wide the curtains. 'Windows open or closed today?'

'Closed. I don't want to freeze while I'm at the wash-stand.'

'Sorry, ma'am.'

'I've asked Peter time and again to have that small bed-room converted into a proper bathroom, but will he listen?' Ada said irritably. 'I can see I shall have to arrange it myself once I'm up and about again.'

Daisy thought that would be lovely. 'My sister works at Cicely Bridge Mill, and the manager there has just had a lavatory put into his spare bedroom. There's a bath an' all, an' a little wash-basin. He says it's a real joy.'

While Ada turned that over in her mind, Daisy brought a clean pair of sheets from the linen cupboard on the landing. 'Quickly, Daisy,' Ada shivered as she came and went through the door. 'You're letting in the cold, child.'

'Sorry, ma'am, I didn't realise.' Daisy went to riddle the fire and put more coal on.

'That's because you haven't got my old bones to contend with, and nor should you.'

'And how are you this morning?' the girl asked in her musical Welsh voice. 'Sleep well, did you, ma'am?'

'No, Daisy. I did not.' Ada watched her go to the big chest of drawers, where she took out a clean white towel which she laid over the rail of the wash-stand; next came a fresh nightie and robe from the wardrobe drawers. 'I did *not* sleep well, and neither, I suspect, did you!'

Discreet as ever, young Daisy made no mention of the noise which had risen to her little attic room and robbed her of a night's sleep; though if the truth be told, she had been shockingly entertained by the goings-on. All the same, she wasn't about to tell her mistress that. 'Whatever do you mean, ma'am?' She could act as innocent as the next one, when necessary.

Frustrated, Ada's troubled eyes followed the girl across to the fireplace, where she poked the embers through the grating and proceeded to catch them in the tray beneath. 'Daisy, will you stop that and come over here? Quickly now, there's a good girl.'

Bright and cheerful as always, Daisy presented herself at the bedside. 'Here I am, ma'am,' she announced. 'What do you want me to do?'

'I want you to be honest with me.'

'Aren't I always, ma'am?'

'Most times,' Ada answered with a smile, 'except when you think I might be hurt by what you have to say.'

'I would *never* hurt you, ma'am!' The bright face darkened. 'You should know that.'

'And I do! That's why I'm asking you to be honest with me now, and not to worry if you think what you say might hurt me. Do you understand, Daisy? Am I making myself clear?'

'Yes, ma'am.'

'Did you hear the master last night?'

Daisy blushed deep crimson. 'Yes, ma'am,' she whispered.

'And the housekeeper?'

She hung her head. 'Yes, ma'am.'

'Did they keep you awake last night?'

'Until gone midnight, ma'am.' Suddenly, she raised her face to look Ada in the eye. 'Going at it hammer and tongs, they were!' Her eyes opened like saucers. 'Then they went quiet. But they were at it again this morning.' Her voice rose hysterically. 'I don't mind telling you, ma'am, I've never heard anything like it in all my life! Not even when my dad used to come home and wake my mam so he could have his wicked way. She used to yell and shout, and then they'd laugh and squeal. Like two young, silly things they were.'

Having blurted it all out, she gave Ada a frightened look and dropped her head. 'Sorry, ma'am, I got a bit carried away.'

For a moment the ensuing silence was impenetrable, then softly at first, Ada began to chuckle. 'Going at it hammer and tongs, eh?' The chuckles got louder until she bent her head to her hands, and collapsed with laughter. 'You're right!' she said. 'Going at it hammer and tongs. I couldn't have put it better myself.'

Daisy looked up, amazed to hear the mistress laughing like that. 'Sorry, ma'am, but you did ask me to be honest.'

With tearful eyes and aching sides, Ada looked at her. 'I did, of course I did, and so you were.' And she began giggling again.

Then Daisy started giggling, and was so mortified she quickly took control of herself and stifled the laughter until later, when she would let it all out in the kitchen where nobody could hear.

In a calmer voice, albeit trembling from the ever-rising giggles, she asked, 'Is that all you wanted, ma'am?' With difficulty, she cleared both her throat *and* the giggles. 'Only I need to get on, or the master will be snapping at my heels.'

Feeling more alive than she had done in ages, Ada took a deep, sobering breath. 'Daisy Morgan, you're such a treasure. What would I do without you?' She took stock of the young girl; envying her in one way, admiring her in another.

Oddly uncomfortable beneath the old lady's eyes, Daisy wondered what she was thinking.

'You're a good girl,' Ada told her. 'I only wish I'd made *you* housekeeper instead of that little gold-digger.'

Daisy blushed. 'Thank you, ma'am, but I'm not ready for that kind of responsibility yet.' At eighteen years of age, Daisy was a mere slip of a thing. Her big blue childish eyes, and straight brown hair parted with a clip on the side of a ragged parting, made her look years younger than her true age. She was trustworthy and obliging, and Ada meant what she said. If she had known how the other was going to turn out, she would have given Daisy the opportunity to prove herself worthy of a housekeeper's position. But no matter, because there was still time, she thought.

Leaning forward, Ada lowered her voice to a more intimate level. 'Will you do something for me, lass?'

'I'll do my best, ma'am.'

'It's not a difficult thing I'm asking,' Ada explained. 'It's just that, well, with my old legs the way they are, and what with being confined to this room, I can't do it myself, you understand?'

'You can rely on me, ma'am.'

'Good! Now then, Daisy, I need you to run an errand, but no one must know – certainly not either of those two.' She grabbed the girl's arm. 'Can you do that for me, dear? Can you get out of the house without them seeing you?'

'I can do that, ma'am.'

Growing excited, Ada pointed to her dresser. 'Fetch me that writing paper and a pen,' she said. 'You can set about your work here, while I write a short note.'

A few minutes later the note was written. After sealing it inside the envelope, Ada called the girl away from the window where she was busy dusting the sill. 'Put it straight into your pocket,' she instructed, fearing the door could fling open at any moment to admit her son, or the other one. Ada watched while Daisy tucked it neatly inside her apron pocket. 'Take it soonever you're finished with your duties. You mustn't lose a minute, Daisy, not a minute!'

'No, ma'am.'

Before she left, Daisy had a word or two of her own to impart. Collecting the tray from the small table, she respectfully noted, 'You didn't eat your supper, ma'am.'

'I wasn't hungry.'

'If you don't mind me saying, ma'am, it's not good to go without your food.'

Ada smiled. 'I've lived a long and busy life, and never worried about what was good or bad for me. But thank you all the same, Daisy. It's nice to know somebody cares.'

Daisy blushed with pleasure. 'I'll be back up with your breakfast tray in ten minutes,' she promised. 'Crunchy toast, and eggs well-boiled the way you like them.'

Ada shook her head. 'No, dear. I don't want any breakfast. All I want is for you to deliver that note.'

'I will, ma'am.'

'Don't cut short your duties though. Finish whatever you have to do and sneak out. I'll cover for you if you're suddenly missed.'

'Thank you, ma'am.'

'Whatever happens, you are not to mention the note to anyone.'

'No, ma'am.'

'Go on then, child. Be quick about it.'

———◦———

So quick about it was Daisy, that she almost fell headlong down the stairs when the master's command caught her unawares. 'Where the devil are you rushing off to, girl?' Up and dressed, Peter Williams discreetly closed the bedroom door behind him. 'I hope the fire's lit and the breakfast ready.' He rubbed his hands in anticipation of a good meal.

Trembling at the knowledge that she had in her pocket a secret between herself and the mistress, Daisy answered in a surprisingly cool voice, 'It's warm as toast in the dining room, sir,' she told him. 'And breakfast is all ready for dishing up.'

'Wonderful!' His sharp, suspicious eyes raked her face. 'What's wrong with you?' Coming down the stairs two at a time, he paused alongside her, his searching gaze sending a shiver through her. 'What's that you've got there?'

'What do you mean, sir?' She felt herself shrinking inside. Oh God! Her heart turned over. He must have seen the letter. But how could that be, when she'd pressed it deep down inside her pocket?

'The *tray*, you silly girl. Whatever's the matter with you?'

Relief flooding through her, Daisy answered with a desperate smile, 'It's the mistress's supper-tray, sir, and not a crumb eaten, as you can see.'

'Is she ill?' *Dead* would be better, he thought cruelly.

'No, sir. She just wasn't hungry.'

He shrugged his shoulders. 'Oh well, if Mother chooses to starve herself, who am I to intervene?' With that he ran on ahead. Having satisfied one appetite, he was about to satisfy another. 'Hurry up, girl!' His voice sailed back to her. 'I'm as hungry as a hunter, and I'm in no mood to be kept waiting.'

'Hmh. You're a pig, you are!' Out of earshot, Daisy could say what she liked, and she did. Marching into the kitchen, she emptied the tray onto the wooden draining board. 'I ought to poison his fried eggs, then we'd all get some peace – some sleep too, I shouldn't wonder.' In fact, she wondered how she could look him in the face and not recall the noises and grunts of last night, and then again this morning. 'Hammer and tongs,' she chuckled. 'It's a wonder the bed isn't in bits after that little lot!'

When her imagination began to run riot, she dashed into the scullery, shut the door and laughed out loud, knowing full well she couldn't be heard, not through these thick walls.

I N N O T I M E at all, the breakfast was served – a full dish of eggs, bacon, sausages and tomatoes for the master, along with fried bread and heaps of thick buttered toast.

'I don't know how you can eat such a pile of food!' Having set Daisy a list of duties in the kitchen, Ruth had taken a moment to peer in and peck her lover on the cheek. 'Especially not after last night, and more especially after this morning.'

Enraged, he thrust her away. 'Get out, you bloody fool! I've told you . . . what goes on between the sheets is one thing, but I am still master in this house and you, like Daisy, are an employee.' Peter's smile was evil. 'So you see, my dear, my place is here, enjoying my breakfast, and yours is in the kitchen, doing whatever it is you're paid to do.'

Looking down at his plate, he forked up half a sausage and rammed it into his mouth. Waving the fork at her, his partly-chewed food spitting out across the table, he gave the order. 'Didn't you hear me? I want you out of here . . . NOW!'

Hating him with all her heart and soul, Ruth Clegg departed the room. Out in the hall, she leaned on the coat-stand. 'You bastard! You arrogant bastard!' she seethed, her voice low and trembling.

After a while, she calmed down. Raising herself to her full height, she admired her reflection in the mirror. She was the image of youth and beauty . . . slim and shapely, her green eyes alight with fury, and her wild red hair framing a perfectly formed face.

'Come on now, Ruth,' she told herself encouragingly,

'you've got the bugger where you want him. You've nothing to worry about where *he's* concerned.'

Her gaze travelled up the stairs towards Ada's room. '*She's* your problem,' she said thoughtfully. 'As long as he gets his fair share, the son should be easy enough to deal with, but not that one. That old boot's as tough as they come, and sharp as a tack with it.'

She chuckled. 'Been around, by all accounts, has old Ada Williams. Had a few enemies – and seen 'em off, I've no doubt. But she ain't come up agin somebody like me afore, I'll be bound.'

After preening herself, she strode into the kitchen where Daisy was wiping Ada's supper-tray; the untouched food was on the draining board waiting to be put out to the midden. 'What's that?' Ruth poked at the plate with a fork. 'The old biddy didn't even touch her supper, did she?'

When Daisy was slow to answer, she took her by the ear, making her wince. 'I didn't realise you were deaf!' she shouted.

'Yes, miss!' Daisy's ear stung. 'It's the mistress's supper gone cold. She wasn't hungry.'

'Hmh! More like she thought I'd poisoned it.' With a cruel twist of her wrist she flung Daisy aside. 'When you've cleared the breakfast things and finished in here, get upstairs and change the master's bed.'

'Yes, miss.'

'After that, you'd best get on and polish the tiles round the sitting-room fireplace. They're a disgrace!' With that she flounced out, leaving Daisy making a rude face behind her; until Ruth suddenly turned to glare at her, when Daisy gave a weak smile. In that moment she wished the earth would open up and swallow her.

S LIPPING ON HER clean nightgown after washing at the basin, Ada instantly recognised the tap on the door. 'I'm not to be disturbed right now,' she answered sharply. But Ruth came in anyway.

'Oh dear, I am sorry,' she lied. 'I didn't realise you were dressing.'

'Hardly dressing!' Ada flung her robe round herself. 'I won't be confined to this room for very much longer,' she said, tying the robe at the waist. 'I've felt so much better these past few days. Indeed, I half expect I'll be able to venture down to the sitting room tomorrow, or the day after.' The sooner the better, she thought, before the pair of them laid claim to everything she owned.

Boldly closing the door behind her, Ruth offered the old lady a hand to help her back into bed. 'You may feel better,' she said, 'but you must still be careful. You know how many times that hip has let you down.' She gave a small wry laugh. 'We can't have you falling down and breaking bones, now can we, eh?'

Thrusting her away, Ada gave her a damning glance. 'I'm not getting back into bed, not yet anyway. Daisy will help me in, when she comes back to change the sheets.' With that she sat in the chair, her face grey with pain. 'I'd like you to leave now.'

But Ruth remained where she was. 'I spoke with Daisy in the kitchen just now,' she told Ada, scowling. 'I'm very angry with you . . . with *both* of you!'

Thinking of the letter and its damnable contents, Ada's heart skipped a beat. 'What's the poor girl guilty of now?'

'It seems you didn't eat your supper?'

'That's right.' She was so relieved she could have cried out. Instead she carried the deception bravely. 'I didn't eat my breakfast either. Did she tell you that?'

'I see. And may I ask why?'

'You may ask, but you'll get no answer. I eat, or I don't eat. That is my privilege.' Wishing to God she had the strength to get up and give this brazen young woman the hiding she deserved, Ada told her sharply, 'I think you must not have heard. I asked you to leave my room.'

That was the second time this morning she'd been told to leave the room. Choosing to ignore her, Ruth put her hands on her hips, and peered down at Ada like a mother might peer at a naughty child. 'Lost our appetite, 'ave we?'

Recalling what her son and Ruth had been up to, and Daisy's wonderful description of it, Ada had to stop herself from laughing out loud. She noticed how flushed the young woman was. Her mass of fiery red hair was tied back, and her eyes were alive with the glow of youth, and something else . . . a kind of wonderful arrogance that drew both Ada's admiration, and her anger. 'You and Peter . . .' She hardly knew how to put it.

Ruth smiled. 'You heard, didn't yer?'

'How long have you and my son . . . ?' She felt the hot flush run up her neck.

Now it was Ruth laughing out loud. 'Don't be embarrassed. I'm not.'

Ada was shocked. 'I can see that.'

'He's my man and I'm his woman. If I'm clever, I daresay all this will be mine some day.' Opening wide her arms she encompassed the room in a gesture that left Ada in no doubt of her meaning. 'He's a good catch is your son, and you ain't gonna live for ever, are yer?'

Enraged, Ada sat bolt upright, her eyes boring into Ruth's. 'GET OUT!'

'Temper! Temper!' Stepping forward, Ruth leaned towards the old woman. Meeting her angry stare with defiance, she said quietly, 'It wouldn't be clever to open your mouth to Peter about our little chat. For one thing I make a very bad enemy, and for another, he wouldn't listen to anything you said. Your precious son hates your guts, did you know that?'

Disgusted, Ada turned away, but Ruth continued to taunt her. 'That's it,' she jeered, 'keep your mouth shut. It's the best way. You see, I know him better than you do. I can twist him right round my little finger.' Taking Ada's plait of hair she twisted it hard round her hand until the old lady squealed out. 'That's what I mean,' she whispered. 'See how easily you can be hurt?' With that she departed, her voice bursting into song as she ran down the stairs.

Feeling old and used, Ada began a slow, painful path across the room. The lino was cold to her feet, making her shiver. 'I'd best ask Daisy to build up the fire.' Her gaze went to the fire grate; like her life, she thought bitterly, it was growing cold and empty. How many days was it to Christmas now? She began to mutter, 'What does it matter? One day's the same as the next to me.'

As the chilly daylight spilled through the window, she moved closer, peering down into the street, her heart uplifted as she watched the children going from door to door, singing their hearts out, hoping for a penny, but being sent on their way. 'It's too early in the day. Come back tonight when my husband's in.' That was stingy Mrs Butterworth from number ten.

Ada tutted. 'Shame on you, Nan Butterworth,' she murmured. 'There is no "husband". He passed on some ten years back. Moreover he left you well provided for, and now you're too mean even to give a poor kid a penny.' Wasn't it always the way, she mused.

Dejected, the children walked slowly away, all muffled up against the cold and looking like snowmen beneath the relentless curtain of snow. Ada painfully lifted the window and called to them, before scattering a handful of threepenny pieces, pennies and ha'pennies in their direction. The cold took her breath away. Shuddering, she pulled the window down.

Casting her glance round the room, she noted the beautiful things she had collected through her life; china and silver, displayed to perfection on antique furniture whose value had spiralled over the years. Every piece gained through hard work and sacrifice. Precious, exquisite things she had once cherished, long ago when she knew no better.

The whisper of a smile bathed her once pretty features. 'Things!' She looked away, her voice hardening with bitterness. 'They mean nothing to me now. They can't keep me warm at night. Nor can they wipe away my tears when the loneliness becomes too much.' More than that, they could never ease the guilt in her heart. Only she could do that and, if it wasn't done soon, it would be too late.

With this in mind, she hobbled over to the mirror, pausing to gaze on her reflection. She wondered how she could have grown so old. 'What would they say now,' she asked whimsically, 'all those young men who thought you the loveliest creature on earth?'

She peered deeper into the mirror. 'Who is this old woman, eh?' There was no regret, only astonishment, and a rush of amusement. 'The mirror never lies – isn't that what they say?' But it was always a shock to see herself as others must see her.

Pinching the flesh beneath her chin, she gave it a little shake, laughing when it trembled like jelly. 'Poor Ada Williams! You look every one of your sixty-nine years.' She shook her head. 'Sixty-nine years. My God, where's it gone?'

The thought brought her up tall and proud, and for a time she remained like that, her bright eyes taking in every facet of herself; the long, grey plait and the flabby skin, the high forehead and the still high cheekbones which alone had carried the shape of beauty. She liked what she saw. She *loathed* what she saw.

With a resigned smile, she dismissed the sagging jawline and the limp folds of flesh lying over her quiet eyes; instead she concentrated on the eyes – hazel in colour, still bright and quick. Like my mind, she thought thankfully. While I have my faculties, *he* can't hurt me! Instinctively she glanced towards the door, but Peter wasn't there, and her heart grew calm.

Curious, she returned her attention to the image in the mirror once more, noting how well-dressed it was in the pink silk nightgown and matching robe, and the once long, fine fingers, gnarled and bent, bedecked in the trophies she had won . . . an emerald ring, a single diamond mounted on glinting gold, filigree shoulders, each ring worth a small fortune. Her wrist was adorned with an entwining bracelet of white platinum, threaded with small perfect sapphires. At her throat a single row of humble seed pearls.

'Bertie gave me these.' Tenderly she fingered the hard cream-coloured pearls. A tear shone proud in her eye. 'I might have married again after him.' A sadness scarred her voice. 'If anyone had asked. But no one ever did. *None* of them did.'

Trailing a slim hand over the long grey plait that hung gracefully over one shoulder, she moved away, her eyes now fixed on the small, circular table by the window. Peter had placed it there, at the furthest distance from her bed. Another little ploy to make her life more difficult.

A few more steps and she was there.

Softly, she picked up the receiver. With trembling fingers she began to dial, saying the numbers aloud as she did so. 'Three, four, six . . .' Here she paused, momentarily unsure, before going on again: 'Two, one.'

After a series of ringing tones there was a click at the other end, then a man's voice, authoritative and crisp. 'Carter here!'

Realising that her son might come into the room at any minute, Ada lost no time. 'There's something I want you to do,' she told her solicitor. 'Right away!' Attentive as always, he remained silent while she outlined her plan.

Downstairs, Peter Williams held the receiver to his ear.

Careful not to breathe too loudly, or make a sound, he listened intently; his dark eyes tightly closed, his handsome face contorting with rage as he followed the conversation.

After a while, Ada brought the exchange to a close. 'My son knows nothing of this,' she warned. 'It must remain a secret between you and me, for now at least.'

'Of course.' The solicitor was an old friend. 'You can rely on me.'

Shaken by what he had heard, Peter Williams softly replaced the receiver. The conversation only confirmed what he had long suspected.

For a time he paced the floor, his mind unsettled. Presently, he stopped by the window, his face a mask of loathing. 'I'm sorry, Mother.' He smiled, a not unpleasant smile – *unlike his thoughts*. 'I can't allow it,' he murmured. 'It simply won't do.'

His dark eyes stared upward, towards the spot where he knew she was standing. His voice was harsh, unforgiving. 'No, Mother dear. *It won't do at all.*'

Chapter Four

COMFORTABLE IN THAT cosy little parlour, Jim Bolton laid out his work before him – two small pairs of boots to mend, a bag of tacks, some large, some small, a half dozen strips of leather, and the hobbling shoe left him by his old dad. 'D'you know, lass, I'm never more content than when I'm tapping away with the leather,' he told Sylvia. 'There's a kind of pride for a man, in mending his childers' shoes.'

When Sylvia didn't answer, he glanced up, saw that she was resting in the armchair and chatted on. 'I don't mind telling you, I feel tired. Staying up chatting till the early hours takes it out of a man my age,' he chuckled. 'If you recall, there was a time when I could stay out half the night, then come home and make love with you, right here on the rug afront o' the fire. Can you remember, lass, that time when young Larry caught us at it on the floor? He were eight year old an' innocent as the day were long.'

He laughed aloud at the memory. 'We told him we were play-fighting and he believed us, bless his little heart. I don't mind admitting, it gave me a real fright, him coming up on us like that. After that we were allus very careful. "It won't do for the lad to see the wrong thing", that's what you said, and you were right.'

Her mind elsewhere, Sylvia didn't hear a word he'd been saying. For some inexplicable reason, she had been on edge all day. There was something troubling her, something she couldn't quite put her finger on. *Something that would not let her rest.*

So now, while the house was quiet and she had time to gather her thoughts, she sat beside the fire, her mind far from easy, her troubled gaze following the leaping flames in the grate.

'*Hey!*' Jim's voice cut through her thoughts. 'Wake up, m'beauty!'

Startled, she looked up. 'Sorry, sweetheart. I was thinking.'

Ever patient, he shook his head. 'Musta been summat pressing, 'cause you've not heard a bloody word I've been saying.' He peered at her, curious. 'Look, lass, I know it's Christmas Eve an' you've been run off your feet, but you've only to ask an' I'll help where I can, you know that.'

Sylvia thanked him, but: 'It isn't that,' she told him tenderly. 'I love Christmas, you know I do.'

'So, tell me what's plaguing yer. You'll feel better if you get it off yer chest.'

Hesitating, she wondered if he would understand. 'Have you ever felt afraid,' she began, 'only you don't know why?'

Frowning, he shook his head. 'No, lass. Can't say I have. Ee, you're a funny little thing an' no mistake. Happen your old Grandma were right when she said you had a bit o' the gypsy soul in you . . . seeing things where others can't, an' all that.' Still, gypsy or not, he loved her like no man ever loved a woman.

'Jim, can I ask you something?'

'Ask away.' He didn't look up. Marrying the tacks to the leather took a measure of concentration.

Getting out of the chair, she dropped to her knees before him. 'Can you stop what you're doing, just for a minute?'

Glancing up from beneath his eyebrows, he breathed in a great noisy sigh, held it for an age, then blew it out in a series of loud tuts. 'Can't it wait, lass? I'm almost done.' Leaning over the hobbling shoe he was in the process of stretching a square of leather over the worn sole. 'A few more tacks in place and I'm ready to cut it to shape.'

'Please, Jim! A minute of your time, that's all I ask.'

He seemed not to have heard. 'When I've finished, it'll be good as new, you'll see. *And* I'll have saved you a shilling into the bargain.'

'Huh! Blowing your own trumpet now, is it?' Yet she was so proud. Jim was a good man, hard-working and handsome with it. And she considered herself very fortunate.

'I reckon I've earned the right to blow my own trumpet,' he chuckled. 'In twelve years since the lasses were born, we've only ever bought them one pair o' boots, and even *they* didn't last as long as the ones *I* make.'

That said, he resumed his work but continued chatting. 'Mind you, I don't suppose it'll be long afore they're gazing in shop winders, wanting summat prettier than their old dad can create. More expensive too, I'll be bound.' He paused, his gaze falling on Sylvia, and his eyes filled with love. 'Bonny lasses the pair of 'em.' He gave a wink. 'But then, what else could they be, with a Mammy as lovely as you?'

Sylvia remained silent for a time, content to watch his quick fingers as they felt their way along the rim of the leather, tapping here, smoothing there; until out of chaos emerged the creation.

It was a fascinating thing to watch. Comforting somehow. Yet even now in this cosy parlour, with Jim beside her and the thought of her two lovely daughters warming her heart, she could not settle.

'Jim?' She tugged at his sleeve.

He paused, looking at her from beneath his long dark eyebrows. 'All right, love, I can see you won't give me no peace till I've heard you out.' Making sure the boot was still pressed down hard over the hobbling shoe, he placed it aside. 'Right then.' Taking her face between his large workworn hands, he kissed her softly on the mouth. 'I'm all yours.'

For a long moment she didn't speak, and he didn't urge her to. Instead, he was content simply to look on her loveliness. After a while though, he grew apprehensive. 'Look, lass, I promised young Ellie her boots would be ready for Christmas morning, and in case it's slipped your notice, that's tomorrow. You asked me to stop work, and I've stopped. So what's on your mind?'

'I don't know.' She shrugged her shoulders. 'I'm worried about something.'

Drawing his head back in surprise, he studied her for a brief moment. The rising heat from the fireplace had bathed her face in a warm, pink glow; her green eyes shone up at him, her beauty taking his breath away. 'What d'you mean, lass?' he said fondly. 'What's to worry about?'

Sylvia looked away, her quiet gaze going to the fire-grate, where she was momentarily mesmerised by the flames – long, licking tongues of red, dancing up the chimney in a frenzy. She answered in a whisper. 'I can't explain. I just feel troubled, that's all. I've been like it all day.'

'I hope yer not gonna tell me you're having another bairn!' His eyes widened. 'Three's enough to be going on with.' When she merely smiled, he took her by the shoulders. 'Yer not, are yer?'

She laughed. 'Not as far as I know.'

Reaching out, he took hold of her hand. 'Are you feeling poorly, is that it?'

'No.'

'The children all right, are they?'

'You know they are,' she said fondly. 'They're in the front parlour, gathering the presents for the tree.'

'You haven't got yerself another bloke on the side, have you?'

She dug him playfully in the ribs. 'Don't be daft! One's enough, thank you.'

'There you go then!' He kissed her soundly on the mouth. 'Like I said, there's nowt to worry about. You and me are still daft over each other. We're all disgustingly healthy. I've a good job, with good money coming in. The larder's full, and the rent's paid up.' He chucked her under the chin. 'Unless you've been squandering it away behind my back, have yer?'

''Course not!'

'Right then.' He took up his tacks and hammer again. 'Happen you might let me get back to me work now? After which I mean to go and get meself a well-earned pint down the pub.'

While he tapped away at the leather soles, Sylvia remained on the rug, eyes closed, the heat of the fire warming her through. Jim's plain, honest words had made her realise how lucky she was.

'I'll tell you what though, lass.' Once again, Jim's voice cut through her thoughts. 'I've been thinking about it for some time now. You, me and the twins should get away for a few days. Oh, not yet, but when the weather turns – Easter mebbe

– we should get off to the seaside. It'll do us both good, and the twins will love it. Larry'll be all right on his own. I mean, he's a capable enough fella, and I've no doubt he'll welcome a bit of peace and quiet, after the twins an' all. Besides, with him looking after it, at least the house will still be in one piece by the time we get back.'

Once an idea took hold he wouldn't let it go. 'Look, as I'm off to the pub tonight, I'll ask the landlord if we could rent a room in his cousin's pub on the coast. What d'you say?'

'Why not.' It was an age since they'd been to the seaside.

'Right then, lass. Consider it done!' He kissed her softly on the mouth, his fingers walking down the opening in her blouse. 'I'll not be out late, if you know what I mean?'

Smiling knowingly, Sylvia took him into her arms.

'And now, love, will you stop all this worrying?'

She nodded. He was right, she thought. When all was said and done, there was really *nothing* for her to worry about.

⇒►◦◄⇐

THAT NIGHT, AFTER she and Jim made love, Sylvia slept like a bairn, and rose to the day a contented woman. By mid-morning she had cleaned the house, plucked and gutted the cockerel and got it in the oven, done all the Christmas vegetables, and finished the ironing, though her mam had always told her you should never iron on a Christmas Day.

Now, after enjoying the sandwiches which would carry them over until the evening, she left Jim and the twins to their own devices, and returned to the kitchen where she busied herself with the Christmas dinner. There was still much to be done, though thankfully, there was no one to interrupt her for the time being. Larry was having a nap; the girls had gone upstairs to play at dressing up, and Jim was lazing in front of the fire.

From the armchair, he called out to her, 'I hope you've done enough food. What with the five of us, then young Mick and Grandad Bertie, you'll need a lorryload of it.'

'There'll be more than enough,' she replied. 'There always is. Come and look for yourself. I've peeled a bucketful of potatoes and veg. I've made two large brandy puddings, there's a mountain of a cake I made weeks ago, an army of pork pies from the butcher's, and I've bought an extra chicken, just in case. So, you can stop your moithering, 'cause you'll not starve.'

The sound of his chuckling filled the kitchen. 'I'll tell you what, our Sylvia. If it tastes as good as it smells, I'll not complain.' The whole house was bathed in the succulent aroma of mince pies, freshly cooked meat, sausage rolls, and big bumpy scones oozing with raisins and browned with the white of egg.

'That's the last batch.' Satisfied with her day's work, for that was how long it had taken on and off, Sylvia placed the hot food on wire racks, before arranging the racks on top of the cupboard. 'Out of reach of you two!' she told the girls, who by now were hanging around the door licking their lips and hoping to cadge a morsel or two.

'Oh, Mam! Can't you even spare one mince pie?' Betsy groaned.

And back came the answer. 'No. You'll be having your Christmas dinner in no time. You don't want to spoil it.'

'Surely *one* mince pie won't hurt.' Her bottom lip was thrust out, always a sign that she was about to throw a tantrum.

Ellie suggested a compromise. 'What if we just have one

between us?' she asked. 'That won't spoil our dinner, will it?'

'Mebbe not.' Trust Ellie to make the peace, Sylvia thought fondly.

So the twins sat at the table with one mince pie and two plates, and were satisfied.

When they returned their plates to the kitchen, Sylvia told them to get washed at the sink, which they did. She then brought them towels and afterwards they ran upstairs to change for their Christmas dinner. 'Quick as you can,' she said. 'I'll need your help to get the table set.'

'And what d'you want from me, lass?' Jim asked jokingly. 'A white shirt and black tie, and a look at my nails to mek sure they're clean?'

'Away upstairs with you!' Flicking the tea-towel round his ear, she suggested, 'You might wake Larry and tell him dinner will be on the table in half an hour. He went up there ages since. "I'll only be having forty winks," he said, and he's still out like a light.'

'Aye well, the lad worked an extra shift yesterday, so he could have today off. It ain't fair, you know, lass. Most folks have Christmas Day off *without* having to do extra hours in lieu.'

'What would you do if *I* had today off?'

'What?' He was taken aback.

'Don't you think *I* should have today off? I worked yesterday, and I'm working even harder today, but I don't expect I'll be paid, will I?' With Jim staring at her like she were gormless, it was all she could do to keep a straight face. When she could no longer pretend, she laughed out loud. 'By! *That* made you think though, didn't it?'

Jim was not impressed. 'Hmh! All it made me think was

that you'd lost your marbles. You *like* cooking and baking, and ironing and all that stuff. I've heard you say so yourself.'

'Maybe I do. But I wouldn't mind being paid for it.'

He ran at her, making her squeal with delight. 'You argumentative little bugger! Are you looking for a fight, or what?'

When, still giggling, she sought sanctuary in the kitchen, he ambled off upstairs to get cleaned up, though he mumbled and moaned the whole way. 'What's so different about Christmas dinner, eh? One dinner's the same as the next. It all goes down the same hole, don't it? Causes the same amount o' washin' up, an' all. But I'll not be dipping me elbows in no grease, 'cause I'll be off down the pub, and Larry alongside me. Grandad Bertie too, if I know that old bugger. Anyway, she's got the twins to help her. They better had an' all, or they'll feel the flat o' my hand against their arses, so they will!'

As he went upstairs, the girls came down. 'Can we put the presents round the table now?' That was Betsy, being impatient again.

Sylvia poked her head round the door. 'No. You know very well we get our presents *after* we've had our main meal of the day. It's family tradition – allus has been.'

'Oh, Mam!'

Out came the bottom lip again, and this time it was Sylvia, not Ellie, who put a stop to the threatened tantrum. 'If you're going to keep moaning, mebbe you'd better go back upstairs and stay there.'

It was only a quiet suggestion, but it did the trick. 'Well, can we pile them all together, ready for afterwards?'

'I thought that was what you were doing before?'

'We were, only we smelled the mince pies.'

'Go on then, and be careful with your Grandad's. It's

breakable.' As she turned back into the kitchen Sylvia warned, 'You'd best be quick about it, because everything's cooked and waiting to be strained. I'll need you to help in five minutes.'

In fact it was *ten* minutes before she called them.

Betsy insisted on putting the best tablecloth over the big old table. Ellie set out the knives and forks, while her sister arranged the spoons and condiments. 'Don't forget to put the block of wood in the centre of the table,' their mother called out. 'I think your dad said it was in the stairhole cupboard.'

As always there followed a little argument about who should fetch it out and, as always, Betsy won the day. 'It's too heavy for you to carry,' she told Ellie importantly. 'You're too skinny and you'll only let it drop.'

'Stop arguing, you two!' Sylvia came in with the plates, and handed them out, three to Betsy and three to Ellie; the seventh one she set down in their father's place at the head of the table. 'Now, see if you can do that without arguing!'

She did the same with the crackers, and the napkins – an old white towel cut into squares, each square sewn neatly round the edges.

When Grandad Bertie arrived half an hour later, the meal was on the table. Taking off his coat he flung it on the nail behind the door, sniffing at the air like a dog after a bone. 'By! I couldn't have timed that better if I'd tried.' Reaching over Ellie, he squeezed a small brussel sprout between his finger and thumb, and promptly popped it into his mouth. 'Done to perfection,' he told her with a wink. 'Like everything else you turn your hand to.'

Sylvia rapped him sharply on the knuckles with the serving spoon. 'I'll turn my hand to *you* if you don't keep your fingers out of the food,' she warned. 'What's the use of me telling the girls not to touch, if you go and do the very opposite?'

Like a scalded boy, he went and sat by the fireside, making faces at the girls and causing them to laugh out loud. One severe glance from Sylvia soon put a stop to that. Larry showed his face, then Mick, and five minutes later, Jim came down from having a short nap. 'Right, lass. Lead me to the cockerel.'

The two of them went into the kitchen and a moment later they came out again: Jim in front carrying the cockerel, and Sylvia behind with the carving knife. Manoeuvring the block of wood so it was central enough to take the big plate, she reminded Jim, 'Don't forget last year, when the plate was lopsided and the chicken almost landed on the floor.'

'By! That's a real beauty.' With eyes like saucers, Grandad Bertie was slavering at the mouth. Basted brown and dressed with bacon strips, the cockerel was big enough to feed an army on the march.

Soon all seven were seated round the table. 'I've not seen a spread like this since our Mam . . .' Mick's voice tailed off miserably. 'All water under the bridge,' he said with a brave smile. 'You're a good cook an' no mistake, Mrs Bolton.'

'Well, thank you.' Sylvia glowed with pride, though her heart went out to him. Twenty years and more he might be, but he was obviously still missing his mam.

'Don't heap too much praise on her,' Jim warned. 'You haven't tasted her cooking yet.'

Sylvia gave him the 'look'. 'No – and neither will *you* if I get much more of your cheek!'

Everybody laughed, and Jim set about carving the cockerel. 'There'll be no fighting over the legs,' he announced. 'Being as we're the eldest, there's one for me, and one for Bertie.' Giving his father-in-law a cheeky wink, he added, 'I'm sorry an' all that, but I've yet to see a chicken wi' four legs.'

When the cockerel was sliced and the meat dished out, it was time to send round the bowls of vegetables; all piping hot and steamed in their own juices. Next came the gravy, rich and brown. 'I'm looking forward to this!' Clapping his hands, Grandad Bertie would have tucked in there and then, until Sylvia discreetly reminded him. 'We haven't said grace yet, Dad.'

'Sorry.' Lowering his gaze, he joined his hands and closed one eye, while the other continued to stare appreciatively at the food on his plate.

Jim didn't have much to say, except, 'Thank You, Lord, for what we're about to receive.' He glanced from one to the other. 'Amen,' he concluded, and no sooner had he finished, than Grandad Bertie was already cutting up his meat.

The crackers were pulled and everyone put on their hats, and made short work of their meals. Sylvia was praised, and then the teasing started. 'How come we only ever get napkins on a Christmas night? The rest of the time it's the cuff of your sleeve.' That was Jim, full of mischief and cockerel.

'And why isn't there a bowl of fruit on the table, like they have in the big houses?' Larry asked, tongue in cheek.

The bantering went on with young Ellie enjoying every minute, though Betsy got annoyed when her cracker fell into the gravy. 'I don't want it now!' she whined, quickly smiling through her tears when Sylvia gave her the one remaining.

Next came the brandy pudding and custard, and, when that was eaten, the girls gave out the presents, which were torn open to cries of delight. 'Just what I wanted!' Larry received the same tie as last year but was too polite to say so.

Jim was given a box of men's hankies with the initial 'J' from the girls and a smart cravat from Sylvia. 'It's grand, love,' he said. 'I'll wear it every chance I get.' As good as his word, he promptly put it on.

Sylvia was given a cameo brooch in return. 'It's not a real one,' Jim apologised, 'Mebbe next year, eh?'

His wife gave him a fond kiss. 'It's lovely,' she said, and meant it.

Larry and the girls had clubbed together to get her a beautiful vase, which she adored. Grandad Bertie gave her a scarf and socks. 'They'll keep you warm on a cold night,' he said gruffly. 'If you don't like 'em, the shopkeeper said you could tek 'em back and choose summat different.'

Sylvia put a smile on his face when she protested, 'I wouldn't dream of changing them, Dad! They're lovely.' The brown clay pipe she had bought for him was accepted with a cry of, 'Oh, lass! It's just what I want. The old one's cracked wide open, as you know. By! That must have cost you a pretty penny!'

Turning it over and over in his hands, he admired the short stubby bowl with its fancy carvings and long flat stem. 'By 'eck, lass!' he kept saying. 'By 'eck!' And he gave her a big sloppy kiss that left her with a face full of spittle.

'I wasn't really sure what to get you.' Mick handed her a small, square box. 'My mam used to like this kinda thing, so I thought it might suit.'

Opening the parcel, Sylvia found the prettiest table decoration. With a base of polished wood and a cloth robin perched on a branch, it brought a gasp of wonder from the girls. 'Oh Mam, it's so bonny!' Ellie held out her hands. 'Can I hold it, Mam? Please?' Though, when Sylvia passed the bird carefully from one girl to the other, they were too excited about their own presents to hold it for more than a minute.

They had a thick roll-necked sweater each from Sylvia and their dad. To Sylvia's relief, Betsy seemed delighted with hers; red and wide-ribbed, it suited her colouring a treat. Ellie's was blue; her favourite colour. The girls also received a game of Snakes and Ladders from Larry and Mick, and a pack of Snap cards from Grandad Bertie. 'I bet I can beat you at Snap!' Betsy could never accept being a loser, even to the point of being the occasional cheat.

'Come on then!' Ellie never shrank from a challenge.

While the girls enjoyed their Christmas presents, the young men cleared the table. Sylvia went into the front parlour, where she got out the glasses and a bottle of mulberry wine that was left over from Jim's birthday a month back. Placing that on the mantelpiece, she then collected a big, brown earthenware jug from the cupboard. Giving it a wipe with the tail end of her apron, she made certain there was no dust inside. That done, she made her way back.

Awaiting the final Christmas night treat, Jim and his old father-in-law retired to the armchairs on either side of the fire. 'The lass allus does us proud,' Bertie sighed, patting his over-full stomach. 'I'm not even sure I've got room for the wine.'

'Get away with you!' Jim replied. 'It'll be a sorry day when a man can't find room for a drop o' the good stuff.' With Bertie agreeing, the talk moved on to pubs and darts.

When Sylvia returned, Jim gave up his chair and drew another from the table. 'Get in here, you two!' he called out to Mick and Larry. 'We're about to warm the wine.'

'Can't miss that, can we, Mick?' Larry emerged from the kitchen with Mick in tow, each of them tugging on the same tea-towel with which to wipe their hands.

When everyone was seated, and the two girls watching as always, Jim thrust the poker into the fire. When it was red-hot, he plunged the poker-end into the heart of the wine, making it sizzle and dance. Before it went cool he quickly filled everyone's glass. They raised a toast and drank it down; then another, and another until it was all gone – except for the small measure Sylvia saved so the girls could have a taste each.

Afterwards, they sat round and listened while the twins gave their usual Christmas treat. Betsy recited a poem she'd learned at school. When she'd finished, everyone clapped and so did she. 'That were lovely, lass,' Jim told her, and the others all said the same.

When it was Ellie's turn, she bowed like a princess and looked like one as well. Her long fair hair hung over her shoulders like sunshine in motion, and her dark blue eyes shone with excitement. There was a pause, when everyone settled again, while Betsy came to sit at her mother's feet.

When Ellie began to sing, the room was hushed, all eyes and ears on her. The voice was magical, a plaintive, haunting voice that tugged at their heartstrings:

'Oh, Danny boy, the pipes, the pipes are calling . . .'

When the last note of the beautiful Irish ballad died away, the silence was thick with emotion. The young men were quiet, heads bowed, while Sylvia and Jim glanced at each other, amazed at the child they had raised.

Grandad Bertie wiped away a tear. 'Aw, lass, that were beautiful. It don't matter how many times you sing it, you mek me cry.' Taking out his hankie, he blew his nose and woke everybody up.

The girls were hugged and praised and the furniture put back where it belonged. 'I've never heard anyone sing so lovely.' Mick was deeply moved.

'She gets it off her grandma,' Bertie murmured, then, when everyone's eyes were on him, he looked away. 'By! I'm a lucky man, with two such bonny grandchildren.' Discreetly changing the subject, he took them one in each arm. 'I'm proud o' the pair of youse.' He gave them each a kiss and sent them back to their games.

Aware that her father had come close to mentioning her mother, Sylvia watched him for a moment, but he never once glanced her way, and she knew the moment had passed.

Her mind still singing with Ellie, she went to the kitchen where she made a start on washing up the rest of the dinner things, while the girls could be heard laughing and arguing from the other end of the parlour.

The young men sat at the table, making plans for the evening. The older men lounged by the fire, talking and laughing, with Bertie puffing at his old pipe and filling the room with smoke.

To Sylvia it was a wonderful scene; the cheery fire in the grate, and everyone so content. *It seemed too good to last,* she mused. No sooner had the thought passed through her mind than she felt the same disturbing sense of danger that she had experienced before. 'Take a hold of yourself, Sylvia,' she said bossily. 'You've had too much wine. It's got you imagining things.'

Jim's voice sailed through to her. 'Talking to yourself now, is it?' he chuckled. 'I can see I'll have to fetch the men in white coats.'

A moment later, her dad came into the kitchen. 'All right, are you, lass?'

'Of course I am.' And, after Jim's light-hearted comment, so she was.

Dipping his finger into the custard pan, Bertie licked

it clean though at the same time keeping a wary eye on her. 'You're not still worried about that Peeping Tom, are you?'

'No, Dad.' Wiping her hands, she filled the kettle and put it on to boil.

'Will it be all right if I stay here tonight?' he went on.

Sylvia smiled at him. 'You feel the need to protect me, do you?'

Bertie didn't answer. Instead, he told her, 'I'll have to go back and fetch the old dog, if that's all right. He's never been left on his own at night afore.'

''Course it's all right, Dad,' Sylvia told him. 'Besides, it will be nice to have you stay over. Larry won't mind sharing with you.'

Bertie shook his head. 'No, love, I won't disturb the lad. I'll be happy enough bedding down on the sofa.'

Jim was consulted, and the arrangement was quickly made. 'I'll be going to the pub in a while,' he told Bertie. 'The landlord's son's got himself a little car; it spits and bangs and frightens the life outta the cats, but it goes forrard and backarrd and that's all as matters. Show him a bob or two, an' he'll have you out to your place and back again afore you can say "How's yer father".'

Having got ready to go out, Larry suggested, 'If you like, I'll ask him. Me and Mick are off there now.'

Getting out of the chair, Jim gave a long, noisy stretch. 'Aye, go on then, son. Tell him me and your grandad are on our way, an' he'll be needing to leave in the next hour.'

Sylvia was astonished. 'What's all this?' Looking from one to the other she asked, 'Since when has the landlord opened his pub of a Christmas night?'

'There's a darts match . . . private like. There'll not be any old Tom, Dick or Harry invited, I can tell you that.'

'Me and your Larry have been asked to make up the numbers,' Mick chipped in. 'With a bit o' luck, we'll give that lot from The Navigation a run for their money.'

Hands on hips, Sylvia looked at Jim with narrowed eyes. 'You never said you'd be going out tonight,' she teased. 'Don't tell me *you've* been asked to play as well? Because if you have, they'll not stand a cat in hell's chance of winning.'

Grabbing his coat, her husband retorted, ''Ere! Less o' that, my girl. I might be rusty now, but in my prime, I could throw a dart through the eye of a needle.' Turning to Bertie, he urged, 'Get your coat, Grandad, afore we're made to finish the washing up.'

Sylvia persisted. 'You didn't answer me . . . *have* you been asked to play as well?'

Shoving the other three men out the door, Jim said, 'Well, as it happens, I haven't, no. But the lads need somebody to cheer 'em on, don't they?' With that he grabbed a quick kiss and was down the passage and out the door before she could catch her breath.

Going after them at the run, she called out, 'Tell that landlord's son to mind how he goes wi' my dad!'

A smile and a wave, and they'd already rounded the corner. 'Little boys at heart,' she sighed and went back to see what the girls were up to.

'Betsy won't come down the snakes,' Ellie complained.

Betsy had a complaint too. 'It's not fair when she keeps landing on the ladders. How can I win if I have to come down the snakes every time!'

Sighing, Sylvia left them to it. In truth, the men weren't half as much trouble as the girls!

Deep in her work, Sylvia's quiet thoughts turned to Mick and his estranged father. 'It's such a pity Mick won't forgive his dad,' she mused. 'Losing his wife must have taken its toll on him. Still, God moves in mysterious ways, they say. Happen He'll find a way of bringing them back together again.'

Feeling contented in the bosom of her family, and with the business of the Peeping Tom out of the way, Sylvia found herself echoing Ellie's song: *'I'll be here in sunshine or in sha-a-dow. Oh Danny boy . . . oh Danny boy, I love you so.'*

When, from the parlour, Ellie's beautiful, clear voice joined in, she felt a surge of pride and something else too – something she had never really felt for Betsy. She felt the deepest, warmest bond. From the moment they were born, Ellie first, Betsy next, she loved both girls, but Betsy had never really let her get close, while Ellie was instantly part of her own soul, and always would be.

Going to the kitchen door she looked out across the parlour. Betsy saw her and looked away without acknowledgement. Then Ellie turned, her pretty eyes shining. She smiled at Sylvia, and returned to her game. But that quick, warm smile had lit her mam's heart, as ever.

Returning to her work, Sylvia wondered how two children – twins, at that – could be so very different.

SOME FEW MILES away, at the north end of Blackburn, a lone man stood by a window. Big in stature, small in courage, he stood, glass in hand, his face haggard from too many sleepless nights. From the way his head was drooped low into his neck, and the forward stoop of his shoulders, it was plain to see that he carried the weight of the world on his back.

As on every Christmas since he and his son had gone their separate ways, Mick's father was filled with thoughts of what might have been. 'Will you never forgive me, lad?' His quiet voice echoed through the cosy but plainly furnished room. 'Drinking and womanising, sullying your mam's memory, it's no wonder you threw me out. But oh, lad. If only you'd find it in your heart to let me into your life now, I'd never let you down again, I swear to God!'

No one answered, because there was no one there to hear him. Freda, his common-law wife, had gone out to the local to replenish their supply of drink.

Raising his glass to the wintry scene outside, he declared, 'Merry Christmas, son.' Gulping down the last remaining dregs of booze, he gave a small, cynical laugh. 'It's no use feeling sorry for yourself, Ernie Fellowes. If you've no life and no family, you've only yourself to blame.' It was a sorry truth and one which he bitterly regretted.

He was still standing there, shoulders hunched and eyes filled with tears of self-pity, when Freda came into the room. 'Huh! So there you are – I might have guessed.' Her sharp eyes found him out. 'Still hankering after that bloody son o' yours, are yer? Even after he threw yer out on the streets – not once but twice!' Her flaming red hair was full of pin-curlers with a net over, even though it was Christmas Day, and the look on her face said, 'I'm after trouble.'

Ernie saw how she was clinging onto the back of the chair, her small eyes glittering with too much Christmas booze. 'You're drunk!' he reproached. 'You're always drunk these days.'

'You don't say.' Laughing, she fell into the chair. 'You're right, I *am* drunk. An' if I feel the need, I'll be drunk again tomorrer, and the day after that.' Swallowing the last drop, she then flung the glass across the room. When it smashed on the wall only inches from his face, she laughed out loud. 'Get us another, will yer?'

He didn't answer. Instead, he looked away, his gaze and his thoughts going to the world outside. First he had lost his wife, and then, because he couldn't see straight, he had lost his son. A good son – a lad who was also suffering the loss of that good woman. Now it was too late. His life was here. With her, God help him.

'Hey! Did you hear me? I said get me another drink.'

He didn't turn round. Too often lately he had looked at her and been riddled with shame and disgust. 'Get it yourself,' he said quietly. 'And see if you can clean up this mess while you're at it.' Shuffling the broken glass at his feet, he limped slowly across the room, his face contorted with pain as he gingerly put one foot before the other.

'Still hurts, does it?' her taunting voice called after him. 'Serves you bleedin' right, you silly old bugger!'

When he closed the door behind him, he could still hear her ranting at him. 'What kind of coward are you, peering in windows, hoping to catch a glimpse of him? Instead of believing your lies, how you were only resting for a few minutes after some wall fell on you, them coppers should have locked you up where you belong! I dare say if it hadn't been so near to Christmas, they'd have took longer in quizzing you.'

'SHUT UP.' At the end of his tether, he could control himself no longer. 'FOR CHRISSAKE, WOMAN, SHUT UP!'

'And what would your precious son have thought if he'd known you were sneaking about like some old tom cat outside in the dark? That you weren't all there in the bleedin' head, that's what he'd think! And he'd be right an' all. Lord only knows why I let you persuade me to come here and live with you, paying half the rent an' all. But I'm here now, and I've as much right as you. So if anybody goes, it'll be *you*, not me. Have you got that, you gormless bugger?'

Her mocking laughter followed him up the stairs, made him feel more of a failure than he already did. She was right about one thing though. Going to the house in Buncer Lane was a damned stupid thing. Yet he had done a far worse thing when he let that scrag-end come here to live with him.

In spite of all that, Ernie knew he wasn't being fair. Freda was a good sort in many ways, and it wasn't her fault he was estranged from Mick. And no wonder she drank like a fish. It couldn't be much fun, living with a gloomy so-and-so like him.

Ernie gave a deep sigh.

He had made his bed and, for now at least, he must lie on it.

Chapter Five

ELLIE WAS RESTLESS.

She heard the downstairs clock striking ten, then came the sound of her mam as Sylvia went out of the back room and into the front room, and now again as she returned and closed the parlour door behind her.

Quietly now, so as not to wake Betsy beside her, Ellie got out of bed. Gasping when her bare feet alighted on the shockingly cold lino, she drew her nightie tighter about her. Going across the room, she softly drew the curtains all the way back, letting the lamplight in to create eerie, sneaking shadows on the walls and ceiling.

Pressing her nose against the window-pane, she watched the night-life down below. For a while she was intrigued by the courting couple in the doorway opposite. First they stood apart, holding hands and smiling up into each other's eyes, then they were locked in an embrace, growing more amorous by the minute, when suddenly the young man's hand slid down the girl's buttocks, causing her to step back and slap him hard across the face.

A few heated words were exchanged, and a moment later the door opened from within to show a fat woman with a bright, flowery turban over her curlers. Wagging a finger at the pair of them, she then grabbed the girl and yanked her inside, leaving the young man to wander desolately down the street. He glanced back once, thinking maybe his sweetheart might reappear, but he was disappointed.

Ellie recognised the girl as Marcia Walker. 'Poor Marcia,' she murmured. 'I'm glad *I* haven't got a bad-tempered mam like that.'

She smiled wistfully. 'I wonder if *I'll* ever have a sweetheart?' When her mam once told her she was pretty, Betsy said afterwards that she wasn't. 'You're a mess!' she claimed. Since then, Ellie believed no boy would ever want her. Turning her head, Ellie glanced at Betsy. Through the incoming light, she observed her sister's features, wondering how they could be twins and yet be so different. She had always thought Betsy was the pretty one, with her fine brown hair and strong hazel eyes.

Ellie loved her sister dearly. She could never hurt her, though there was no doubt Betsy could be cruel . . . like the day she teased Ellie about how thick and wild her hair was, and how she looked just like their grandad's scruffy old dog. Her spiteful taunts had hurt Ellie so much, she had taken the scissors from her mam's sewing box and cut great lumps off her hair, in an attempt to make it look more like Betsy's. When Betsy saw it, she laughed till she cried, but soon stopped when their mam gave them both a good telling-off. Afterwards she trimmed Ellie's hair into shape, so their dad would never know.

There had been many instances like that, when Betsy had a go at her and Ellie would cry. But that was a long time since, and Ellie didn't cry any more. Betsy's mean comments always hurt, but she had learned not to show it.

Returning her gaze to the window she was relieved to see

Marcia Walker running down the street, and the young man swinging round to greet her. She ran into his open arms and all was well.

Now, as she turned away, Ellie caught sight of someone lurking by their own front wall. Because the figure was in the shadows she couldn't quite see who it was. Then suddenly it was gone down some back alley, and the street was quiet again, save for a mangy old dog which cocked its leg up the lamp, sat a moment to have a good scratch, then trotted off through the patchy snow in the direction of Old Preston Road.

Mindful of the man who had been loitering earlier, Ellie stretched her neck and peered this way and that, but could see no one. She shrugged her shoulders. 'Some old drunk, I expect,' she muttered with a smile. 'Can't find his way home in the dark.'

Tiptoeing back to bed, Ellie quietly climbed in and drew the warm covers over her. One glance at Betsy told her the other girl was still sleeping. ''Night, God bless,' Ellie murmured, and was soon fast asleep herself.

Outside, the figure hid in the mouth of the alley. Aware that Ellie had been watching, it stayed until the coast was clear before venturing out again.

———◦———

S TARTLED OUT OF a deep sleep, Ellie sat bolt upright in bed. Something had woken her, and she didn't know what.

Betsy gave her a dig in the ribs. 'Keep still. You're making me cold!' Drawing the blankets round her, Betsy turned away; in less than a minute she was out to the world again. But not Ellie. She had heard something . . . voices maybe? The sound of a door opening? She wasn't sure. But it was something different from the usual. And it made her curious. Sitting back against the pillow, she listened.

Downstairs, Sylvia had been catching up on some ironing when the knock on the door disturbed her. 'Whoever can that be?' Both Jim and Larry had their own keys. 'It might be Dad,' she mused. 'Happen Jim's dropped him off with the old dog, and gone back to the pub himself.'

On the way up the passage, she suddenly remembered: 'O' course – they won't allow dogs in the pub, not since them two bull terriers got scrapping and bit the landlord's hand.'

When she opened the front door, she was surprised to see there was no one there. She peered into the darkness and even came out to look up and down the street. But there was no one to be seen. 'Pranksters!' she muttered. 'Little sods, I'll tan their arses if I catch hold of 'em – even if it is still Christmas Day!' Lately, there had been a spate of young 'uns running loose till all hours, banging on doors then racing away. Still, it must be around eleven o'clock by now – too late for kids to be out and about. Closing the door she made her way back to the parlour.

It was when she turned to close the parlour door that the stranger pounced. Clapping one hand over Sylvia's screams, he pinned her arms behind her back and pushed her hard against the wall. His face was pressed close to hers, his eyes glittering with excitement. 'Don't struggle.' His voice was soft, almost endearing in a sinister way. 'You'll only prolong it,' he whispered, 'and we don't want that, now do we?'

Eyes wide with terror, Sylvia looked up, silently pleading. All manner of questions raced through her frantic mind. Who was he? Why was he here? Dear God, the twins . . .

did he know they were upstairs? WHAT DID HE WANT FROM HER?

Seeming to read her mind, he leaned forward, whispering in her ear, taking pleasure in her terror, 'Somebody wants you *dead*.' Tenderly flicking her hair from her face he tutted, 'All I can say is, you must have been a real bad girl.'

Shocked to her roots, Sylvia could hardly take in what he was saying. Somebody wanted her dead? *Somebody wanted her dead!* The words echoed through her brain, spurring her into action. With an almighty effort she brought up her knee and aimed for his groin; when he reeled back in pain, she took her chance and made a dive for the door. All she could think of was her girls.

She had seized the door handle when the intruder caught hold of her by the hair and yanked her viciously back. 'You stupid bitch!' With the flat of his hand he hit her hard across the mouth, sending her slamming against the wall, then before she could recover her senses, he had her by the throat, squeezing the life out of her; and all she could think of was her children.

Upstairs, Ellie heard the commotion. Shaking Betsy by the shoulder, she whispered harshly, 'Quick! There's something going on . . . we'll have to go down. Betsy, wake up!' But her sister was dead to the world and could not be roused.

Afraid to go down, but even more afraid not to, Ellie got out of bed for the second time that night. She went silently down the stairs, her instinct telling her there was something not right. There was a moment of silence, then a crash, and muffled cries. She thought of the man who had been taken away by the police, and the other man who had been lurking about outside. And she knew her mam was in some kind of danger.

Pausing on the bottom step, she held tightly onto the banister; leaning forward, she prepared to sneak a peep into the parlour. The door was open and that in itself was odd. Always, after they'd gone to bed, their mam would close the parlour door, in case her pottering about woke them up, and besides, the draught from the front door blew down the passage and made the room cold.

With her heart thundering in her chest, Ellie looked into the parlour – and gasped in horror at what she saw. Her mam was lying over the back of the sofa and, bending over her, his hands round her throat, was a stranger.

Without thinking of the consequences, Ellie launched herself at him. 'YOU LEAVE MY MAM ALONE!' she screamed.

Startled, the man swung round. 'Jesus!' As he turned he loosened his grip on Sylvia, who slithered to the floor, half-senseless. Frantic that he would hurt Ellie, she dragged herself up by the fireplace, where she grabbed the smoothing iron and took a swing at him, but she was weak and her aim went wild.

Enraged, the intruder threw Ellie aside, then, bunching his fist, he smashed it into Sylvia's face, laughing when the force of his punch sent her crashing against the tree, which then swayed and threatened to fall over, but ended up slumped against the wall, like a drunken man against a lamp-post. Sylvia lost her footing and went down, at the same time striking her head on the fender. Through blurred vision, she saw her daughter making for their attacker. 'No, Ellie!' Summoning every ounce of her strength, she warned her off. 'Run! *Get away from here!*'

The terror in her mam's voice caused Ellie to stop. As she looked up at the stranger, he was smiling. 'She's done for, little girl,' he murmured. 'Now it's *your* turn.'

In two strides he had her by the arm, but Ellie was not

so easily overcome. Fighting like a tiger and slithering like an eel, she squirmed out of his grasp and wrenched the parlour door open. But he was right behind her. Positioning himself in such a way as to stop her from going out the front door, or back through the scullery, he left her no alternative but to make for the stairs.

Cursing, he thundered after her. 'I can't let you get away, you little vixen. Not now you've seen me!'

In the parlour, Sylvia struggled to recover her senses. Taking hold of the tree she tried to haul herself up, but it wouldn't hold her weight. As she went down, the tree came with her, the tip of its greenery tickling dangerously close to the fire's edge.

Upstairs, Ellie was screaming at her sister. 'Wake up, Betsy! Help me!' Pressing herself against the door, she turned the key, and still he came at it from the other side, throwing his considerable weight against it, intent on breaking into the room and killing her.

'What's going on?' There was more anger in Betsy's sleepy voice than curiosity. She never liked being woken up, not at any time, nor for any reason.

'There's a stranger in the house,' Ellie sobbed, 'and he's hurt our mam. We have to get out – we have to get help.'

'What d'you mean, he's hurt our mam?' When suddenly there came a creaking sound from the door, as though something was wrenching it off its hinges, Betsy leaped out of bed and cowered in the corner, her face a picture of terror. 'Don't let him in, Ellie,' she whimpered. 'Please don't let him in.'

Downstairs, Sylvia lay unconscious, unable to help anyone, least of all herself. She didn't know of her children's cries, nor of the intruder's determination to leave no one alive in this house.

Mercifully, she was beyond all that.

Only an arm's length away from where she lay, the tree had taken hold of the flames, which in turn were licking at the mantel-cover, its long green tassels already dancing in the intense heat.

Desperate to get help for her mam, Ellie rang out instructions to Betsy. 'I can't do it on my own. I need you to help me.'

'Leave me alone!' Shivering with fear, Betsy remained in the corner and would not be persuaded out of it.

'Open this door!' the man shouted. When there came no answer, he put his shoulder to the wood and, using all his formidable strength, began to slowly inch the hinges apart.

From the other side, Ellie pushed frantically against the door with all her skinny might. 'Go away!' she screamed. 'Our dad will be home any minute. He'll kill you for what you did to our mam!' Her voice breaking with emotion, she pleaded with Betsy. 'Go out the window,' she said. 'Climb down the roof and get help. Go on, Betsy! It's the only way!'

Betsy shook her head. 'I can't do it, I'm too afraid!' Hysterical, she began screaming, 'I can't do it, Ellie, I can't!'

Her sister despaired. 'Then I'll have to go. Come here, quick! Push against this door as hard as you can. Don't listen to anything he says, and I'll be as quick as I can.'

Betsy's answer was to shake her head and crouch down even lower. 'I can't,' she wept. 'Don't make me, Ellie. Please don't make me.' Her whole body shook uncontrollably.

Ellie had to make a split decision. Should she leave the door unprotected and climb out of the window, or should she stay with her twin, and do all she could to stop the man from getting in? She looked at Betsy, afraid and whimpering, and knew she could not leave her.

Suddenly, she felt the door giving way; one of the hinges

had snapped off and it was only a matter of time now before he had them both at his mercy. 'I won't hurt you,' he lied. 'You might as well open the door, there's a good girl.' Beneath his continued onslaught, the door began to split and break. *Any minute now, and he would be in the room with them.*

———⊱•⊰———

S OME DISTANCE DOWN the street, the three men made their way home. Filled with merriment and a few pints into the bargain, Jim and Larry meandered along, arm in arm, their voices raised in song.

Bemused, Bertie Hill straggled behind, talking to his old dog, and laughing at their antics. 'They're a daft pair o' buggers an' no mistake,' he chuckled. All the same, it was good to see how close were father and son.

Breathless, Jim gave up the singing, and made Larry do the same. 'We'd best not wake up the whole street,' he laughed. 'We don't want Maggie Arkwright emptying her pisspot on us heads, do we now, eh?' And, by the way he stopped mid-song, neither did Larry.

'Did *you* see where Mick went?' Larry had lost sight of his mate some time during the evening. When he went to look for him on leaving, there was neither hide nor hair of him to be found.

'If I recall, he went off with that dark-haired lass – a nice bit o' stuff she were an' all.' Jim beamed, proud of his own 'bit o' stuff' waiting for him at home. 'Mind you, she ain't half the cracker yer mam were when I first clapped eyes on her. By! She had every bloke in the street after her.'

'So what made her choose an ugly bugger like you?' Larry asked cheekily.

They were still laughing fit to bust when the cry went up from Bertie. 'Jesus Mary and Joseph, the house is afire. Look! THE HOUSE IS AFIRE!'

Startled, the two men looked up and were shocked to their souls. 'God Almighty!' Already at the run, Jim screamed out to his son, who had gone like the wind before him, 'For God's sake, lad, GET THEM OUT OF THERE!'

Even as they ran down the street, the flames had burst through the windows, shattering glass in their wake and bringing the street alive. Somebody had gone to telephone for the fire engine, while others ran in and out of their houses with buckets of water and ladders, but all to no avail. The flames spat out at them, driving them back, making them fear for their own lives. But not the two men. Their loved ones were inside that inferno and, if it was humanly possible, they would get them out.

The old man would have gone in after them, but strong arms held him back. 'Not you, Grandad,' they said, and so he remained outside and prayed. His whole life was inside that raging hell. His whole life, and his past with it.

The draught had blown the parlour door wide open. 'Upstairs, lad – quick as you can.' Finding it hard to breathe in the dense smoke, Jim covered his face with his arms and plunged into the back parlour. 'SYLVIA!' His voice reached into every corner. 'Are you in here, lass?' Coughing and choking, he pushed forward.

While Larry fought his way upstairs, he caught a glimpse of someone near the landing window – a fleeting figure through the brightness of the flames. 'MAM?' But it wasn't his mam, and in the winking of an eye the figure was gone.

In the back bedroom he found the girls.

Crazed with terror, Betsy was hiding under the bed. On

hearing Larry call her name, she scrambled out and threw herself into his arms. 'Ellie's dead!' she screamed. 'He would have killed me too, only I wouldn't come out from under the bed and he couldn't get me. Ellie fought him. I told her not to, but she wouldn't stop. He killed her. The man killed her!'

'Ssh. It's all right. I'm here now. It's all right.' Thinking she was gabbling out of fear, Larry kept her safe while he looked for Ellie.

He found his other sister lying face down by the wardrobe. She wasn't dead as Betsy had claimed, because when he picked her up, she soon came to her senses. 'Mam's downstairs,' she croaked. Dazed and hurt, she had only one thought. 'We've got to help her.'

'Here!' Ripping apart the bedsheet, Larry gave them each a thick, folded piece. 'Keep this across your mouth.' By now they were all three heaving and choking on the acrid smoke. 'Hold hands and stay right beside me,' he warned. The roof could go at any minute, and he didn't want them inside when that happened.

The flames had followed him up the stairway. There was no escape that way. 'Keep close!' Inching his way through the horror, he led the girls towards the front window. With every step, he prayed to God they would be saved.

Outside, the crowd prayed too. 'They'll never get out of there alive!' someone said for them all. A sad comment but realistic because now, the flames had eaten into the roof and the whole house was engulfed. 'What's taking the fire engine so long?' one angry voice asked.

'Another few minutes and it'll be too late for fire engines!' said another and, knowing it was true, Bertie Hill fell to his arthritic old knees and wept.

Suddenly a cry went up. 'Look! The upstairs window! It's Larry. He's got the lasses!'

None of their ladders would reach, and there was nothing they could do, except to call up, 'Let the girls go, lad, we'll not let them fall. Trust us. For God's sake, lad, let them go!'

Knowing he could do no other, Larry helped the girls to climb out, first Betsy, because she was nearest, then Ellie. He held them by the arms, easing them down the wall as far as he could, before being forced to let them drop.

The men below were as good as they said, and the girls were caught clean, though Betsy screamed hysterically for a full minute after they had her safe.

'Now you!' they called up, and the flames were already licking at his back. 'Jump, Larry! Come on, lad . . . JUMP!'

Larry searched the faces below, but couldn't see the two he most wanted to see. All he could do was pray that his mam and dad had found a way out.

Crawling out to the window-sill, he sat on the edge; below him he could see the men with arms outstretched, watching his every move. 'Careful, Larry, lad,' he told himself, and twisting round, he held on to the sill, hung motionless in the scorching air for a moment, and then let himself go.

No one could say, later, just how or when it happened. One minute they were looking upward, ready to catch him, and the next minute it was mayhem as a section of the roof slipped away and they ran for their lives. Dislodged by the falling debris, Larry hit the ground with a dull, heart-wrenching thud, as behind him the whole house began to cave in.

In that same moment, a moment already too late for some, two fire engines and an ambulance arrived and everyone was cleared back. 'Keep away,' they were told. 'You've done all you can.'

But it was not enough.

Ellie saw how twisted and hurt Larry was, and how he cried with pain when they lifted him into the ambulance. She heard Betsy screaming for her mam and dad, and saw her grandad demented, pacing the street and muttering, 'They're all gone . . . all gone.'

When they brought her parents out and laid them side by side on the pavement, she would have gone to them, but they wouldn't let her. 'Come away,' they said. 'Come away, child.' So she held Betsy, who had seen and was uncontrollable.

On that night, with her whole world falling apart before her eyes, she clung to her sister, and sobbed as she had never sobbed before. After all, like Betsy, she was just a frightened child.

Chapter Six

T HE GRUBBY BACK street ran alongside the canal. There was a cotton mill and a cloth factory, and a small wooden hut used by a night-watchman whose lot in life was to keep a wary eye out for any roaming thief.

Some way down towards the bridge was a large, dilapidated warehouse – a place that ran with rats and stank of damp where all manner of goods were stored, to be sold later on Blackburn market. Above the warehouse was a room, and in that room resided a man fallen on hard times and eager to make his living by any means available.

In the late hours of Christmas Day 1932, the light was still shining in this upper room. Through the grimy window could be seen the figure of a man as he paced feverishly back and forth. Every now and then he would pause to peer through the window, watching for someone, waiting for his reward for having carried out his terrible task.

From the distance the Town Hall clock struck once, then twice, and now it was nearing three and still he watched, his pacing growing more frantic, his peering out the window more frequent.

'Come on! Come on!' For the umpteenth time he stared

out into the night, his eager eyes roving the street, his temper rising when he could see no one approaching. 'Where the hell are you?'

With his fist he rubbed a circle of film from the window-pane, bending his body to see out yet again. 'I did what you asked and more,' he grumbled. 'I want paying, or I swear to God I'll do for *you* an' all!'

Death was still on him. He had use for it yet.

Shivering, he turned to the fireplace. In this tiny godforsaken room he didn't have far to reach any part of it. No bigger than a large shoe-box, it held a narrow bed, a tattered sofa and a sideboard. There was a sink of sorts in the corner and a gas-ring for boiling a kettle on. Hanging at the window was a pair of faded curtains; too short by far, they had long ago seen their best. The lavvy was downstairs, at the far end of the yard beyond the warehouse.

Muttering and moaning, the man counted the knobs of coal onto the fire. 'Did the job, just like you asked, and nearly finished meself into the bargain. I want paying! I should get a bonus for what I've been through!' Enraged, he flung the last knob of coal with such force that the sparks flew out in all directions. When one landed on the scabby rug he quickly stamped it out, sniggering when he thought of the spectacular fire he had caused down Buncer Lane.

Now, when the door was flung open, he almost leaped out of his skin. 'Bloody hell, man! Did you never learn to knock?' White-faced and breathless, he confronted his visitor. 'It's done,' he announced, and his pride was visible to see. 'From what I can make out, the house is gone an' all.' He shrugged. 'It went a bit wrong, but the result was the same. More than what you wanted, I'd say.'

The visitor kept his back to the door, his voice harsh as

he reprimanded the other man. 'I said the *woman*, that was all. "Do it quick and keep your mouth shut," that's what I said. I didn't tell you to burn the bloody house down.'

'That was an accident, nowt to do wi' me! Besides, if I hadn't got out that window, I might have been burned to death. As it is, I took a few cuts and bruises climbing out of the landing window . . . twisted my damned ankle when I dropped into the yard.' Hobbling forward a few steps to make his point, he leered up at his visitor. 'I reckon I've earned a bonus, don't you?'

'Don't push it!' Producing a handful of money from his coat pocket, the man dropped it onto the dresser. 'That's all you're getting – it's what we agreed. And you can thank your lucky stars I'm paying you at all!'

Grabbing up the money, the murderer counted it greedily, checking that he hadn't been cheated.

'And keep well away from me,' the other man warned him. 'I'm not involved. I know nothing about any of it. And he who says otherwise might find his throat cut one fine day. Do you understand what I'm saying?'

Thrusting the money into his back pocket, the man nodded, but he wasn't afraid. Fear had no meaning for someone of his sort. 'You know where I am if you ever want another job doing,' he grunted.

'Just remember what I said.' With that the visitor departed, desperate to fill his lungs with clean cold air after breathing in the foul atmosphere of that awful place.

Behind him the man counted his money time and again. Satisfied it was all there, he took one half-sovereign from the pile; the others he wrapped in an old piece of rag, which he then tightly rolled into a brown paper bag. This he hid inside a slit under the mattress.

Chuckling to himself all the while, he whipped off his shirt to expose a thin, bony chest and a grimy tidemark round his neck. 'I reckon I've earned myself a woman.' Licking his lips, he imagined himself lying alongside some fat, juicy flesh. 'Whoo!' Trembling with delight, he made for the sink in the corner. 'I ain't had a shag in ages!'

Outside, the visitor waited a few minutes, shivering a little in the cold, crisp air. When he felt it was time enough, he went back inside. Going silently up the stairs, he softly turned the door handle, then paused a minute waiting for the door to be snatched open from the other side, or maybe for a voice to call out and ask who was there. Instead, all was quiet, and he knew the moment was right.

He eased the door open. A quick glance inside told him he would have no trouble. His man was at the sink, singing while he lathered his face and neck, ready for a shave. His back was to the door, and there was no mirror in front of him with which to see anyone creeping up.

On tiptoes, the intruder crossed the room, took a pillow from the bed and, reaching over the other man's bent head, pressed it hard to his face. Forcing him close to the sink, he was able to minimise the inevitable struggle that followed.

It took only minutes.

Afterwards, the intruder coolly replaced the pillow on the bed. He searched the man's pockets but found only one coin there. He then looked in every cupboard and every other likely hiding-place. He raised the mattress but there was nothing there. He even took up one or two floorboards, but to no avail. The money seemed to have vanished into thin air.

He stood still for a moment, his eyes roving the room. 'It's got to be here somewhere.' Again he raised the mattress, but this time he saw the narrow slit, cunningly hidden by a seam of stitching. The brown paper was inside and, on drawing it out, he saw how the money had been tightly rolled into it, so as not to chink.

He smiled down at the still figure on the floor. 'You weren't so cunning after all, were you?' When the wide open eyes stared back at him, he quickly turned away. Emptying the money into his palm, he then dropped it into his coat pocket. The cloth and brown paper bag he let lie where they had fallen. Next he took a few minutes to leave the place how he had found it, making doubly sure that there was nothing there to link him with this unfortunate fellow.

Nauseated by the stench on his hands, he washed them at the sink and wiped them on his handkerchief. He then left, closing the door behind him. Quickening his footsteps he hurried to the main road, and was lucky to hail a cab. 'Lytham Saint Anne's,' he instructed the driver, 'Summerfield House, West Gardens. As fast as you can.'

He had done a good night's work and silently congratulated himself. The Bolton woman was out of the way for good, and all was well.

There was nothing to stand in his way now.

Nothing and no one! Not even his own mother.

>—⊙—<

H AVING FINISHED HIS night-shift, the old watchman locked up the hut and ambled down the street. 'That's a funny thing an' no mistake,' he muttered. 'I ain't never seen a gent down this alley afore. Looking for a cheap bit o' skirt, I shouldn't wonder.'

As he went on his way his jolly laughter echoed down the alley. 'Wouldn't mind a bit o' skirt meself — but what self-respecting woman would want a shrivelled up old fella like me, eh?' He used to worry about his failing manhood, but not any more. Because these days, he was happier with a nice mug o' tea and his old baccy pipe. They didn't give a man half so much trouble!

Chapter Seven

I<small>T WAS A</small> week since the fire.

From every corner of the land, there was much talk and speculation, but no real answers as to what exactly had gone on in that house, or why. Rumour had it that a stranger had attacked the family; some claimed it must have been the same man who was loitering round the back yards some time before.

There was a fight, they said, when Sylvia Bolton fought for her life against the intruder. Apparently the Christmas tree had toppled over to start the fire, but more than that, nobody knew for sure.

The consequences however, were dreadful.

Sylvia and Jim, two good people, had perished in the fire. Grandad Bertie had suffered a breakdown and was in a nursing home. Larry was laid up in the Infirmary, both his legs broken, and his back so badly injured it was feared he might never walk again. The house in Buncer Lane was boarded up as it was now structurally unsafe and would eventually have to be demolished.

Sadly, because there were no close relatives to offer them a home, the two girls, Ellie and her sister Betsy, had been taken into foster-care.

Today, on the first day of January, 1933, their mam and dad would be laid to their rest.

———————

As on every other night since the tragedy, Ellie had not slept. Instead she had lain awake, the haunting questions careering through her mind and breaking her heart. Why did it happen? What would she and Betsy do now, without their mam and dad, and what about Larry? And Grandad Bertie?

And who was the stranger who had brought such devastation into their happy home?

Deep in thought, Ellie was not aware that Betsy had climbed into her bed. It was only when a cold hand touched her shoulder, that she was jolted back into the present. 'Ellie?' Still in shock, Betsy was like an infant, afraid of everything and everyone except her twin sister. Ellie was her rock, the only person to whom she could open her heart.

Drawing her close, Ellie kissed her on the forehead. 'What is it?' she asked gently. 'Did you have another nightmare?' Not a night had gone by when Betsy didn't wake up in a sweat, screaming and thrashing out, as if fighting off an attacker.

Moving away, Betsy sat on the edge of the bed. 'I don't want to go,' she whimpered. 'Don't make me go.'

Clambering out of bed, Ellie came to sit beside her. 'I won't make you do anything you don't want to do,' she said tenderly. 'But where is it you don't want to go?'

'To the church,' she whispered.

Ellie was shocked. 'Are you saying you don't want to go to the funeral?'

Nodding, Betsy couldn't bring herself to look into Ellie's face. She couldn't bear to witness the pain in her eyes. She knew her twin was suffering badly. She had heard her crying in her sleep; she had seen how sometimes, she would go to the window when she thought no one was watching, and there Ellie would close her eyes and visibly tremble at the memories that tortured them both.

If Betsy had been able to console her sister, she would have, but it was not in her nature. And so Ellie silently suffered, while Betsy leaned on her, seeking solace, yet unable to return it.

'I don't want to see Mam and Dad in a coffin.' Her voice broke and she could say no more. Instead she bowed her head into the palms of her two hands and wept.

A wise head on young shoulders, Ellie let her weep. She wrapped her loving arms round her sister and held her close until the tears subsided. 'It would help you to go to church,' she murmured. 'You need to say your goodbyes.' Swallowing hard she said huskily, 'We *both* need to say our goodbyes, or we might regret it later. That's what Peggy said, and I believe she's right.'

Betsy shook her head. That was another thing. Peggy Walters was their foster-mother, and at present they were living with her and her husband Ted. 'I don't want to stay here. I want to go home.'

'We can't go home. You know that.'

'Grandad Bertie will look after us.'

Ellie squeezed her hand affectionately. 'You're forgetting. Just now, poor Grandad can't even look after himself. And our Larry is in hospital in a bad way.'

'Ellie?'

'Yes?'

'That man . . . it was all his fault, wasn't it?'

'Yes.'

'Why did he come to our house?'

97

'I don't know.'

'Did he mean to kill us all?'

'I don't know, Betsy.'

'Will the police catch him?'

'They *have* to!' Whenever she thought of him, Ellie wanted to hurt him, like he had hurt all her family. 'We've told them all we know,' she said. 'What he looks like and everything. It's up to them now.'

'What if they don't catch him?' Betsy's voice was becoming hysterical. 'What if he comes after us again?'

Ellie stiffened. 'Let him. I wish he would.' Clenching her fists she saw his face in her mind as clear as day. 'If he came after me, I'd *kill* him!'

Betsy was shocked rigid. In all her life she had never known her sister to be violent. 'Don't say that, Ellie. You're frightening me.'

Regretting that she had let her deeper emotions show, the other girl regained her composure. 'I didn't mean to frighten you,' she said contritely. 'I was just thinking out loud.'

'You didn't mean what you said, did you?'

'I think you'd best get back in bed now, love, or you'll be so tired later on.'

'You *didn't* mean it, did you, Ellie?'

'Ssh. Get back to sleep. We've got a hard day ahead.' As for her need to kill that man, yes, she *had* meant every word. He had taken her parents, and crippled her grandfather and brother. She wanted to hurt him in the same way. If ever she got the chance, she would take it, right or wrong, and may God forgive her.

Betsy was watching and saw the hatred in Ellie's face. 'You *did* mean it!' she cried. 'If you say it again, I'll tell our Larry.'

'Listen, Betsy. You mustn't talk about that man to our Larry, nor to Grandad Bertie. We mustn't do *anything* to upset either of them.'

A pause, then: 'Will Larry get better?'

'I pray every night that he will. Grandad too.'

'Will we have to stay here until they get better?'

'Would it be so bad?'

'Yes.'

'But Mr and Mrs Walters are nice people. We should be glad we weren't put with somebody who was unkind to us.'

'I don't like being here.'

Ellie sighed. Sometimes Betsy was so difficult. 'Nobody could look after us better than they do,' she answered. 'We're in a nice house, Stephen Street is a lovely little street, and people are being really kind.'

'It's not as nice as Buncer Lane, and the house isn't as big, and this room is too cramped. I don't like it, Ellie. I don't want to stay here!'

'We'll have to stay here.'

'I'll run away.'

'If you do, they'll only fetch you back and then you might be put into the council home. You wouldn't like that, Betsy.'

'I might!'

'You should remember what Larry told us. He said we were lucky to have found Mr and Mrs Walters, and that they were good to have us. If we went into a council home we'd have to share a big room with lots of other girls, and it wouldn't be like a proper family. This nice couple treat us like their own.'

'They're old!' Betsy wept.

'No, they're not, or they wouldn't be allowed to look after us.'

'Well, they *look* old!'

Sighing, Ellie took her arm away. 'Don't be unkind, Betsy.'

Walking across to the window, Ellie gazed unseeing at the morning sky. In her mind's eye she could picture her mam and dad in the scullery; her mam was up to her armpits in soapy water, laughing at something Dad had said. Then he tickled her under the arms and she flicked the soapy water at him. The memory brought a sad smile.

For a time she let the pictures play in her mind, and when it became too painful she turned away, the tears rolling down her face, and her heart aching. 'We'd best get back to bed now, Betsy,' she began. 'Peggy will call us when it's time to get up.' When she turned, it was to see how Betsy had fallen asleep, not in her own bed, but in Ellie's.

Gently, her sister drew the clothes over her. 'We'll be all right,' she murmured. 'You'll see.'

Going to the other narrow bed, she climbed in and covered herself over. She was so tired. But, unlike Betsy, she found that sleep did not come easy tonight.

———⟞⟐⟝———

WHEN PEGGY PEEPED in some two hours later, both girls were fast asleep. A plump little soul, with tiny face and feet the same, she had a mess of brown hair that stuck out like string on a mop, and a face that resembled that of a squashed-up teddy bear. But she had a heart of gold and a pantry always filled with goodies with which to delight her visitors.

Now, as she stood at the foot of the two beds, her heart went out to these lost orphans. 'Bless their little hearts, I thought I heard them talking in the early hours. Couldn't sleep, I expect, and who could blame them?'

Having had a sheltered upbringing with parents who lived until she was well into her forties, Peggy Walters couldn't begin to imagine what Betsy and Ellie must have been through. 'I'll let them sleep for another half hour,' she decided. 'There's time enough before we need to set off.'

She was about to leave, when Ellie stirred. 'I'm sorry,' she apologised, her voice thick with sleep. 'Is it time to get up?'

'It's all right, lass,' the little woman assured her. 'You go back to sleep. I'll call you in a while.'

'No, Peggy, thank you all the same.' Ellie was already out of bed. 'But if it's all right with you, I think we should leave Betsy for now. She's been really upset.'

'Very well, dear. You get washed and dressed. By the time you come down, I'll have your breakfast on the table.' And off she went, like a mother hen minding her chicks.

Deeply moved by the woman's kindness, Ellie lingered a moment. What Peggy had said just now was what her mam used to say whenever she and Betsy overslept. 'Get washed and dressed, and I'll have your breakfast on the table by the time you're ready.' She could almost hear Sylvia saying it.

When the tears threatened, she took another long look at Betsy who was sleeping peacefully. 'Get hold of yourself, Ellie Bolton,' she told herself firmly. 'Betsy needs you to stay strong.' But it was hard. So very hard.

Going into the bathroom, Ellie thought she had never seen such luxury. In Buncer Lane, they'd had to wash at the sink in the scullery, but here was a bath in the corner, a toilet under the window and a basin against the side wall; all of it stark white and sparkling clean.

Peggy had told her that, before too long, every house in

Blackburn would have a bathroom and inside toilet. Recalling how Sylvia had nagged at Jim to get a bathroom put in, Ellie believed it was so. All the same, seeing it for herself was a real surprise.

Betsy, however, had not been impressed. 'I still don't like it here,' she had declared, and nothing Ellie said would change her mind.

While Ellie was washing upstairs, Peggy made herself and her husband Ted a cup of tea. 'I want to ask you something,' she said. Sitting before him at the table, she crossed her arms and looked at her husband with a gravity of expression he had not seen in many an age.

'Best get it off your chest, my dear.' Ted Walters was a good man, content with his lot. Long and skinny, with a balding head and bright blue eyes, he had the exact opposite appearance of his wife. In fact, when they were younger, people used to call them 'the long and short of it all'.

Taking a deep, noisy breath, his wife burst out, 'It's them poor lasses upstairs.'

'Go on.' Peering at her from beneath dark, hairy eyebrows, Ted urged, 'Say what's on your mind, then we can get on and enjoy our tea.'

'Well, I . . . I mean . . . I think . . .' She stuttered and sighed and started again. 'I think we should ask to keep them with us longterm. I don't just want them here for a month or two, love, like the others. I'd like them to stay until they're grown and can spread their wings. It'll give them that measure o' stability. What d'you say?'

He stared at her for what seemed an age. 'So we'd have 'em with us for several years . . . three at least?'

'That's right, Ted.' Having got over the first hurdle, Peggy gained a degree of courage. 'They're two lovely girls. They've lost their mam and dad; their grandad has gone out of his mind from the shock of losing half his family, and their only brother lies in the Infirmary, nearly every bone in his body broken in the fall. The lasses don't seem to have much of a future. We could give them security, right here with us, if only you'll say yes.' Allowing that to sink in, she went on, 'We've always wanted a family, Ted, but the childer never came along. Why don't we ask the authorities if we can keep the twins? We're in a position to give them a good home, a new start after what they've been through. It's the least we can do.'

When deep in thought, Ted Walters had a habit of pushing out his thin lips and working them backwards and forwards, as though chewing. To his wife it was a sign that he was at least considering her suggestion. 'Can we, Ted?' she asked eagerly. 'Can we?'

'We'll see.' And that was all he was prepared to say, except, 'We have a funeral to attend in a short time, m'dear. Don't you think we should pay mind to that before we go making other plans?'

'Yes, you're right.' She became flustered. 'But don't forget what I said.'

He smiled. 'As if you'd allow me to.'

By half-past eleven, they were ready to leave. Neither Betsy nor Ellie could do more than nibble at their fried breakfast. 'I'm sorry, Peggy.' Ellie spoke for them both. 'It's a lovely breakfast, but we're just not hungry.'

'Not to worry yourselves.' Considering what lay ahead of them, the little woman was not surprised they had no appetite. 'Happen you'll have something later.'

Betsy made no comment. She was happy to let Ellie speak for her.

A knock on the front door told them the woman from the

authorities had arrived. 'I'll get it.' Ted went smartly down the passage, a moment later reappearing with a prim little woman of pretty features and sympathetic expression. She spoke to Ellie and Betsy with kindness. 'Are you all right?' As a mother herself, Mrs Potton felt the urge to hug them, but the uniform of authority held her back.

'Right then, it's time we were off.' Peggy had on her new belted brown coat and her best brown hat – the one with the little feather that hung over her face as if it had just dropped from a flying duck. 'Are you sure you've got everything?' She looked from Betsy to Ellie. 'Because once we get in the cab, it'll be too late to come back.'

'Thank you, we've got all we need.' Betsy carried the flowers for Larry. Ellie had the two smaller bouquets for the church; the wreaths were already there. 'Have you got Grandad's chocolates?' Ellie asked the little woman.

'In my bag, quite safe.' Peggy urged them to hurry. 'It's time to go now.'

In his dark suit and bowler hat, Mr Walters looked splendid. 'If it's all right with you,' he told Mrs Potton, 'when we get to the church, I'd like the girls to walk between us.' Like his wife, he knew it must be a shocking thing for these two innocent lasses.

He wouldn't tell his wife until he had made up his mind properly, but already he was beginning to think of the girls as family, especially Ellie. He had taken a real liking to her. The other one was a selfish little devil, all take and no give but then, in view of what had happened, they must make allowances.

The journey to St Peter's was not a long one, but to Ellie it seemed to take a lifetime. Even now, she could not believe where they were going, or the reason for it. Inside she was shaking, and though she would keep them in for Betsy's sake, the tears were never far away.

Betsy sat beside her, stiff and still, except for her hands which were trembling. Ellie reached out to hold her, but Betsy shook her off. 'No!' That was all she said, but her rejection cut Ellie to the core.

On arrival at the church, Ellie arranged with the driver to leave Larry's flowers on the seat until they returned. 'That's no problem at all,' he said, and took them gently from Betsy.

Handing her sister one of the smaller bouquets, Ellie told her quietly, 'You're not to worry. Just follow me when we get inside.' They had already been instructed what to do, first by Mrs Potton and then by Peggy Walters – though each time Betsy chose not to listen.

Afterwards, they walked up the path, just as Ted had requested: he and his little wife on the outside and the girls between them. Mrs Potton walked ahead.

The path was lined with people from all over Blackburn town, all weeping, all murmuring their endearments as the girls went by. 'God bless you,' they said. 'You've a lot o' friends, should you ever need them.'

Her dark blue eyes bright with tears, Ellie acknowledged their blessing with the twitch of a smile and the slightest nod of the head. Betsy, however, looked straight ahead, her grief already giving way to crippling bitterness. She didn't want to look at any of them. They had no business being alive, not when her mam and dad were lying in that church!

Mick was waiting in the doorway. 'Are you all right?' he asked softly, kissing them one after the other. He had wanted to escort them all the way here, but the authorities in their wisdom had decided otherwise.

As they entered the church, the people from outside followed them in, until the place was full to overflowing.

On a gentle prompting from Mrs Potton, Ellie walked to where her mam and dad lay, surrounded by winter flowers at the foot of the altar. With immense tenderness, she laid her bouquet on her mam's coffin; Betsy followed to lay hers on their dad's. Heads bowed, they made their way back.

In that beautiful church, Ellie was aware of nothing, except the two narrow boxes lying at the foot of the altar. All around her, people were singing and praying, and she could do neither. The pain of losing her parents was excruciating; it would never go away. She felt lost and alone. Starting out on a journey and not knowing where it might end, she would have to do it all, without her mother to guide her, or her father to lift her spirit.

Standing strong, she kept the tears back as long as she could. Then slowly, when emotion began to overwhelm her, her face slowly crumpled and her lips trembled uncontrollably. In a minute, there was no holding back the awful pain inside.

The sobs came quietly at first, smothered and controlled. Then they were echoing round the church, touching every soul there, until Mick took her in his arms and held her tight. 'It's all right, lass,' he murmured. 'You've every right to cry.' And, though he had vowed not to, he cried with her. He had lost two good friends; one of them being the kindest person he had ever known. His best mate was crippled, maybe for life. It was a terrible thing.

Betsy stood beside them. She had done her crying. Seeing her mam and dad lying there had made her realise they were gone for ever. They could not help her any more. From now on, she would have to lean on her sister. Ellie was good. Ellie would look after her, she knew.

When the service was over, they all gathered in the churchyard, to pray and say their last goodbyes at the double grave. Afterwards, earth was thrown on top of both coffins, and when everyone had gone, Ellie stayed to say her piece. *'I won't always be a child,'* she told her parents. *'One day I'll be old enough to make my own way. I'll find out who the man was, and I'll make him pay for what he did.'* The promise was given in a calm, quiet voice; and etched on her soul like it was branded in hot iron.

Falling to her knees, she leaned into the ground where they lay, her fingers reaching out to them, and her voice breaking. 'I love you both so much. I'll *always* love you, for as long as I live.' With Betsy watching from a distance, she cried for a while until her heart was calm and she could face the others. When she walked away, she did not look back. It would have been too much.

Peggy greeted the young girl with open arms. 'You'll want to visit your grandad now.'

They bade goodbye to Mrs Potton. 'I can come with you if you'd rather,' she offered, but Ellie refused.

'It's best if me and Betsy go in alone,' she said. 'He's very poorly, and he's easily frightened.'

When they arrived at their grandad's house in Accrington, where Bertie was recuperating after his stay in the nursing home, Ellie and Betsy were taken to the door. The kindly neighbour answered and they went inside, while the foster-parents returned to the cab. 'Take your time,' they said. 'We'll be right outside.'

A portly soul with silver-white hair and a permanent smile, Widow Partridge had been Bertie Hill's neighbour for nigh on twenty years. Even before the tragedy, she had often cooked for him. They sometimes ate together in his house, and sometimes in hers. They talked about any-thing and everything, and laughed at the same silly things; occasionally they would go down the street for a pint at the local. They were good friends, nothing more – though even now, when he was ill and needed a nurse rather than a wife, Tilly Partridge would have been the happiest soul on God's earth if Bertie had asked her to be his partner in marriage.

'It's grand to see you both,' she told the girls. She had known them a long time. Tears hovered in her eyes but wisely she thrust them away. 'Come in and let your grandad know you're here. He'll be that glad to see the pair of youse, so he will.'

Leading them down the passage to the parlour, she chatted all the way. 'He's nicely tucked up by the fire, and I've just made him a bowl of his favourite soup.'

Ellie could hardly believe her eyes when she went in. In the short time since she had last seen him, on Christmas Day, Grandad Bertie was older by twenty years or more. His hair had turned snow-white, and even seemed to have thinned on top. He had lost a deal of weight, the consequence of which was a sagging jaw and baggy jowls. Gone was the cheeky grin and chubby cheeks, and that look of devil-may-care that so endeared him to her.

The old man didn't hear them come in. These days he was aware of very little. Instead, he sat very still, with his hands wrapped round the tray on his lap. The bowl of soup was untouched; the bread broken but not tasted.

'Sometimes he escapes to a little world of his own,' Tilly informed them. 'The doctors have said he'll recover, but it could take months yet, and o' course he ain't as young as he once was.' Going over to her old friend, she touched him on the shoulder, 'Bertie, here's your lovely granddaughters come to see you.'

Spying the chocolates in Betsy's hands, she teased, 'They've brought you chocolates, but I'm not sure if I can let you have them. You haven't even touched your soup, you bad lad.'

Taking the tray from him, she told the girls, 'Sit in that sofa opposite – he'll see you there. Talk to him.' She paused. 'Although happen you shouldn't tell him about the church an' all. Not unless he asks.' Seeing Betsy's scowling face, she addressed her nervously. 'Is that all right, lass? Am I speaking out of turn?'

When Betsy turned away, it was Ellie who answered. 'We understand,' she said. 'And you're right. It might be as well if we don't say anything about it.'

'I'm so sorry, lass. I don't know what to say.' Taking out her hankie, she blew her nose.

Ellie told her she didn't have to say anything at all, that she was a good friend. 'You're so kind to be taking care of our grandad.'

'Well, they wouldn't keep him in the Infirmary once he began to show signs of some improvement. They don't let you occupy a bed when there's some other poor soul waiting for it. But I'm happy to look after him.' Her smile was so pretty. 'I'll allus be here for Bertie,' she said proudly. 'He's all I've got.'

Taking the tray into the scullery, she carried on talking. 'The nurse calls in every morning to wash and dress him. He has his medicine and a check-up. Then me and him have our breakfast together, right here in this little parlour. I allus have a cheery fire on. O' course, I need to make sure there's a guard round it in case he slips or some such thing. At night, the nurse comes back and washes him – gets him ready for his bed an' all that.'

Returning, she put a tender hand on Bertie's shoulder. 'Between me and the nurse, he's well looked after. And, I have to say, he seems to be getting a little better every day.' Her face beamed with pleasure. 'It's no hardship looking after your grandad, not at all. I'd have to do it if we were wed, but o' course we're not, and that's a shame.'

Having said her piece, she offered to fetch them each a glass of sarsaparilla. When it was accepted, she went off to the scullery, where she could be heard bustling about, even at one stage, talking to herself, saying, 'I'll make Bertie a cup of cocoa . . . he likes cocoa, does Bertie.'

Betsy shook her head. 'She's daft as a brush. Silly old cow!'

Ellie rounded on her, horrified. 'She's no such thing – and well you know it! She's a dear old soul and we ought to be grateful to her. If it wasn't for her, Grandad would probably be put in a home.'

But Betsy could see how bad Grandad was; chunnering and moaning to himself, he didn't even seem to know they were there. 'He might be better off in a home.' Betsy seemed to have lost all sense of compassion.

Ellie turned to the old man. 'Grandad?' He didn't look at her, so she spoke to him again. 'Grandad, it's Betsy and Ellie. We've come to see you.'

He glanced at her and looked away.

'*Please*, Grandad.' Ellie needed him to look at her again. She needed him to know she was there for him, that she and Betsy loved him so. 'Look – we've brought you some chocolates. Give him the chocolates, Betsy,' she urged her sister. 'Let him see.'

Betsy thrust the box into her hand. '*You* give them to him.'

Inwardly making every excuse for Betsy's behaviour, Ellie held the chocolates out. 'Look, Grandad. These are for you.'

Again he turned and looked at her. His sorry gaze shifted to the box of sweets in her hands. Ever so slightly he shook his head. Then his eyes locked onto hers, and agonisingly slowly the recognition was like a small light dawning. His smile was beautiful to see, sad yet filled with wonder; his voice the same. 'Ellie . . . ?'

He gave a long, trembling sigh, then tears filled his old eyes. 'Oh, Ellie!' Then he saw Betsy and his chin began to dimple, his voice dropping to a whisper. *'Betsy.'* Like two round clear raindrops the tears rolled down his cheeks. 'My lovely lasses.' He opened his arms and they went to him, Ellie on one side, and Betsy on the other.

From the door, his old friend watched, her heart full at that very special sight. It was a wonderful reunion, with each one needing the other, even Betsy. They cried, and laughed and clung to each other, but all too soon, it was over. Like Widow Partridge had said, 'Sometimes he escapes into his own little world', and that was exactly what Bertie did now.

Gently he eased them away. 'All gone,' he muttered, his eyes glazing over. 'All gone now.' He began rocking backwards and forwards, arms folded, eyes vacantly staring into the flames, 'All gone . . . all gone.'

Overcome with sorrow at the sight of her grandad like that, Ellie fell to her knees before him. Taking his hands into hers, she squeezed them tight. 'Listen to me, Grandad. Mam and Dad . . .' Swallowing hard, she looked up at the old woman, who seemed to understand. When she gave her blessing with a nod, Ellie continued, 'Mam and Dad have died. It was too late to save them.'

She had to pause for a moment or she would not have been

able to go on. Memories of the churchyard were too fresh in her mind. 'We took some flowers to the church – some from you and some from us. Larry is in the Infirmary – he's badly hurt but he's alive, and you know him – he's a fighter. He'll come through it. He'll be all right, I know he will.'

She pointed to Betsy. 'Betsy's here for you, and I'm here for you. We love you, Grandad. So you see, they're not all gone. *We're* here, so is Larry . . . and so are you, Grandad. We're still a family. We still have each other.'

Suddenly, the old man stopped rocking. He didn't look at her, nor did he seem to acknowledge what she had been saying. Instead he began to murmur, as though talking only to himself, 'Larry . . . . Larry.'

Thrilled, Ellie knew that she had somehow got through to him. 'That's right,' she whispered, giving him a kiss. 'Your grandson's in the Infirmary. He's not well enough to leave yet, but he'll get better, you'll see. And when he does, he'll want to visit you, show his support, won't he? And so will Betsy and me. We *need* you, Grandad. We love you.'

For a few minutes he seemed not to have heard. The rocking grew frantic, then he suddenly stopped and turning to Ellie, he whispered, *'I'll ask Ada. She knows.'*

He didn't speak any more, nor did he look at her.

'He's wandering again,' Widow Partridge sighed. Suddenly she looked worn out. 'Happen he's best left alone now, eh?'

Before the girls departed she told them: 'It's been so good for him, having you here like this.' To Ellie, she said, 'You did right, lass, telling him about Larry an' all. I was afeared it might upset him, but when you talked to him like you did, I swear he seemed better than he's done in ages. I think he'll dwell on what you said. I'm sure it's bound to help him.'

Hugging her tight, she murmured her thanks again and again. Then she hugged Betsy, and waved them all the way back to the waiting cab. She had a feeling Bertie might not say it any more – that terrible, desolate phrase 'all gone'. Not now that lovely young lass had opened her heart to him.

———⋙•◦•⋘———

LARRY WAS WAITING for them. In his mind he had been there at the church, part of that congregation. He had shared every hymn, every prayer, and when they walked to the churchyard with the coffins, he was there with them.

He could see his mam and dad, not as they were now, but how they had once been, laughing and teasing, and loving each other as they had done for all their married life and some time before. He saw his Grandad Bertie, and the girls, and was as much a part of the occasion as if he had really been there.

Now, when his sisters came running down the ward, his eyes lit up like beacons. 'By! You look right bonny, the pair of you.'

'We brought you some flowers,' Ellie said, and laid them on the side-table.

'They're beautiful, just like my two sisters. Leave them there on the table,' he said. 'The nurse will put them in a vase later, I'm sure.' Smiling, he opened his arms. 'Let's have a look at my girls.'

They hugged and kissed and talked about everything but the service, until suddenly Betsy said, 'I wish you'd been there, Larry.'

Solemn-faced he nodded. 'I know, lass.' He had intended not saying too much about it, but now he let his emotions show. 'I wish I could have been there too.'

More than that, he wished to God it had never happened in the first place. If only he could turn back the clock! He and his dad would have come home earlier than they did. They would have been in time . . . they might have caught the man described by Ellie, the same man he had seen fleetingly as he ran up the stairs. Over and over it played in his mind like an old film.

Ellie fell silent. She didn't know what to say any more. She didn't know how much more she had to give, or how much longer she could go on being strong. She could hear Betsy telling him everything; about the church and all those people, and how she hated being in a foster-home, and why couldn't he get better quicker so they could all be together again.

It was thoughtless talk, yet Ellie didn't seem able to intervene. What with seeing Grandad in that pitiful state and now Larry trussed up to some iron contraption, and both his legs in plaster, it was too much to take in all at once. His upper body and face still bore the dark, yellowing bruises and every time he turned his head, pain was visible on his face.

Ellie felt paralysed. It was as if she had lost the use of her limbs and wasn't able even to move, or open her mouth to stop Betsy's whining tirade. Instead the babble of words just washed over her – until she heard Betsy telling Larry how Grandad had 'gone out of his mind – a babbling old man who didn't even know them'. When she heard that, her senses reeled in anger.

'NO!' Her intervention took the other girl by surprise. 'That's not the truth. Grandad *knew* we were there. He knew what I was telling him, but he's been ill – like Larry but in a different way.'

Betsy didn't argue. Instead she leaned back in the chair and lapsed into a sulk. The other two knew the only way to deal with it was to let her stew for a while, when she would come out of it on her own.

All the same, Larry was concerned, asking Ellie, 'How is Grandad . . . really?'

Ellie was honest with him, though gentler than Betsy had been. 'He's very poorly, and like Betsy said, sometimes he doesn't even know you're there, but he's *not* out of his mind. He's confused and frightened. He thinks we were all . . . you know?' She couldn't bring herself to say it, and Larry wisely ignored her stuttering.

'So he wasn't well enough to go to the church?' he asked. 'I was told there might be a possibility he could go to the service at least.'

Ellie shook her head, 'I'm glad he didn't,' she said simply.

'And what about you two?'

'We're all right, Larry, you mustn't worry about us. Just concentrate on yourself, and get better.'

'But I do worry about you,' he said. 'I want you to be with good people. They told me you were with a lovely couple – Mr and Mrs Walters, isn't it?' When Ellie confirmed it with a nod, he went on, 'Are they nice to you?'

'Yes. They're very kind. They're outside now, waiting.'

'Do you think I should talk to them? See what kind of people they are?'

Ellie was adamant. 'No, Larry. Me and Betsy are tiring you out, I can see. Maybe they'll come and visit another time, when you're stronger. If you really want them to?'

Amazed at how she had seemed to grow up all in an instant, he reached out to her, wincing in pain as he did so. 'You're a good lass, Ellie. You too, Betsy. Come here, sweethearts, both of you. Give your old brother a hug, eh?'

At first Betsy hesitated. She hadn't quite forgiven Larry for getting hurt and deserting them to foster-parents. But then she saw how Ellie curled into his arms, and not wanting to be left out, she did the same. '*When* will you be better?' she asked tearfully.

He groaned. 'I'd be better tomorrow, if only I knew how. But I have to put my faith in the doctors, love. I don't know how long it might be before I'm better, and neither do they.' His voice trembled slightly. 'The truth is, I don't even know if I'll ever walk again, but I'll try my damnedest, you can bet on that!'

The three of them held each other for some long time. There were no tears, not now. Tears would not bring their loved ones back. Nor would it mend their grandad, or make Larry walk.

Only time and determination could say whether the two men would regain their strength, albeit in different ways. And no one knew that better than Larry and Ellie. Betsy, however, wanted it all right now. She had neither time nor patience for waiting.

The nurse's voice cut through their thoughts. 'It's time to go,' she whispered. 'We'd best let your brother sleep now.'

Shocked, Ellie realised he'd gone fast asleep with his arms round them, and she hadn't even noticed. Betsy was all for waking him. 'He won't like it if we go without saying goodbye,' she pouted.

'I'll tell him.' The nurse was a small, smiling thing. 'I'm sure you'll soon be in to see him again.'

Betsy asked her the same question she had asked Larry. 'When will he get better?'

Taking them away, she answered, 'Did you ask your brother that question?'

'Yes.'

'And what did he say?'

'He said he might never walk again, but that's not true, is it?'

The nurse knew of the family's tragic background, and her heart went out to these two young girls. 'I can't discuss it with you,' she said, 'but I understand that Mrs Potton, the lady from the authorities, has already spoken with the doctor. I'm sure she'll explain it all.'

'I don't want *her* to explain it!' Betsy had a difficult mood on. 'I need to know now!'

Sensing it might develop into a confrontation, Ellie quickly intervened. 'Leave it for now. We'll ask her tomorrow.'

On the drive home, Betsy was very quiet. 'Are you all right, young lady?' Ted Walters asked. He had watched Betsy for a time, thinking how he might regret having taken this one on. Her sullen moods were already beginning to annoy him.

Betsy surprised them all when she asked abruptly, 'Can I have a dog?'

Drawing back his head, he laughed out loud. 'A *dog*?' The smile fading, he shook his head. 'I don't think so, my dear.' Gesturing to his wife, he explained, 'Peggy won't have a dog in the house, you see. I've been trying to persuade her for years, but she won't budge. I'm sorry, but you'll have to think of some other pet. How about a cat? We used to have one, but she got run over, poor thing.'

Betsy made no comment, but her mind was working furiously. When she wanted something badly enough, she always got it, by one means or another.

LATER THAT AFTERNOON, when Mr Walters was fast asleep in the chair, Ellie went upstairs to write in her diary. This past week she had not been able to concentrate, so now she had a lot to catch up on. It helped to ease her spirits a little, to write it all down.

When, an hour later, she returned to the parlour, it was to see Betsy seated on the sofa beside Peggy Walters. They were smiling at each other in a quiet, intimate manner that made Ellie's heart feel glad.

'Oh, here you are, Ellie!' Clambering off the sofa, Betsy hurried across the room to her sister, her face wreathed in smiles. 'Peggy says we can have a dog, after all. Imagine that!'

Ellie looked at the woman with surprise. 'That's very kind,' she said. 'I thought you didn't like dogs?'

'Ah well,' their foster-mother said, 'it's no time to be selfish, is it? It's true to say I've always been a bit wary of dogs, but it will do us a power of good to have an animal about the place. And your sister can be very persuasive when she needs.'

Her kindly gaze swept back to Betsy. 'It's so nice having you two young girls living with us, and Betsy's right, of course. It might be very nice indeed, having a dog. Yes, I've quite taken to the idea.'

And she even woke her husband to tell him so.

PART TWO

SUMMER 1935
THE JOURNEY

Chapter Eight

'Look, Bertie, there she is. Half-past two on the dot, same as ever.'

'Aye, she never lets me down, does our Ellie.' He had already seen her. 'By! She looks all grown-up these days, don't you think, Tilly?'

'All grown up and prettier than ever.' Tilly Partridge had nursed her neighbour through the worst of his illness and now, a couple of years later, he was much more like his old self. 'I'd best get inside and make sure everything's ready.' She wagged a finger at him. 'And don't you dare tell her, Bertie. I want it to be a surprise.'

It seemed to take her a little longer these days to get out of a chair, especially when it was the most beautiful day of summer, and the sun was warm and friendly on her face. Groaning and creaking a bit more than she used to, she hoisted herself up. 'I'll not be a minute!' she said and, softly singing as was usual, she ambled into the house.

Bertie watched his lovely granddaughter approach. Swinging down the street, Ellie Bolton looked every inch the young lady. A slim figure but taller now, she wore a sky-blue dress whose generous hem danced round her legs as she hurried along. The pretty dark shoes she wore made a quaint tapping noise against the pavement as she quickened her steps towards him. 'All grown-up and lovely with it,' he murmured under his breath. And he was oh, so proud of her.

'Grandad!' Waving at him, she broke into a run, her long wild hair flowing behind her like ripe corn in the breeze. 'Hello, Grandad!' Her blue eyes laughing, she fell into his open arms. 'Oh, it's so good to see you. You look so *well*!'

'It's good to see you an' all, lass,' he said, holding her at arm's length. 'And just look at you.' Her dark blue eyes were shining and all the shadows gone. 'Oh lass, you're so grown-up these days, I can't believe it.' It seemed only minutes since she was a little girl playing with her dolls, and now here she was, a beautiful young woman.

'Where's Tilly?' Since she had no real grandma, Ellie had adopted that dear woman as her own.

'I'm here, lass.' Emerging from the passage, the Widow Partridge gave her a hug. 'You're looking bonny,' she said. 'Same as always.'

Seeing Tilly wink mischievously at Grandad, Ellie sensed there was something going on. Being as both her grandad and Tilly had on their best clothes, she couldn't help but wonder if a little romance was in the air. She suspected they might be planning an outing together – maybe a tram ride into Accrington town, or a pint down the corner pub. But then, as she recalled, they didn't normally get all dressed up for that.

'You look bonny an' all,' she told Tilly. 'I like your new dress.' Fitted at the waist with a lightly flared hem, it was a pretty brown thing, with white spots and big floppy collar.

Flattered, Tilly beamed from ear to ear. 'Thank you, lass, that's very kind of you to say,' she cocked a thumb at Bertie, 'especially as your man over there never thinks to pay me a compliment. I could be wearing coal-sacks or fig leaves, for all he notices.' She laughed out loud. 'Fig leaves, eh?' She curled up at the thought. 'By! That'd be a sight for sore eyes an' no mistake.'

Try as she might, Ellie couldn't quite conjure up such a frightening image. 'Be draughty too, I shouldn't wonder,' she teased, and set Tilly off again.

Looking at Bertie, Tilly winked. 'Hey, but, doesn't your grandad look smart, eh? He looks a real dandy, in his white shirt and blue tie, so he does.'

'Give over, woman.' The old man blushed pink. 'Anybody would think you'd never seen a man in his best togs afore.'

'Aye well, it's a rare occasion to see *you* in your best togs. What! If I so much as ask you to put on a clean shirt, you mek a right old fuss! I've to argue and tussle, and even then you insist on wearing the oldest one o' the lot!' Returning her attention to Ellie, she confided, 'You wouldn't believe the trouble I had, getting the old bugger into that shirt and tie.'

'Aye, well.' Jiggling his shoulders, Bertie told them, 'I need to be comfortable, just like any other man.' Holding out his arms, he complained to Ellie, who was bemused by the whole thing: 'Look at what she's done to me, lass. Trussed me up like a bloody turkey, she has. Though I say it meself who shouldn't, I'm not a difficult man at the best o' times.'

'No, yer not!' Tilly wholeheartedly agreed. ''Cause you're a nightmare, that's what you are, Bertie Hill . . . a bloomin' nightmare on legs!'

Ellie couldn't help but laugh at their light-hearted banter. 'Is it a special occasion or what?' she asked Tilly. 'Are you planning to go out somewhere?'

'Only so far as the parlour, lass,' Tilly told her. 'Me and

your grandad, we've a little surprise for you.' Taking her by the hand she winked at the old man. 'Come on then, Bertie.' To Ellie she said, 'Close your eyes, and don't open them till I tell you.'

Ellie did as she was told, and was led down the passage, with Tilly holding her hand and giving instructions all the way. 'Mind the aspidistra.' Being over-cautious, she held the big broad leaves back with her free hand; that beautiful plant was her pride and joy. 'Keep straight, lass, an' don't dare open your eyes till I tell you.'

Ellie felt herself being guided through the parlour door. 'Careful, lass. No, you're not to open your eyes just yet.' Tilly's voice was soft in her ear.

A moment later, Ellie was brought to a halt. 'Stand still, lass.' When positioned in the right direction, she was urged, 'Go on! You can open 'em now.'

Curious, Ellie opened her eyes. Taking a split second to acclimatise, she gave a gasp of delight on seeing what Tilly had done.

'It's wonderful!'

Set out on Tilly's big old table was a splendid feast. The array of goodies included little sausage parcels, sandwiches of every kind, great hunks of cheese, pork pie slices, and savoury pastries. Here was a plate of scones, heavy with raisins, and there a wicker dish filled with ragged chunks of fresh-smelling bread; a platter of little tarts oozing with home-made strawberry jam, and a trifle the likes of which she had never seen before.

Set proud in the centre was a huge cake, tied with a ribbon and set on a fancy white doiley. Fit for royalty, the table was set with Tilly's best cutlery and starched white napkins standing up from the plates like miniature pyramids.

'My old granny taught me how to do that,' Tilly imparted proudly. 'She were in service at Yardle Manor, right from when she were a lass up to when she got wed at the age of thirty-nine. After that her husband was too proud to let her work. Anyway, soon after they were wed, she had my mammy, and that were that.' She leaned closer. 'Don't let it be said, but there *was* talk that the babby turned up a bit quick. But then, some folk will allus find summat to gossip about in my experience.'

Ellie agreed. 'She sounds like a fine woman to me.' Observing the table and the manner in which it was laid out, she imagined Tilly's grandma to be of creative mind, with a flair for entertaining. 'And you say she was taught how to do all this?'

'Aye, lass. An' she taught me the very same. She were a good teacher too, 'cause I've never forgotten how to lay a table and how to place everything just right. She allus had white napkins at special times – starched gently because otherwise they'd be too stiff to wipe your mouth on. Like I said, special times such as christenings and birthday parties. That were the only time her best china came out of mothballs.'

Gesturing to the beautiful white china and big old cutlery adorning her own table, she confided, 'This was hers – the cutlery, plates and dishes. Every last piece was my granny's, even the chenille tablecloth.'

Ellie thought the tablecloth most striking. Crimson in colour, with long silk tassels falling from plump, round bobbles, it was a work of art. Now, in the warmth emanating from the fire, the tassels danced and leaped, almost as if they were alive.

'She allus said it would all come to me one day, and there it is, shining and cherished for such an occasion as this.'

Ellie was amazed. Fancy the old lady bringing all this round to her grandad's house! She could hardly contain her excitement. 'So what's the occasion today? It's you and Grandad, isn't it?' She had already suspected it, right from the minute she'd seen what trouble they'd taken to look especially nice. '*That's* why you're all dressed up. He's asked you to marry him, and you've said yes. I'm right, aren't I?' To see them married would be wonderful, she thought. The couple were made for each other.

Tilly was wide-eyed with astonishment. 'What! By! That'll be the day, when your grandad asks me to wed him, child. He's happy enough to be waited on and pampered, but talk about marriage, and he'll skulk in the corner for a week and more.' Tilly's hearty laugh echoed round the room. 'Did you hear that, Bertie?' she asked. 'The lass thinks thee and me are to be wed. Fat chance, eh?'

When Bertie made no comment and instead shuffled guiltily to the armchair, she teased, 'It's all right, you don't have to wed me, not today nor any other day neither . . . unless you want to.' She winked at Ellie, while telling Grandad, 'Besides, I might find meself another handsome fella – and then where would you be, eh?'

Ellie did love these two, and she had to smile when Bertie replied, 'Will you give over, you daft bugger! I've said I'll wed you, only I'm not sure if I'm ready yet.'

'It's all right. I'm only teasing, so don't get all riled up.' Laying a hand on Ellie's arm, Tilly gestured to the table. 'It's your birthday treat, lass,' she declared proudly. 'Yours and Betsy's.'

Ellie could hardly believe it. 'But our birthday's not until Saturday!'

Bertie chipped in, 'We know that, but we thought being as

you're going to Blackpool with the family, we could have our own little treat today . . . you and Betsy, me and Tilly. That's all right, ain't it, lass?' He glanced at Tilly, who was already beginning to wonder if she'd done the right thing after all.

Ellie soon put their minds at rest. Flinging her arms round Tilly she told her, 'It's the best present I've ever had. Thank you! I love it, and so will Betsy!'

Crossing the room, she knelt at her grandad's feet, her arms folded on his bony knees while she told him the same thing – and something else, which touched his heart and made him proud.

'It's true me and Betsy are being taken to Blackpool for a birthday outing by Ted and Peggy,' she murmured, 'but kind as they are, they're not our family, Grandad, and they never will be. You, Larry, Betsy, and Tilly. *You're* our family.'

'Eh, God bless yer, lass.' He put his hand over hers. 'But I'm too old and worn to look after yer. You an' Betsy need somebody as can tek care of you the way you deserve.' His brows furrowed in a frown. 'I thought you were content enough with Mr and Mrs Walters. Are you telling me different, lass? Are you and Betsy unhappy? Is that what you're trying to say?'

Ellie put his mind at rest. 'No, Grandad, I'm not saying that. All I'm saying is that nobody can ever take the place of my family . . . however much they might want to, or however hard they might try. And that's no fault of theirs. It's just a plain and simple truth.'

She looked into his old eyes and there she saw her mam and dad, and all that had gone before. And when his eyes began to mist over, she kissed him fondly and held on to him, as though she would never let him go.

Tilly watched the two of them and was choked with

emotion. Bertie was right; like her, he was too old and worn to take care of the girls, though they would if they had to.

After a moment, she intervened in her own inimitable fashion. 'Come on, you two, stop all that canoodling. Tea's almost ready.' She had the cups and saucers to put out, and thirty candles to set round the cake; fifteen red one side and fifteen blue the other, so the twins could each blow out their own.

She also had another three places to set, though she would have to be careful, because Ellie might notice. It was another surprise, and one which she would love more than any other. Careful not to draw attention to herself, she quickly put out the extra places. 'Another minute or so, and we'll be ready to start.'

'Can't you see we're talking important stuff here?' Bertie chided; he had here two of the dearest people in the world. 'Come an' sit yer arse down, woman. There's time enough yet.'

Scoffing, Tilly told him she didn't have no time to 'sit her arse down'. Instead she went about her business, and left them to talk between themselves.

'She's a good woman, is Tilly.' Bertie followed her with his eyes into the scullery. 'She doesn't know it yet, but I've every intention to wed her . . . when the time's right.'

'Better make it soon, Grandad,' Ellie warned with a smile. 'You heard what she said about some other handsome fella whisking her away.'

'Ah! She'll not leave me,' he answered softly. 'Same as I'd not leave her. We're a pair, like bread and butter, me and Tilly.' Absent-mindedly stroking Ellie's long hair, he smiled when it bounced back, wild and undisciplined. 'I'll never understand why you were given hair thick and wayward as this,' he ran a strand of curls through his fingers, 'while Betsy's hair is fine, and straight as a tramline.'

Bringing in some teacups, Tilly placed them on the mat beside the birthday cake. 'That's a funny thing to say,' she commented. 'Whatever d'you mean by it?'

'What I mean is this. The hair should suit the person, and I reckon Betsy and Ellie have it the wrong way round, 'cause Ellie has a straight, fine nature, while Betsy is . . .' He sighed. '*Betsy*!'

Troubled by his remark, Ellie leaped to her sister's defence. 'Betsy's all right, Grandad, you mustn't worry about her. She's just a bit . . . defiant, that's all. She'll come good with time, I know she will.' Or rather, she hoped she would!

'Aye, happen she'll be all right in time, though I swear I can't think of who she might take after, with her funny moods and secret ways.' His mind went back to his own youth, and the woman he had adored, and then wed, Betsy and Ellie's grandmother, Ada. She had been a bit of a wayward creature, and he had suffered because of it when she ran off and left him in the lurch with their infant daughter. Yet she had not been deliberately spiteful, nor cruel; not in the way Betsy was.

Thrusting Ada and the past from his mind, he glanced towards the door. 'Where *is* young Betsy anyroad?'

'She'll not be long, I'm sure.' Ellie offered to go out in the street to see if she could spot her. 'She was late getting ready. She told me to go ahead and she'd catch the next tram. I'll just go and see if she's coming down the street.'

As Ellie went down the passage and out the door, Bertie spoke his mind to Tilly. 'Nobody knows how much I love them two lasses.' He glanced at the door. 'I hope she's right about our Betsy.'

'Oh, I'm sure she is,' Tilly answered fondly. But he wasn't convinced and, in her deepest heart, neither was Tilly. On the few occasions Betsy had been here, she had never once shown any real affection for her grandad, and it was obvious she had no liking for Tilly herself. More worryingly, there were moments when she was positively cruel to Ellie, though the latter never once buckled under her nastiness. Ellie might be a little thing, but she could be firm when she had a mind to.

Outside, Ellie was running down the street to meet Betsy, who had just rounded the corner. She had obviously taken trouble with her appearance and looked very smart. Taller and of bigger build than Ellie, she was dressed in a dark skirt and white blouse. These days, her brown hair hung to her shoulders. She and Ellie had never been much alike, and over the years any slight similarity there might have been seemed to have altogether disappeared.

Running alongside her was the dog, a light-coloured Labrador of some three years old. Puffing and panting, the poor thing was being taken along at a pace too fast for her liking.

Catching up with her, Ellie walked alongside. 'Grandad looks well,' she told Betsy. 'Tilly too. They've got a surprise waiting.'

Betsy wasn't impressed. 'What is it?'

'I'm not telling. It would spoil it.'

'How come you know what it is and I don't!'

'Because I was here first, that's all.'

'I hope he hasn't been and bought me anything babyish. He forgets we're all grown-up now.' When the dog seemed to draw back on the lead, she gave it an almighty yank, making it wince.

'Let me take her lead,' Ellie offered. 'You can go on ahead, if you like.'

Betsy refused. 'I'll take her. She's my dog, not yours!'

Ellie's hackles rose. 'Don't treat her like that then. She doesn't like it, and anyway, she's with pup.'

'Pups or no pups, she'd better do as she's told.'

After that there was no need to yank on her neck, because from then on the bitch kept pace. Though her mouth frothed and her paws hurt, she was wise enough to know that in Betsy, she had a hard mistress.

When she saw the party-table, Betsy put on a show of appreciation. 'It's lovely,' she told Tilly and gave her a swift peck on the cheek. When Grandad called her over for a birthday hug, she kept the dog between them and her kiss was fleeting and given grudgingly.

'Happy Birthday.' Bertie gave them each a small silver locket. Ellie loved hers and put it on immediately. Betsy shoved hers in her pocket. 'I'll wear it later,' she said airily. But it was clear she didn't think much of it.

Bertie hid his disappointment and showered his affection on the dog, which settled at his feet and enjoyed the attention.

It was then that Ellie noticed the extra places. 'Hang on – the table's set for seven,' she observed. 'Who else is coming?'

When in that moment the front door was opened, Tilly suggested with a wink, 'There's your answer. You'd best go and see, hadn't you?'

When she saw who was coming down the passage, Ellie gave out a squeal of delight. 'Larry!' Wheelchair-bound, but looking every inch the old Larry she knew, her brother was being pushed by Mick, the loyal friend who had stood beside him all this long time.

'Hello, sweetheart.' He held out his arms. 'Ellie! You're as pretty as ever.'

Going at a run, she threw herself into his arms, hugging him so hard, he cried for mercy. 'Oh Larry! I didn't know!' Laughing and crying all at the same time, she kissed him then ran ahead to tell Betsy. 'Look who's come to our party!' she cried, bounding into the parlour. 'It's Larry and Mick.'

Betsy seemed happy to see her brother. 'I thought they wouldn't let you out of the convalescence home on your own?'

'I'm not on my own,' he said, pointing up at Mick with a grin. 'I've got my very own chauffeur.'

Tilly took charge as always, bustling and fussing, and making everyone feel wanted. 'Set him here,' she said, and led them to a space nearer the fireplace. 'Mick, you can sit over here, aside o' me.'

When the two young men were settled, she put Grandad on the opposite side next to Betsy, knowing he needed to talk with her, then Ellie and herself opposite Mick.

The girls had some news. 'You tell them, Betsy,' Ellie said.

Bertie looked up. 'What's all this then, eh?' He didn't like surprises.

'Me and Ellie are not going to college after all.' By the look on her face, Betsy was obviously angry about it.

Tilly gave a little cry of disappointment. 'Oh, what a shame. And you were both looking forward to it so much.'

'I had it all planned,' Betsy said peevishly. 'I wanted to be a teacher. You get respect from the pupils, and nobody challenges your authority.' The idea of being in charge of forty and more children appealed to her sense of superiority.

'So, why the change?' Larry wanted to know. 'I thought it

was all settled. You've had the home teacher in since you left school at Christmas, and next September you'd go to college and make summat of yourselves.'

'It's to do with money,' Ellie told him. She too had been disappointed, but for different reasons. 'What with the home teacher and books and everything, it's taken most of Peggy and Ted's savings. Going to college would mean Ted working overtime every night. It would have been too much for them, and that's why the plans were changed.'

Betsy rounded on her. 'We could still have gone,' she said sourly. 'If only *you* hadn't said we could go out to work and forget college.'

'I had to, sis. It wasn't fair to them, and besides, they've done so much for us already. It's time we paid some of it back.'

'Well, I think you'll both do very well, whatever you turn your hands to.' Tilly always looked on the good side. 'Now then, we've a party to enjoy. What's say we get started, eh?'

Bertie led the example by clasping his hands together, his head bowed. 'We thank the good Lord for the food on this table,' his voice dropped to a whisper, 'for them we love, and them who can't be here.' No one round that table doubted his meaning.

'Happy Birthday, girls!' Tilly cried, and by starting the singing, she wisely carried the mood away from things best forgotten.

When the singing was over, everybody cheered and the party was on. Tilly poured tea for everyone and, made hungry by the feast before them, nobody needed telling to tuck in.

Ellie was curious. 'Is there somebody missing?' she asked, indicating the empty place. 'Looks like you've set a place too many.'

All eyes went to Tilly.

'I hope you don't mind, but my sister's grandson, John, is in the area today,' she explained. 'Bertie will tell you, he was here earlier but then he went off in search of a job. I told him we wouldn't wait, but that sooneer he got back, he was welcome to come and eat with us.' Looking flustered, she turned first to Betsy then to Ellie. 'I hope that's all right with you both? Because if not, I'll head him off at the door and make some sort of excuse.'

Betsy swallowed the knob of bread before answering. 'I don't like strangers much,' she declared ungraciously. 'But it's Grandad's house, so it's up to him.' It was a cruel dig.

Stunned by Betsy's unfeeling remarks, the others looked embarrassed, but not Ellie, who told her in no uncertain terms: 'Tilly has gone to a lot of trouble for us to enjoy this party, and as far as I'm concerned, John is welcome to share it. Besides, the more the merrier.' Turning to Tilly, she smiled warmly. 'It's my party too, and he's very welcome. In fact, I'm looking forward to meeting him.'

Bertie nodded. 'The lad will always be welcome in my house.'

Realising she was the villain, Betsy grudgingly retracted her words. 'I suppose it's all right if he comes. Besides, you've made so much lovely food,' she cooed, 'it would be a shame to waste it.'

Relieved, Tilly thanked them both. 'He's a quiet lad,' she explained. 'An only child, and now with his parents moving away down South, he'll be all alone in the big bad world. You'll like him, I'm sure.'

So now, the conversation turned to this stranger.

'How old is he?' Larry wanted to know.

'I'm not altogether sure, but to my reckoning, he'll be

coming up to twenty or so.' Having given the answer, Tilly concentrated on buttering her slice of bread.

'What kind of work is he looking for?' Mick was curious.

Tilly shrugged. 'I'm not sure about that neither,' she admitted. 'Anything that pays well, I expect.'

Bertie had a few words to say. 'He's not a tradesman or owt like that. In fact, I don't reckon he's all that bothered what he does. He drove a truck some time back, I do know that, 'cause he called in here once on his way back to Darwen. Like Tilly said, he needs a wage, 'cause he's after a place to live round 'ere, and they don't come cheap.'

Licking the butter off her fingers, Tilly told them, 'I'd have the lad to stay with me, but I'm past all that.' She smiled at Bertie. 'The only company I can put up with these days for any great length of time is Bertie's. We understand each other, you see.' Winking at Larry, she made them all laugh. 'The truth is, I'm the only woman that *would* put up with him. I'd wed him tomorrow, but d'you think he'll put a ring on my finger? Will he heckaslike!'

Calm as you please, Bertie cut himself a slice of pork. 'I might think about it,' he said cheekily, 'if you promise to put a spread on like this every week.'

The talk soon shifted to Larry. 'I watched him do his exercises today,' Mick disclosed. 'He's doing well.' Gesticulating with his arms he said, 'They put him between these narrow rails and held him up. Then, just for a second or two he was on his own. It was grand to see.'

'Yes, and I can tell you, it was the longest minute of my life,' Larry admitted.

'And when will they let you loose?' Bertie wanted to know.

'Oh, I've a long way to go yet, Grandad,' came the answer.

'They'll not let me out till I can fend for myself.' A glint of determination lit his eyes. 'It won't be easy, but I'm determined to walk again. I *have* to!'

Mick had some good news. 'I've already told Larry that when he's able to, he's welcome to come and live at my place. It'll be better than him being on his own, and I'll be glad of his company. He'll not even have to go upstairs if he doesn't want to, 'cause I never use that big front parlour. And we've got a downstairs lavvy off the scullery.'

Larry had been overjoyed when Mick told him of his plan. 'I can't tell you how much it would mean to me,' he said now. 'If I'm near all I'm used to, with Mick to urge me on, I'd be out there in no time, like Tilly's John, looking for work and a chance to get my life back.' He looked at Mick with gratitude. 'I've a good mate here,' he said. 'The best.' He gave a deep-down sigh. 'But, like I say, there's a way to go yet.'

'You'll do it.' Mick had no doubts.

Neither had Bertie. 'I'm sure you will, lad,' he said stoutly. 'You've done wonders already, and we're all proud of you.'

'And are they hopeful,' Tilly loved Larry like her own, 'about you walking again, I mean?'

'They won't commit themselves.' How many times had he himself asked that same question, and each time been given that same answer.

Greatly encouraged, Ellie gave him a goal. 'If you're not standing on your own two feet by this time next year,' she announced, 'you're not coming to our birthday party!'

Tilly raised her glass. 'We'll all drink to that. So there you are, Larry . . . think on what your sister said. You're to be out of that contraption by this time next year.' And they all tipped up their glasses and toasted the dream.

Ellie discreetly closed her eyes and said a little prayer. When she opened them again, it was to see Mick looking across the table at her, his kind brown gaze resting on her face with such tenderness it startled her. *For the longest moment of her life she could not break the contact between them. Nor did she want to.*

He smiled then, a warm, wonderful smile that sent the blush up her neck and into her face. Seeing her embarrassment, he felt ashamed and looked away, hurriedly engaging in conversation with Bertie.

The all-too brief incident had left Ellie shaken and excited. She had always liked Mick, right from when she was a little girl. He made her laugh, and he was the best friend in the world to all of them. But Mick was just Mick, and nothing more. Now though, she had seen him in a different way. When he looked at her through those quiet, loving eyes, she had seen something wonderful. Probably without even knowing it, he had awakened something in her that she had never known was there, a kind of need. A rush of exhilaration. It was a frightening thing, and yet so natural.

She covered her nervousness by gabbling on to Tilly. All around her she heard them talking, about how Grandad missed his old dog, after losing it to an illness. She heard Betsy reveal how her own dog was in pup and how she meant to sell the pups for a good deal of money. 'If they're not sold I'll have them put down,' she announced, provoking a volley of protest from everyone round her.

Ellie heard it all, the chiding and the laughter, and the inevitable bantering that happens round a table when friends and family get together. She heard it all, and yet she heard nothing, because all the time she was thinking of Mick. Though she dare not look at him, she was acutely aware that he was only an arm's reach away; a smile, a word, and she would be the happiest soul on earth.

She was tempted to glance up, to see that quietness in his brown eyes. *And feel the strange, trembling excitement he had caused in her.* Instead she avoided eye-contact, yet just occasionally she felt his gaze settle on her, and her young heart beat fifteen to the dozen.

While the food was still plentiful and the home-made elderberry wine still flowing, a resounding knock came on the door. 'That'll be our John!' Scrambling out of her chair, Tilly hurried down the passage to let him in, returning a moment later with the young man in question. 'This is John,' she said. 'Come to join us, if you please.'

John was nothing like Ellie had expected. Tall and wiry, with a long mop of brown hair, he seemed rather brash . . . a bit too full of himself. Not at all like Tilly.

Mick got out of his chair and shook hands; so did Ellie. 'Nice to meet you all,' the young man said. His attention went to Ellie in particular; he thought she was the prettiest thing he had ever seen. 'I hope you don't mind me busting in on your party like this?'

'I'm Betsy!' Drawing his attention, the girl smiled up at him. 'We don't mind you coming to our party one bit.' Looking at her sister, she asked boldly, 'That's right, isn't it, Ellie?'

'You're very welcome,' Ellie told him, and he thanked her kindly.

Tilly was delighted. 'There you are, son.' She introduced him to everyone and showed him to his seat. 'We're all glad to see you. You've missed the start, but you'll not miss the finish. The girls will blow out the candles and cut the cake in a while, but for now, tuck in and if there's anything you'd like that isn't on the table, you've only to ask.' Looking at the twins, she suggested timidly, 'Happen the girls won't mind if we save a little slice of cake for you to take back to your grandma?'

The girls agreed, and her thank-you smile enveloped them all. John, too, showed his gratitude. 'Grandma will like that. She loves a nice bit of cake, and Auntie Tilly bakes the best cakes ever.' In truth, he thought it would make him a nice little snack on the way home.

Tilly explained, 'I've never been quite sure what John should call me. Being his grandma's sister, I'm not really his auntie, but that's what I've been known as, since he were this high.' She demonstrated a height just above the table leg.

Larry said he thought the correct term was 'great-aunt', but Mick argued that it was too much of a mouthful anyway.

Bertie approved. 'Auntie sounds right enough to me . . . especially for a young 'un.' With his own mouth full of chewed scone, a stern scowl from Tilly made him swallow the piece whole.

When John was settled with a loaded plate of food in front of him, Larry asked, 'Tilly said you'd been out looking for work. How did you get on, if you don't mind me asking?'

'No, why should I?' Taking his time, he bit off a chunk of pork pie and ate it reflectively. 'If you must know, I got absolutely nowhere!' he admitted. 'I must have walked miles! I trudged round God knows how many cotton mills and foundries. I must have been to half a dozen coalyards. I even went to the tram depot to see if they needed any drivers.' He shook his head. 'Nothing doing!' Picking up another slice of pie, he told them, 'I'm working out a week's notice where I am now, so I'll have to be off soon and catch the train. I'll come back next week and try again. You never know, I might strike lucky next time.'

Mick said little, but he couldn't help but wonder if this

fella-me-lad was telling the truth. As far as he knew, there were umpteen jobs going spare in Blackburn; in fact, there was even talk that the coalyards were desperately short-handed. 'Did you try the coalyard down Henry Street?'

Swilling down a glass of elderberry wine, John answered, 'Tried them all. Like I said – there was nothing doing. Why – where do you work?'

'I'm the foreman at Brindle's Shoes in Blackburn town. We often need people in different departments. Why don't you call in one day?' Mick said, trying to be helpful.

But John would not be drawn further on the subject. In fact, he seemed more interested in listening than talking, and more in looking at Ellie than he did at the food in front of him.

Ellie felt an instinctive dislike for him, and that was unusual, because as a rule she got on with everyone, friend and stranger alike. Where Mick had made her feel good when he smiled on her, this one's smile made her skin crawl. But, seeing as he was the lovely Tilly's guest, she would treat him as such.

Two others had seen the way John looked at Ellie. One was Bertie; the other was Mick.

Bertie had never really taken to the lad. Like Ellie he put up with his company for the sake of Tilly, that dear soul who could see no wrong in anybody.

As for Mick, he suspected John was a lazy good-for-nothing, and an out-and-out liar into the bargain. So far, he had not been able to figure out what John was after, but he definitely knew he was a bad lot. Moreover, when he saw how taken John was with Ellie, his eyes shifting over to her every minute, he was not only uncomfortably jealous, but uneasy on her behalf.

When it came time to cut the cake, it was given to Larry to light the first set of candles, which he did by leaning right over the table and touching the wicks with the long taper Tilly lit from the fire.

'Right!' When they were all lit, the candles were blown out; first by Betsy, who did it all in one big breath, next Ellie, who had two goes before all her fifteen candles were put out. A great cheer went up and they all sang 'Happy Birthday' again. And now it was time to cut the cake.

'Betsy was first to blow out the candles,' Bertie declared, 'so it's only fair that Ellie makes the first cut.'

Telling her to be careful, Tilly handed her the knife, a long wide-bladed thing that she kept out of sight under the sink at home.

'I never did like them blessed things,' she had told Bertie some time back. 'If the house is ever broken into while I'm abed, I wouldn't want the burglar to get his hands on that knife. By! Like as not, I'd get me throat cut!'

After that, though he didn't tell her, Bertie began giving serious thought as to whether he should wed this lovely woman after all, so he could fetch her here, where she might be safer.

Ellie had the knife raised, ready to cut into the cake, when John sprang out of his chair and sidled up to her. 'Let me help you, eh?' He wrapped his fist over hers and, pressing her hand down, sliced into the cake with ease, at the same time gripping her knuckles so hard, it was painful.

All too soon, the party was over. John was the first to excuse himself. 'I'd best get off and catch an early tram.' He kissed Tilly first, then Betsy, and, taking a little longer than was necessary, put his arms round Ellie and kissed her too. 'I'm sure I'll see *you* again,' he said in a whisper, his eyes smiling into hers.

Unsettled by his unwanted attention, Ellie instinctively glanced at Mick, who was looking at her from the far side of the room. He nodded and smiled, and she was calmed by his presence. She had no idea of the hostility he felt towards the stranger in their midst.

Clutching his box containing the piece of cake, John was soon gone, with the promise, 'I'll see you some time next week, Auntie Tilly.'

In those few precious minutes when only close friends and family remained, the talk inevitably came round to the awful incident that had taken loved ones and put Larry in that wheelchair. 'I still can't understand it,' Larry began. 'Why did they never find the man who I saw running along the landing that night?'

Bertie had his own theory. 'There's plenty o' folk who say that man and the fella they found murdered in that grubby room down by the river were one and the same.'

'I don't see it, Grandad. There was nothing to point that way . . . no evidence to tie the two together, so what makes you think that?'

Shrugging his shoulders, he could only say: 'It's just a feeling I've had all along, that's all. But, like you say, there was no evidence to tie them together, so happen it was just a sick old man's imagination.'

Ellie had a question. 'You're not sick any more, Grandad,' she said thankfully. 'So now, do you still think it was him?'

He shook his head. 'Happen not.' All the same, there was something about that business – something that had nagged away at him, and yet he couldn't quite put his finger on it. But then, like Ellie said, he had been very ill. After what had happened, it was a wonder he could turn his mind to anything at all!

The talk went on, but nothing came of it; nothing could. Too much water had gone under the bridge. 'I wonder if we'll ever know the truth,' Mick said quietly, and they all had to ask themselves the same question.

Soon, Larry and Mick were ready to leave. 'Take care of yourselves,' Larry told his sisters, after an exchange of kisses and cuddles. 'Come and see me when you can, and we'll talk about what you mean to do with your future, eh?'

Mick gave Betsy a kiss, then, not trusting himself, he kissed Ellie just fleetingly. 'See you soon,' he said, and afterwards thanked both Tilly and Bertie for a wonderful time.

Ellie waved them away from the doorstep. Even when they'd gone out of sight she stayed at the door, her mind still on Larry, and the reason for his being in that wheelchair. 'I'll find out, Larry,' she murmured, the tears rolling down her face. 'I promise you . . . I'll find the man who killed our mam and dad and did that to you. He'll pay for what he did!' After a moment, she wiped away the tears, put on a smile and returned to the others.

As they made their way to the station, Mick glanced back, hoping to see Ellie, yet knowing he couldn't. He felt all kinds of a fool. Here he was, some ten years older than her, and he felt like a schoolboy in love. But no, it was more than that. He had seen the goodness in her when she talked about others, and the way she had bowed her head to say a little prayer for her mam and dad. In that moment when she looked up and caught him gazing on her, he was embarrassed, yet elated. His heart had turned over, in a way he had never experienced. He loved her. That was all he knew. He loved her, and wanted to keep her safe. But it was impossible. *Impossible!*

Larry's urgent voice broke into his thoughts. 'Get a move on, mate. I need the toilet.'

Mick quickened his steps. 'Why didn't you go back there, at your grandad's?'

''Cause I'm a proud bugger, that's why.'

Mick chuckled. 'Proud nothing. You knew Tilly would have insisted on giving you a helping hand, ain't that the truth?'

Larry admitted it, and the two of them had a good laugh.

<hr>

SOME SHORT TIME later, Ellie and Betsy prepared to leave. 'Can I ask you something, Grandad?' Ellie asked.

''Course you can, lass. Ask away.'

'Who's Ada?'

The colour bled from his face. 'What d'you mean?'

'When you were ill, you cried for someone called Ada.' Ellie was persistent but gentle. 'Who was she, Grandad?'

Slowly, the colour came back to his old face. 'Somebody I once knew,' he said. 'I've already forgot her. Now get yourselves off, or you'll get a wagging from Peggy.'

Only half satisfied with his explanation, but realising he didn't want to talk about it, Ellie said her goodbyes and so did Betsy. 'Don't be too long afore you come to see us, now,' Tilly said, and Ellie promised they'd come again soon.

When they were gone, Bertie winked at Tilly. 'You did us all proud, lass. Thank you. And now I reckon you've earned a nice cuppa tea. I shall do the honours. You just sit there – you must feel that worn out.'

For a long moment Tilly lingered. 'Do you want to talk about it?' she asked tenderly.

'Talk about what?'

'This woman called Ada. I saw how you changed colour at the mention of her name.'

Bertie laid back his head and sighed. Should he tell, or should he not? He decided to confide in her. ''Twere a long time ago,' he began, and as he spoke his memories carried him back.

'We were just kids really. She were smart as a tack, and pretty as a picture . . . the lass every fella wanted. But it were *me* as won her over. We got wed and had a child – a lovely little girl.' He paused, his voice faltering. 'We called her Sylvia.'

Tilly gasped. 'Are you saying this woman . . . this Ada . . . is the twins' grandmother?'

'Aye, lass. God forgive me. That's what I'm saying.'

'Is she still alive?'

'As far as I know. We were divorced a long, long time ago. I never told no one, mind. 'Tweren't none of anybody else's business.'

'But you let Sylvia believe her mam died when she were young?'

'Because as far as I were concerned, Ada was as good as dead!'

Anger flooded his features, his fist pounding the chair as he explained. 'She walked out on me and Sylvia, when that bairn were only three months old. Thank God I had my sister Margaret to help me with the kiddy while I was at work all those years. She raised Sylvia like one of her own. I don't know how I could have got through without her coming in every day!'

'So, your Sylvia never knew her mam was still alive?'

'No, she never knew, and neither will the girls, not if I can help it. If I were to tell them now, they'd never forgive me for deceiving my lass. They knew how much she wanted to know about her own mam. They might even try to find her.' Fear marbled his voice. 'I don't want that, Tilly. Ada was a bad lot. She went off to make her fortune and, from the stories that came back, she was doing all right, bedding the well-off, and making them pay heavy for the privilege. The last I heard she was in some sort of set-up with a fella who died and left her with a son in tow. Filthy rich, she is. And no doubt as wicked as ever into the bargain!'

'So, the girls could be in line to inherit a lot of money?'

'I hope to God they never have to lay a finger on her dirty money! *I'll* not tell them, and I'm trusting you to keep this to yourself . . . for their sakes, lass.' His voice dropped to a whisper. 'I couldn't trust her. *You see, I know how she can get you to love her – and then break your heart.*'

Chapter Nine

'COME ON NOW, Ada.' The nurse was a cheerful sort. Small and round she had the smile of an angel and the strong arms of a wrestler. 'Your son's coming to visit today, so you'll want to look your best, won't you, eh?'

From her bed, Ada shifted her gaze to the nurse. In her mind she smiled at her, but in reality she could no more smile than she could move. Already weakened by illness, the shock of her daughter being killed in the fire had not only paralysed her body, but impaired her brain, until now she was at the mercy of others. Yet she could see, and she could hear. And she was alive; but only just.

The two nurses turned her over and washed her back, then they rolled her the other way and washed the remainder of her body. 'We'll have you looking so beautiful, your son won't recognise you,' the round one said. 'By the time I've finished with you, you'll shame the film stars.'

The nurse was as good as her word. By the time Peter arrived, Ada was bright and shiny, with her long grey hair fanning the pillow beneath her, and even a touch of pale lipstick tracing her mouth. 'My, my! Look at you. Sleeping

Beauty, no less.' He laughed, a soft, cruel sound that sent a chill through her soul.

'Good evening, Mr Williams. Don't you think your mother looks lovely?' Coming up behind him, the nurse's voice cut through his malicious tirade. 'She has such beautiful skin. I'm sure there's many a young woman would be proud of it.'

'Yes, she does look lovely,' he agreed. 'Thank you, Nurse.' He waited until the woman had gone to the other end of the ward before he began his vicious taunting again. 'It's such a shame you have to stay in this ward with all these sick old people,' he said sweetly. 'I couldn't be doing with all that moaning and shouting myself, somebody being sick and waking me all hours of the day and night. But then *I* wouldn't have to put up with it, because if it were me who was bedridden, I'd be in a private place, with nurses at my every beck and call.'

'Come to see yer mam, 'ave yer?' Bent and balding, the old woman paused on her way to the lavvy. Eighty years old and recovering from a nasty fall, she leaned heavily on her cane. 'Such a lovely lady,' she said, nodding towards Ada. 'Speaks with her eyes, you know.' Smiling at Ada, she said, 'That's right, ain't it, lass?' She spoke slowly and clearly, hoping Ada would understand. 'Such pretty eyes.' Nodding again, she resumed her lonely trek to the lavatory, muttering as she went, 'Poor thing. If I were that crippled, I'd want somebody to put me out me misery.'

'Silly old cow!' Wiping his face as though he had been infected with some kind of disease, Peter stared into his mother's eyes. 'Though she's right, you know,' he whispered. 'Somebody *ought* to put you out of your misery.'

When he saw a flash of fear light up her eyes, he grinned in her face. 'You didn't like me saying that, did you, eh? But it's true! You've lived too long, Ada Williams. And I'll tell you something else: if that stupid bint Daisy Morgan hadn't told you about the fire, and how they'd found the bodies of Jim and Sylvia Bolton, you might never have known. Pity she panicked and sent for the doctor when you collapsed!'

Clenching her hand in his, he groaned. 'Why didn't the silly little cow wake *me*, eh? Why didn't she wake Ruth? I wouldn't have sent for no bloody doctor. I'd have dealt with it myself.'

He smiled into her eyes, softly laughing when she closed them, to shut him out. 'Mind you, she did say how she knocked and banged on the bedroom door and couldn't wake us. Happen she were telling the truth. I wouldn't know, would I? I mean, me and Ruth were fair worn out. We'd had a rough night, if you know what I mean. Oh, but I forgot. You'd know *all* about that, wouldn't you, Mother?'

The rage was like cold heat inside him, searing his insides until the pain was almost unbearable. 'Yes, you'd know all about that – after the life you've led.' Dropping her hand, he bowed his head. 'All those *men*!'

Opening her eyes she looked at him, shocked to see him crying as he recalled the way it had been. 'I was just a boy, locked in the bedroom till it was all over – you and him . . . *them*! *One after the other, night after night*!'

Gritting his teeth, he waited until the images grew fainter. 'I could hear you, Mother, did you know that? Oh yes, I could hear every disgusting sound. It made me sick to my stomach. *You* made me sick to my stomach!'

As he went on, he could see the guilt and regret in her eyes, and it pleased him. 'The other boys thought you were beautiful, but they didn't know. I knew though, and I was so ashamed of you. Underneath, you see, you were dirty – all spoiled.'

His eyeballs stood out like hatpins as he glared at her, his face almost touching hers, his voice low and shivering. 'If Daisy hadn't called out the doctor, you would never have survived, I can promise you that, Mother dear. I would have turned the key in the lock and left you lying there till it was all over.'

Just as quickly as his mood had erupted, it subsided. Taking both her hands in his, he began to stroke them. 'That nurse was right, you know,' he murmured. 'You *have* got lovely skin.' It gave him pleasure to know she could not move her hand away, nor could she cry out at his touch. All she could do was move her eyes from side to side, as she did now, with the hatred alive in them.

He tutted. 'Now, now! Don't look at me like that,' he chided. 'Anybody would think you loathed the sight of me.' He had no illusions on that score. 'You don't even like me coming here, do you? But I will,' he gloated, 'every day until I see you done with – and from what they tell me, it won't be too long before my waiting's over. Oh yes, Mother! Me and Ruth are already counting the days.'

Moving his chair so he could sit even closer, his voice sank to the merest whisper. 'Every time I come here, I expect to see you laid out in the mortuary – gone from my life like the pest you are. Instead I find you still here, looking at me with those pathetic eyes, asking questions – *always asking questions!*'

Leaning forward, he pretended to kiss her. Instead he was making a confession he didn't want anyone else to overhear. 'I *heard* you, Mother. I heard you making arrangements with the solicitor. You meant to leave all your worldly goods to your precious daughter, didn't you, eh?'

The flicker of an eye told him what he had suspected. 'You know, don't you, Mother? You know it was me. But you see, I had to be rid of her. I couldn't allow her to take my inheritance.

It wouldn't have been fair. Not after I helped you build up your property business, working my fingers to the bone – what for, eh? Just so you could leave it all to some little bastard who was there before me.'

Falling back in his chair, he looked down on her. There was no compassion in his heart. No love or respect. Only repugnance, and a loathing that was like a living thing inside him. 'I'm going now, Mother.' Scraping the chair back, he leaned down and kissed her on the face; it was cold to the touch, and grey like new-chiselled marble. One eye was silently weeping. 'Oh, I'm sorry. I've upset you, haven't I, telling you about your daughter and everything?'

He smiled sweetly. 'Never mind. You still have *me*!'

———❖———

U NSETTLED BY HIS meeting with Ada, Peter slid his key in the front door and flung it open. 'Ruth! *Ruth*! Where the devil are you?'

'In here,' came the reply.

Hurrying into the drawing room, he found her lolling on the sofa, a drink in one hand and her feet curled up beneath her. She was neither dressed nor washed. 'I've been waiting for you.' Her voice was slurred with booze. 'Where've you been? Oh, Peter! You didn't go and see your mother again, did you?' She belched. 'Helping the old lady on her way, were you? Telling her a few home truths, is that it?' She held out her arms but he made no move towards her.

Instead he was looking round the room. One of the sideboard drawers was open; there were clothes flung down beside her, and both shoes were tipped over on the rug. In the fire grate, two drained bottles lay on their side, and the fender was littered with empty glasses from last night. The curtains were half-drawn and the smell was overpowering.

Suddenly he was across the room. 'Filthy bitch!' Smacking her hard across the head he took hold of her arm and yanked her from the sofa. 'You're no better than she is. What's more, you stink to high heaven.' Snatching the glass from her hand he smashed it into the hearth. 'Get out of my sight.' He gave her a spiteful push. 'Go on! Get upstairs and don't come down until you're dressed and looking like any decent woman!'

Shocked and dazed, she hobbled across the floor, muttering angrily under her breath, 'You should never have gone to see her. You're always upset when you've been to that hospital.'

'*Daisy!* Get out here NOW!' His voice sailed through the house.

The maid came rushing into the room. 'I'm sorry, sir, I were doing the ironing.'

With his hands behind his back, Peter walked slowly round the trembling girl. 'Do you want to keep your place in this house, Daisy?' His voice was calmer now. His manner charming.

'Yes, sir.'

'Do you carry tales from this house, Daisy?'

'Oh no, sir!'

'And do you recall what I said I would do, should I ever discover you carrying tales?'

'Yes, sir.'

'What did I say, Daisy?'

Gulping, she trotted out the very words. 'You said you'd be sure and find some precious thing missing from the house, and then I'd be accused of being the thief. You would see to it that I was thrown in jail, or something worse.'

'You won't ever forget that, will you?'

'Oh no, sir!'

The silence was thick as he continued to walk round her, his piercing eyes intent on her terrified expression. Stopping right in front of her, he bent his head to see into her face. 'Daisy?'

'Yes, sir?' Keeping her eyes straight ahead, she avoided looking at him.

'Have you seen the state of this room. It's *filthy*!'

'Yes, sir.' When he paused, she gabbled on, 'I meant to clean it first thing, only Miss Clegg wouldn't let me in. She told me to leave it, sir, and that's what I did.' Shifting her stricken gaze to the door, she told him, 'She did that, sir. She threw a glass and it hit me, then it broke on the door.' Turning her face sideways, she showed him the cut right along her cheekbone. 'She wouldn't let me in, sir.' Then, thinking she had said too much, she bit her lip. 'I'm sorry, sir. I'll clean it now. I'll have it shining like a new pin in no time at all.'

He didn't answer. Instead he strode out, leaving her quivering in his wake. 'Mad!' she muttered, rushing to open a window. 'They're both mad as bleedin' hatters.'

Upstairs, Ruth heard the front door close behind him. Going to the window, she looked out to see him striding across the road. 'Miserable git!' Tipping the bottle to her mouth she took a long swig. 'Where's he gone to now, I wonder? Gone to terrorise his tenants into handing over their hard-earned brass, I expect. Can't even take somebody on to collect the rents, in case they steal a penny or two. Tight-fisted bugger!'

She began to snigger, then she was crying, and feeling sorry for herself. 'Allus threatening to throw me out, he is,' she moaned. 'I'll tell you summat, though. If he did throw me on the streets, I'd make damned sure I took a bag o' money with me. I know where he keeps it. He'd never find me, 'cause I'd be away to me mam's.' Falling on to the bed, she took another swallow from the bottle. 'Never mind *him* finding me,' she chuckled, 'I don't think even *I* could find where the old cow lives now. Allus moving on, moving on. I'll find her if I have to, though. I allus have before.'

Returning to the window, she watched Peter turn the corner at the bottom of the street. 'Hey, Mr High and Mighty Big Mouth Williams! I've got enough on you to send you to the bloody gallows.' Stopping to think, she realised the serious position she could be in, should she go running to the police. Who would they believe . . . the housekeeper or the property dealer? Ruth had no illusions. 'Some way or another, it'd be *me* swinging from them gallows, not him,' she knew that for sure.

She pressed her nose to the window, as if seeking some kind of cold comfort. 'You'd best get yourself a plan, Ruth Clegg,' she slurred. ''Cause as soon as he knows you're carrying his kid, he'll want you out on the streets, never to lay eyes on you again.'

That was the sorry truth of it all.

OVER THE FOLLOWING week, Ruth Clegg used her available spare time to try to track down her mother. She had no other family, and nowhere to go if Peter should decide he wanted shut of her; and with his child in her belly, there was every chance that might happen sooner rather than later.

Whichever way it turned out, she had no intention of leaving without filling her pockets from his secret hoard. It was a deadly risk, she knew, but one she would have to take because, even though she carried his child, there'd be no money coming her way from that miserly bastard!

Come the weekend, she had found someone who might lead her to her mother. Having exhausted most avenues, she decided to try a street in Preston where her mam had lived a few years ago after Ruth had left home.

The old man in the corner shop recalled her straight away. 'A bonny, wild thing she were an' all,' he said, laughing. 'Most of us have grown quieter over the years, but not her. She's still got the devil of a temper, has your mam. Must be that red hair you both have. By! I wouldn't like to get on the wrong side of her, I can tell you.'

'Do you know where she went when she moved from this street?'

Concentrating hard, he shook his head, then he paused, and now he was wondering. 'I might at that. Yes, let me think now.' A moment or two of casting his mind back, and he remembered. 'She took up with this fella – sad kinda bloke, they said – fell out with his son and became a bit of a vagabond.'

'But where did they go from here?'

Lapsing into concentration again, he scratched his head. 'Top end o' Blackburn, they said – a place called Mill Hill, but o' course I can't swear on it.' Pleased with himself so far, he took a small ledger out of the drawer and put it on the counter. 'There's something in here . . . let me see now.' He put on his spectacles and flicked through the pages. 'I don't normally give tick,' he said sternly, 'but I bent the rules for your mam – for both of them, in fact. They neither of them went into town to shop.' He grinned. 'Seems they were too tied up in each other to want to move out the house.'

When his remark was met with stony silence, he cleared his throat and scanned the pages, 'Ah! Here we are.' Swinging the book round, he let her read it.

Ruth wasn't sure. 'This is a Freda Morris,' she said, puzzled. 'That's not my mam. Her name were Clegg.'

'Aye, well, that were the name she went under when she lived here in Preston. Freda Morris.' He prodded the page with his finger. 'The bloke's name should be there an' all.'

Ruth followed the line along. 'Ernie,' she read. 'Ernie Fellowes.'

'That's the one.' Taking the book, he scanned the page, scrutinising the figures there. 'By my reckoning, they still owe me one and sixpence.'

Ruth glanced up at the big old clock over the counter. 'My God! Is that the time?'

Following her glance, the old man nodded his head. 'That's right, lass,' he said. 'Half-past five, that's what it says.'

When he turned round, she was already out the door and going at some fast pace towards the tram stop. 'Like mother, like daughter!' he sighed. 'There goes my one and sixpence!' and he ran a pen right through the page.

LOOKING IN THE mirror, Peter Williams struggled to arrange his tie. 'That's twice you've been late back,' he grumbled. 'Where the devil have you been?' From the corner of his eye he watched her pacing the floor. 'What's wrong with you, woman? Stand still, for God's sake! You're making me dizzy!'

Coming to a halt she smiled at him through the mirror. 'Sorry.'

'You've been out every day this week.' He was not a man to miss even the smallest detail. 'Late back Wednesday and again today. What's more, you're wearing too much rouge for my liking.' Suspicion flooded his mind. 'You're not hiding anything from me, are you?'

'I don't know what you mean. You've no reason to be suspicious of me, and well you know it.' She was well versed in sounding hurt.

Having finished at the mirror, he came across the hallway to where she was standing. 'If I thought you had another man behind my back, I'd have to deal with him. You know I'm capable of it.'

Stroking his face she smiled up at him. 'That was a clever move,' she murmured. 'You got him to do the job, then smothered him and took your money back.'

Clapping his hand over her mouth he silenced her. 'Walls have ears!' he warned.

Releasing herself, she reassured him, 'There's only you and me here. Daisy's in the yard, hanging out the washing.'

Smiling wickedly, he put his hand up her skirt and through her knicker leg, making her gasp with pleasure. 'You wouldn't carry on behind my back, would you?'

'You know I wouldn't.'

He played with her for a while, rousing himself. 'I'd best be gone!' As abruptly as he had thrust his hand up, he drew it down. 'There's money waiting to be collected.'

'If you hadn't put your helper in hospital, you wouldn't have it all to do yourself.'

'He stole from me.' His face darkened. '*Nobody* does that to me!'

'Find somebody who's honest,' she said indifferently, 'then you wouldn't have to get out so early of a morning.'

'Easier said than done. They're all rogues when it comes to other people's money. No, I'll do my own collecting from now on.'

'So, you'd rather have money than me, is that it?'

'Of course!'

And try as she might, she couldn't change his mind.

Convinced she was up to something, he had a warning for her. 'If I ever found out you *were* two-timing me, I'd have to teach you the same lesson I taught him.'

'I'm not two-timing you.' Christ, he was stupid. She was pregnant by him, and he hadn't noticed yet.

'You'd be thrown out, with nothing but the clothes you stand up in,' he warned her.

'There's no other man,' she protested. 'There's only you, Peter. I don't want anybody else.'

'Hmh!' Pursing his lips, he took stock of her, quietly nodding with satisfaction. 'That smack across the head the other night seems to have brought you to your senses.'

'Really?' There were times when she hated him.

'I mean, look around here.' Propelling her backwards into the drawing room, he gestured widely. 'Not an empty bottle in sight, and everything in its place.' Pointing to the side-table, he sneered, 'There's even a bowl of flowers on the table. My God, Ruth! You're such a cunning bitch, I can't help but wonder what you're up to.'

'I'm keeping a good house for you,' she smiled knowingly. 'After all, it's what you pay me for.'

His cold eyes raked her face. 'Something tells me you're not to be trusted.'

When she reached out to embrace him, he stepped back a pace, and was quickly gone. Left behind, Ruth couldn't rest. She walked to the window then back to the fireplace, now to the door, and back again, as if she'd forgotten something, but didn't know quite what.

Suddenly she went rushing out of the room and straight

into young Daisy, who squealed with fright. 'Oh miss, yer nearly gave me a heart attack!' Clutching her chest she leaned on the wall to catch her breath.

'Stand up, you stupid girl!'

Daisy stood up straight as a ramrod. 'Yes, miss.' She had felt the weight of Ruth Clegg's fist several times – and it was not a pleasant experience. 'Sorry, miss.'

'I'm going out now. I may not be back for a while.'

'Yes, miss.' Secretly, she wished the pair of them would go out and *never* bloomin' well come back!

'When the master returns – whatever time that may be – I want you to tell him I've only just that minute gone out. Do you understand what I'm saying?'

Daisy nodded. 'You're going out now,' she repeated, 'only when the master comes back, even if it's ten o'clock tonight, I'm to say you've only that minute gone out.'

'And you're to say that I've just gone for a quick breath of air – is that understood?'

'Yes, miss.' Daisy's imagination ran riot. A breath of air, my arse! she thought. More likely you're meeting some bloke for a bit o' tomfoolery, 'cause *he* didn't 'ave yer in his bed last night. Ever vigilant, Daisy kept account of what the couple got up to, in case the information might come in handy some day.

'Remember what I said, Daisy,' Ruth rapped out, seeing the maid's attention wandering. 'Keep it in mind and don't open your mouth before you think what you're saying.'

'No, miss.' She got all flustered. 'I mean yes, miss.'

'Or I may have to look for someone who can do as I ask.'

'I understand, miss.'

'Good. Now be about your business. Go on, girl!'

While Daisy scurried away, Ruth took herself upstairs to get ready. She decided to look her splendid best. 'It's been a long time since she last saw yer,' she muttered, throwing this and that out of the wardrobe. 'The last time you an' her were together you fought like cat and dog. You never got on, and you never will, and now you're thinking of going back to grovel at her feet.'

She sighed, long and hard. 'That hard-faced bugger might take you in and she might not, but one thing's for certain, if she *does* take you in, she'll make you suffer first, then she'll want every penny in your purse.' She chuckled. 'So she won't have to know what I've got in my purse, will she, eh?' A surge of anger coloured her thinking. 'All the same, I want her to know how well I've done. She said I'd never amount to anything, but she's wrong. I've got fine clothes and a few bits of decent jewellery, and what with the odd guinea I've been stealing away from that bastard, it all adds up to a tidy little haul.' Taking a long crimson dress out of the wardrobe, she flung it aside. 'I don't suppose I'll be wanting *that* where I'm going.' But she had worn it time and again, when they'd acted the lady and gent and sat at the table to be waited on by Daisy. Still, better to be alive and wearing sack cloth, than to be dead in a crimson dress.

She paused a moment, filled with all kinds of regrets. 'I *had* intended taking him for a damned sight more, but what with him having his own sister murdered, then killing the man he sent to do his dirty work . . . By! I daren't think what he'd do to *me* if he took a mind.' The idea of being burnt alive or smothered to death was so terrifying, she sat on the bed and gave herself a minute to think about what she was doing.

'You're stealing his money,' she said aloud, 'and you know how he'd repay you for that, if he ever found out. That poor young fella he had working for him was beaten senseless, before being left for dead in some dirty old alley.'

The truth was, Peter Williams was capable of anything and everything. 'Even his own mother isn't safe.'

Realising the danger she herself might be in, she summed up the total of her sins. 'I've lived in his house and slept in his bed, and now I've got myself with child – the very thing he told me not to do. I might have got rid, but I didn't realise till it were too late. And now I'm stealing his precious money, and looking to go into hiding so he can't get his evil hands on me.' It was a catalogue of errors, which sent the shivers down her back.

But she decided, 'I'm not like all the others though. I *know* what he's done, and I could shop him to the police tomorrow, if I had a mind. If he ever finds me, I'll remind him of that.' On the other hand, knowing all that was small comfort. She decided it was best not to tell her mam too much about him. Otherwise, if he found her there, like as not he'd have the whole bleedin' place set afire, with all of them in it!

After washing and putting on clean underwear, she brushed her hair until it shone like gold. Her long, auburn hair was the one feature of which she had always been proud. There had been a time when she enjoyed Peter running his hands through it, but not any more. Not since she knew those same hands had smothered a man to death.

Some short time later, looking stunning in a brown, close-fitting costume and matching court shoes with high, chunky heels, she went to the kitchen and reminded Daisy, 'Don't forget what I told you.'

'No, miss.' Kneeling over her mop-bucket, Daisy drew her hand out of the soapy water and rubbed her nose, leaving a blob of soap-suds clinging to her nose-end. 'I've not forgot.'

JOSEPHINE COX

'Think on it, then. If you let me down, I'll swing for you.'
Trying not to laugh, she told the hapless girl, 'Wipe your nose.
You look like a clown.'

With that she turned away and in a minute was out of the
house and down the street. Behind her, mimicking Ruth to
perfection, Daisy strutted about the kitchen on her tippy-toes.
'Think on now, Daisy,' she said, in her best voice. 'Let me
down and I'll swing for you.' Giving the bucket a kick, she
promised sourly, 'If I wasn't so bleedin' scared, I'd give the
police enough to get the pair of youse put in clink where you
belong!' Another possibility had often crossed her mind. 'Mind
you, I could demand enough money from Peter Williams to set
meself up for the rest of my life.'

When somewhere in that old house a floorboard creaked,
she swung round in terror, one hand clapped over her mouth.
When she realised that it was nothing, she sat down in the
chair, trembling with fright. 'Oh, you silly, silly girl, Daisy
Morgan. When will you learn to keep your mouth shut!'

Resuming her work, she sang at the top of her voice;
anything to shut out the dangerous thoughts. She mustn't
speak of them again; she mustn't listen at doors or peep
through key-holes. Because she, like Ruth, already knew far
too much for her own good.

———⋅◦⋅———

FREDA MORRIS WAS in the back scullery washing out her
smalls, when the knock came on the front door. Swinging
round, she stood, momentarily petrified, as she wondered what
to do. A moment later and the knock came again, this time
more determined. 'That bloody Ernie's never here when he's
needed!' Like a thief in the night, she made her way along the

passage where she sneaked into the front parlour and lifting the curtains, peeped out to the front door.

Oh, thank God. It wasn't the rent man. She breathed a sigh of relief. They were already three weeks in arrears, with still no money to catch up. But who the hell was that? Her curious eyes raked the smart figure at the door. 'No, it can't be!' Then, 'Yes, it bloody well *is*!' It was her daughter, Ruth, and Freda couldn't believe her eyes.

Lifting the curtain, she called out, 'Clear off, you! I said when you left you were never to set foot over my front doorstep again, and I meant every bleedin' word. So bugger off – and good shuts to you!'

Dropping the curtain, she marched out of the room and down the passage to the back parlour. 'Bleedin' cheek! If she thinks I've forgotten the names she called me, she can think again, the little slag! Coming after me like that! How in God's name did she find me, that's what I'd like to know.'

Bubbling with anger, she thrust her two arms into the water, drew out her bloomers and wrung them in her fists, like she might have liked to wring her daughter's neck, if only the silly little bitch was to stand still long enough!

Refusing to go away, Ruth shouted through the letter-box. 'Mam, let me in! MAM! I've summat to tell yer. I'm not on the scrounge neither. I've got money to lend, if you're in need of a bob or two.'

'GO AWAY! WE DID OUR TALKING YEARS BACK.' Money to lend indeed. Huh! That'd be the day.

'Come on, Mam!'

'I SAID GO AWAY!'

'Listen!' If she was to get inside, Ruth knew she would have to do some quick thinking. 'If you send me away now, you'll regret it for ever.'

When only silence greeted her, she went on, 'I've summat important to tell yer, but I'm not shouting for all the neighbours to hear, so you'd best let me in. When I've told you what I've come for, I'll be on my way . . . if that's what you really want.' Taking a breath she called out, 'I'll count to ten. After that, I'm leaving. And you'll allus wonder what it was I had to tell you.'

She began the count. 'One . . . two . . . I mean it, Mam.'

Suddenly the door was flung open, and there stood Freda Clegg, eyes rolling with amazement as she looked her daughter up and down. 'Well, will yer look what the cat's dragged in,' she declared. 'The last time I clapped eyes on you, you were like some scruffy urchin off the streets – down on your luck, with a man friend who used you to bring home the wages, then smacked you senseless when it wasn't enough.'

'Come on, our mam! Will you let me in or what?' Ruth didn't like the way two passing neighbours had slowed their footsteps and were cocking an ear to what her mam was saying.

They soon quickened their steps and hurried off when Freda yelled after them, 'Heard enough, have yer? Come inside, why don't you. Happen I'll tell you how often me and Ernie do it. He might even oblige the pair of youse, if you ask him nicely.'

Ruth laughed out loud, and it felt good. 'You're a tonic, Mam,' she chuckled. 'You never change, do you?'

'Never mind that.' Propelling her up the steps, she gave Ruth an almighty push. 'As for you . . . get inside. I can't believe you've tracked me down. Jesus! I thought I'd seen the last o' you, and here you are – done up to the nines and offering me money.'

That much at least, Freda Clegg would never refuse.

Once inside the parlour, Ruth glanced about and was pleasantly surprised. The furniture was not expensive by any means, but it was good, solid stuff, and even had a shine where Freda had been polishing it. The rug in front of the fire was a bit threadbare, but it was cosy and colourful all the same. The table was laid with a pretty blue cloth, and there was a jug of flowers in its centre.

Though the window was open, the room smelt slightly of booze; but all in all, it was a nice enough room.

'Not what *you're* used to, I don't expect, not by the cut o' them clothes.' Scowling, the older woman defended her modest abode. 'I'm proud o' my little parlour. So you'd best not come here looking down on me, my girl. Don't forget, I knew you when the snot dribbled from your nose and you hadn't got a hankie to wipe it, nor for that matter, a pair o' drawers to cover your skinny arse!'

Ruth thought of the grand rooms, filled with expensive furniture that made you afraid to mark it, and Daisy, who listened at every door, and she knew where she felt safest. 'You're wrong,' she told her mam quietly. 'I was just thinking how cosy the parlour was.'

'Oh! Got your approval, has it?' Freda chuckled. 'You should see it when there's a good supply o' booze about. I don't waste no time on polishing and dusting then. You know your mam. She likes a good time when there's one going. Only, what with one thing and another, good times have been in short supply lately.'

Ruth gave a small, wry smile. 'Nothing's changed then, has it, Mam?'

'Hey! I didn't let you in that door so's you could insult me. Besides, from what I can recall, you're no angel yourself.' She took another good look at her wayward daughter, at the smart brown suit and expensive jewellery, and was astounded. 'Looks like you've done all right though, gal. Lying on your back with your legs in the air, was it?'

Ignoring her mother's attempts to start a row, Ruth took a liberty and sat herself down. 'Look, Mam, I haven't come here to argue, there's no time for all that.'

'What *have* you come for then?'

'I need to ask you summat.'

'Oh, do you now?' Leaning up against the sideboard, Freda folded her arms and kept a wary eye on Ruth. 'You're in trouble, aren't you?'

'Sort of.'

'There! I knew it. I bloody *knew* it!' Shaking her fist she warned, 'I told you when you ran off not to fetch your troubles to my door, and here you are, bold as bleedin' brass! You'd best get out afore I lose my temper – and you know well enough what kinda temper I've got.'

'Please, Mam, it's not like that. Sit down and I'll tell you.'

Temper subsiding, Freda peeped at her from beneath frowning eyebrows. 'You said you had money to lend. Was that just so's I'd let you in?'

Desperate to get back to Summerfield House before Peter got home, Ruth denied it. 'I've money in my bag, but first I need to talk.'

Freda's voice sharpened. 'You'd best not be playing games with me, young lady. Just now, when you came knocking on that door, you put the fear o' Christ in me. Ernie's been off work and we're three weeks behind with the rent. Can you sort it, or can you *not*?'

In answer to that, Ruth opened her bag and took out a wad of notes, which she waved in the air. '*Now* will you sit down?'

At the sight of all that money, Freda could do no other than sit down, or she'd have dropped where she stood. 'My God! Wherever did you get all that? Jesus! You ain't stole it from some man and he's got you on the run, have you? 'Cause I don't want that kind o' trouble here. I'm too old to be doing with all that.'

Ruth lied through her teeth. 'There's no man to worry about. He went off with some woman when he found out I was pregnant. But as you can see, he left me well provided for.'

'Pregnant, eh? I knew you'd get caught one o' these fine days.' Suspicion reared its ugly head, 'What I don't understand is what you're doing here. Looks to me like you've enough money to get yourself a place of your own.'

'I don't want a place of my own, at least not yet. All I'm asking is to stay with you until the baby's born.'

'What!' Freda laughed out loud. 'Don't tell me you're scared of having a bairn. Is that it, eh? You've come home to your mammy 'cause you're frightened to be on your own when it's born. By! I never thought I'd see the day when you were frightened of anything!'

Ruth was secretly delighted. She had been about to make up some other story, but now she pounced on the opportunity. 'That's it, Mam,' she agreed. 'I'm terrified of having a bairn. I can't sleep at night, I'm that worried. I had to find you, Mam. I need to stay with you until it's born. After that, I'll get a place of my own and keep right away, if that's what you want.'

Freda's only thought was to be rid of the rent arrears and line her own pocket. 'How much will you pay?'

'Whatever you ask . . . within reason.' She must remember she wouldn't have unlimited funds; even if she stole enough to set her up later on.

'Five shillings a week.'

'Two.'

'Four.'

'*Three* shillings a week, and an extra sixpence a week when the bairn's born.'

Freda considered it, but it wasn't enough. 'Three and sixpence a week, and the extra sixpence after.'

Ruth hadn't expected her mam to be so mean, but right now, she didn't have time to argue, 'All right, it's a deal.'

Freda couldn't take her eyes off the wad of notes peeping out from her daughter's bag. 'And four weeks' rent in advance, payable now afore you leave.'

While Ruth counted out the money, her mam went to put the kettle on, all the while chatting about her life so far. 'Me and Ernie fight a lot,' she confessed, 'but it wouldn't be me if I didn't want to rule the roost.'

'You're a mean, selfish cow, that's why.' Ruth knew her mam only too well, 'I bet you give him hell, don't you?' she suspected. 'I bet you knock seven bells out of him at different times, especially if you've had a drink or two.'

Returning with two mugs of tea, Freda put one on the arm of Ruth's chair and the other she kept herself. Sitting opposite in Ernie's armchair, she answered Ruth's question. 'Like I said, we fight a lot, and happen I am a bit mean to him, but that's the way I am, and he knew that when he asked me to come here and live with him.'

Ruth took a sip of her tea, only to find it was disgusting. 'It's cold and there's hardly any milk in it,' she complained, setting it down in the hearth. 'Don't tell me you haven't got any milk?'

Freda shook her head mournfully. 'You had the last drop,' she said. 'Me and Ernie have learned to take it any way it comes, but it won't stretch to visitors.' Her face lit up. 'He's back in work now, though,' she reminded Ruth, 'and things are already looking up because you've just given me a month's rent in advance.'

'Don't you think you should clear it with this Ernie first?' Ruth asked.

Freda's eyes almost popped out of her head. 'Why?'

'Because it's *his* house, that's why.'

Freda laughed out loud. 'It might be *his* house,' she declared, 'but *I'm* the boss.'

Ruth might have known. 'Poor sod,' she said. 'I should think he regrets the day he let you move in here.'

'Oh, he does. But he'd break his heart if I were to walk out on him.' Her eyes grew dreamy. 'I do love him though. He's a lovely bloke and you're right, he doesn't deserve a spiteful cow like me.'

'Are you two wed?'

'Good God, no!' Freda seemed astonished at the thought. 'We left it so either one of us could walk out that door whenever we felt like it.' She chuckled coarsely. 'The truth is, there have been times when we've had such awful rows, that I'd have run a bleedin' mile. But when I stopped to think about it, I knew where I was well off, so I stayed.' Leaning back in her chair, she confided, 'He was wed once, you know . . . had a grown-up son too.'

'What do you mean, had?'

'His wife passed on some time back – twelve year or more ago. A while after that, me and him got together, but the son took a dislike to me.'

'I wonder why!' Ruth muttered sarcastically.

'Anyway, there was a God-awful row and they went their separate ways. It's such a shame, 'cause Ernie idolises that lad. He even got arrested some time back, hanging about the street where his son lives, waiting to catch a sight of his lad, he was. It's pathetic really. I told him, "You silly old bugger," I said, "he's turned his back on you. Leave it at that, why don't you?" But he can't. He'll never be content till they've made up their differences.' She grimaced. 'Mind you, I can't see it happening.'

'Where does his son live?'

'Along Buncer Lane – where that poor couple got burned to death.' Oblivious to her daughter's whitened face, she went on, 'They say the son was badly injured – been in a wheelchair ever since.' Suddenly, catching sight of Ruth's shocked face, she peered at her through small eyes. 'Hey! Look at the colour o' *you*. I've knocked you for six, ain't I, talking about them being burned to their deaths?'

Without replying, Ruth collected her cold tea from the hearth and took a great big gulp. *If her mam found out how her own daughter was living with the man responsible, there was no telling what she might do!*

Freda continued her chatter. 'It turns out that poor lad Larry and Ernie's son Mick are the best of friends. They went to school together.'

By now her chatter was washing over Ruth's head. It was a dangerous world she had found herself in. 'Look, Mam, I've got to go,' she said, 'but I'll be back.'

Before she had taken two steps, a loud knock came on the front door. 'Jesus! Get down!' Grabbing Ruth's arm, Freda dragged her behind the settee. 'It's that bloody rent man again!' she hissed.

Ruth couldn't understand it. 'So pay him, Mam,' she urged. 'You've got the money now.'

'Like hell I will!' Freda snapped. 'He can whistle for his bloody rent!' And she would not be budged. 'Stay where you are, till he's good and gone,' she ordered. 'He'll be away in a minute, you'll see.'

It was twenty minutes before she let Ruth get up, at which point Ruth bolted out of the house and took to her heels. 'I'll see you some time soon, then?' Freda called.

'All right, Mam, yes.' Because, however much she dreaded it, Ruth feared she had little choice.

Better the devil you knew, than the devil himself, she thought.

Chapter Ten

I T WAS SUNDAY, Ellie's last day before starting work.

'What's the matter, dearie?' Peggy had been watching Ellie pick at her food. 'You always enjoy your Sunday dinner.'

'Oh! I'm sorry.' Ellie had been miles away, her mind on tomorrow, when she would be out in the big wide world, earning her living at last. 'I was just thinking.'

Ted put down his fork. 'It's a big day for the lasses,' he said. 'They've finished with school, and tomorrow they'll be working folk. It's a bit hard to get used to at first.' Picking up his fork again, he stabbed a piece of red meat, then a small potato and, smiling at Ellie, continued to enjoy his meal.

Betsy had something to say and, as usual, it betrayed her selfishness. 'I'd rather be at school. I don't fancy working at the shoe-factory.' Her comment was addressed to Ted, but he ignored her, so she turned to Peggy. 'I really wish I was going to college. I know you can't afford for us both to go, and I'm sure Ellie's not all that bothered, so why can't you just send *me*? You promised I could go to college!'

'Oh, dearie me.' Peggy began to get flustered. 'That was before me and Ted sat down and worked it all out. The truth is, it would take every penny we've got, and more besides. We would have to borrow, and we've never been in debt in our lives. We probably couldn't pay it back, you see.' In desperation she turned to her husband. 'That's right, isn't it, dear?'

'Beg your pardon?' The lump of carrot bobbed up and down over his tongue.

Realising he hadn't been listening to a word she'd said, Peggy gave a sigh. 'Don't talk with your mouth full, Ted,' she chided. 'It isn't nice.'

'Hmh.' Closing his mouth, he swallowed his food so quickly it made his eyes water. 'What did you ask me, just now?'

'I said we're sorry the girls weren't able to stay on at college. Betsy was saying how Ellie wouldn't mind if we just sent Betsy, but like I was telling her, we can't really afford to do even that.'

Frowning, Ted Walters peered at Betsy from beneath his brows. 'I thought we'd settled all that, weeks since. You know very well, if we'd been able to, we would have sent you *both* to college. But we can't afford it, and all the will in the world won't put money in the bank.'

'You'll be all right, Betsy dear,' Peggy chipped in. 'You might even *enjoy* working at the shoe-factory.'

Ted agreed. 'Moreover, if you're dead set on going to college, you can now begin to save up every penny towards it. Me and Peggy won't charge you much for your keep – just enough to cover the basics, that's all. So, with low outgoings, you should soon be able to build up a tidy sum.'

Ellie finished her meal and pushed her plate away. 'That's just what *I* said. Mrs Potton even promised she would ask the authorities if they could help. But first, Betsy has to prove how dedicated she is.'

Ted shook his head. 'Oh, I wouldn't count on the authorities helping,' he said, pursing his lips in his usual, contemplative fashion. 'Promises are like pie-crust, you know – made to be broken. In fact, it won't be too long now before they wash their hands of the pair of you altogether. In my experience, once you're out and working, they turn their attention to the more needy.'

Peggy was hopeful. 'I'm sure it will all work out very well,' she said. 'I've a feeling you'll like working at the shoe-factory. You'll make new friends and you'll be earning your own money. Once you get over the first day or so, it'll be grand, you'll see.'

'That's right,' Ted declared. 'It'll be good for them. It will make the lasses independent as you say, and give them a sense of responsibility into the bargain.' He was alluding to Betsy in particular.

And it was she who retaliated: 'I'm not looking forward to the journey. It's a long way to the shoe-factory on the tram. I'll be worn out by the time I get home.'

Ellie had a thing or two to say. 'Don't be peevish, Betsy. It's not as if you'll be working at the mill, where they're on their feet all day, and have to start at six o'clock of a morning. You'll be sitting in the office in front of a desk, and besides, you won't have to start till half past eight, so it's not so bad.'

'*And* there'll be a meal waiting for you when you get home,' Peggy reminded her. 'Many of those poor women in the mills have to work all day, then go home and cook the meal afore they can even sit down and take a breath.' Peggy recalled her own mam doing the very same. 'Besides, the shoe-factory is a good place to work. It's clean and well ordered, and they have proper tea-breaks. I think we owe your friend Mick a vote of thanks for mentioning it.'

Ted intervened. 'That's right, love! What's more, when Ellie told us what young Mick had said, about how they were looking for trainees, I went out of my way to speak to the boss. He's a good man. He's promised to look after you, and I'm sure he will.'

Ellie had thanked him before and she thanked him again. 'Me and Betsy know that, and we're very grateful, aren't we, sis?'

'I suppose so.'

Ted was more concerned about Ellie. 'Are you sure you're doing the right thing, love?'

'What do you mean?'

'Well, what I'm saying is, you were both given the option of working on the factory floor, or up in the office. Betsy's gone for the office work, but you've chosen to work on the factory floor. It seems such a waste. You're bright and quick – and so is Betsy, I know – but you'll be making the shoes, while Betsy's selling them. I don't see the sense in that. You would have done so well in the office.'

Ellie defended her decision. 'I'm sorry if I've disappointed you,' she said honestly, 'but I'm not cut out to sit behind a desk all day. I'd rather be with the people downstairs, where I can breathe. Besides, I'll be happier, I know I will.'

He smiled, suddenly understanding. 'You've always been good with people,' he admitted, 'and you're clever with your hands . . . creating things and such. Happen you're right,' he conceded. 'At least you'll be getting the same pay as young Betsy here.' He nodded. 'Aye, happen you're right.'

'Well, I think she's mad!' Betsy had already told Ellie what she thought, and now she told the others. 'They're a common lot who work down there. They wear turbans and slippers and don't care tuppence what they say. I'm glad I'll be upstairs, out of the way.'

Scratching his chin, Ted gave the matter some consideration. 'You've a hard heart, lass. Happen the workers on the factory floor will be glad you're not down there alongside them. What do you think to that?'

Her head jerked up. 'I don't care one way or the other. Besides, I wanted to go to college. I never wanted to work in a factory.'

'So you keep saying. But do you know something? I've a feeling you and Ellie will get on so well at the shoe-factory that the idea of college will have gone right out of your head in no time at all.'

Betsy disagreed. 'Even if I *didn't* want to go to college, I *still* wouldn't want to work in a shoe-factory!'

'Is that so?' Regarding her for what seemed an age, Ted said quietly, 'Well now, I think I see what the trouble is here.'

Peggy was curious. 'What's that then, dear?'

Keeping his eyes on Betsy, Ted scraped back his chair and prepared to leave. 'Why! The lass doesn't want to work at *all*! And if we gave her the choice of going to college, she wouldn't want that neither. The truth as I see it, is that Betsy doesn't want to work and she doesn't want to learn. She wants to be a lady who sits on her arse all day and does nothing!'

Leaving them all in shocked silence, he slammed shut the door behind him and marched upstairs. 'Oh my word!' Peggy had gone white as a sheet. 'In all the years I've known my Ted, I've *never* heard him use that kind of language.' Nervously clutching her throat, she looked at Betsy with tearful eyes. 'Oh, you've really upset him, dear. Go after him and apologise . . . for my sake. Please?'

'No. It wasn't me who did the swearing. It was *him*. So it should be him who apologises.' She then got up from the chair and flounced out of the room.

A few minutes later Ellie and Peggy heard the front door slam. 'Oh dear! I do hate rows of any sort. I'll have to go and humour Ted. I don't like him being in such a mood.' Peggy went out of the room at a trot. 'Ted!' she called his name timidly, but there was no answer.

A moment later she returned to find Ellie clearing the plates away. 'Oh no, dear!' Rushing to help, she told Ellie, 'I can do that. You away and follow Betsy. I'm worried about her. She's taken the dog, and she knows very well that Sunshine's pups are due any day now.' Leaning against the sink she caught her breath. 'Ted won't speak to me.'

Ellie felt sorry for her. 'He will,' she replied. 'Give him time, eh?'

Peggy looked at her foster-daughter, at her kind face and those wonderful dark-blue eyes, and she felt ashamed. 'You're a good girl, Ellie,' she said, 'not like Betsy. I'm sorry to say it, but she does seem to enjoy upsetting people.'

'I'll have a word with her.' And she would, in no uncertain terms!

'Tell her I'm not angry – except that she must bring that poor dog home.'

Feeling the need to be on her own, Ellie jumped at the chance to get out into the fresh air. 'I'll not be long,' she promised. 'I'll just go along the front a little way. I shouldn't be gone more than an hour or two.' The trouble was, once she got down by the sea, it was so wonderful, she never wanted to come away.

'All right, dear. Mind how you go now,' Peggy instructed. 'And take your coat. It looks as if it might shower.' Giving

Ellie no choice, she took the coat from the peg and handed it to her. 'And don't go down to the water's edge. The tides can be unpredictable at this time of year.'

Assuring her that she would be all right, Ellie departed.

———<del>>•○•<</del>———

SHE WALKED FOR a while then, when the smell of the sea filled her nostrils, she began to run. The cool, salty air on her face was exhilarating. There was a kind of excitement in living by the sea, when you could hear the waves at night, crashing into each other, and the soulful cry of seagulls with first light. Ellie loved it. Now that she had lived so close to the sea, she never wanted to live anywhere else.

Rounding the corner, she saw Betsy straight away. Hunched and miserable, she was sitting on the sand, the dog beside her. 'Betsy!' Running across the road, Ellie made for her.

Her sister was in no mood for company. 'Why do you always have to follow me?'

'I'll go if you like.' When Betsy was in this kind of mood, she was impossible.

'I expect *she* sent you, didn't she?'

'She's worried about you. And so am I.' Now, when the dog nuzzled up to her, Ellie tenderly stroked it. 'Hello, girl.' The feel of the Labrador's soft, cool coat was oddly comforting.

'What do you want?'

Ellie was honest. 'I want you to stop being ungrateful to Peggy and Ted. They took us in and they've cared for us every step of the way. They're good, kind people and they don't deserve to have you moaning at them all the time.'

'Hark at Miss Goody Two Shoes!'

Ellie had suspected it wouldn't be too long before the insults came round to her. 'You can call me what you like, it doesn't bother me. But you should have more respect for them, that's all I'm saying.'

'Mind your own business.'

'No, Betsy. When I see you behaving like that, I shall speak my mind. I've told you what I think, and now it's up to you.'

'You're right! It *is* up to me. Ted doesn't like me, and well you know it.'

'And why do you think that is, eh? You always seem to be goading him into some sort of an argument. If you ask me, it's *you* who's made up your mind not to like him. Not the other way round.'

Leaping to her feet, Betsy kicked off her shoes. 'You don't know what you're talking about. Like I said before, mind your own business and get off home. I don't want you here.' Calling the dog, she ran across the sand towards the sea. Reluctantly, Sunshine ambled behind, her soft, swollen belly dragging in the sand.

For a time Ellie watched them. She saw how the foolish Betsy ran in and out of the water, her skirts held high, and time and again she called for her to come back. But she wouldn't, and Ellie knew she could not persuade her.

So she sat there, watching those two, and enjoying the scenery, and life felt good. The skies were big and blue, the sea endless, and the sand was like a carpet of gold before her.

Now, in the early afternoon, people were beginning to arrive; young couples arm in arm and families, settling down on the sand with their colourful rugs and picnic hampers. The sound of laughing children rang in her ears. It was wonderful, Ellie thought, just wonderful!

Her mind was taken back to one Sunday afternoon when her mam and dad had brought them all further down the coast to Blackpool. They had arrived by train, and afterwards taken a ride on an open-topped tram. She and Betsy had ridden the donkeys, and all in all, it had been a day to remember. Tears filled her eyes. But amidst the tears was a great joy, to have known her mam and dad, even if only for such a cruelly short time. She would always miss them; always love them. Yet she gave thanks to the good Lord for sparing her and Betsy. Larry too, and her lovely grandad.

Inevitably, her thoughts turned to the man who had been in the house that night. She hadn't forgotten him; she never would. So far, no one had been able to find out who he was. But one day in the future, Ellie would find out. She was sure of it.

Lazing there, with the September sun on her face, she closed her eyes and thought about Mick, and how very soon she would be working in the same building. The other week, at Grandad's house, she had not been fully aware of her feelings towards Mick. Now though, after giving it much thought, she knew only one thing; she needed to see him again and again. She needed to find out what was going on inside her; she needed to know how he felt towards her.

But it was early days yet, and she was too young to be thinking of love and suchlike. All the same, the thought of seeing him tomorrow made her smile, made her happy.

Suddenly aware of a dog barking, people shouting and others running across the sand, Ellie's attention was drawn to where she had last seen Betsy. At once she realised something was wrong. Going at a run she fled the short distance to the water's edge, and there, being cradled in a towel, wet and shivering and in floods of tears, was her twin. 'She must have fallen in and got out of her depth,' the man who had rescued her said. 'Fortunately, I'm a strong swimmer. She was lucky I was close by, or the tide would have swept her out.'

When Betsy had calmed down, the man's wife told Ellie, 'She'll be fine, but she needs to get home and into some dry clothes.' And, while her husband called a cab and paid for it too, Ellie walked Betsy back to shore, the pregnant dog trailing wearily behind.

<hr>

PEGGY GOT INTO a right state when she heard what had happened. Within minutes she had Betsy in a hot bath with a pile of clean clothes waiting beside her. 'You bad girl!' she scolded Betsy. 'How many times have I told you! The waters there are unpredictable. You could have been drowned!'

'It wouldn't have mattered if I *was*!' Bolting the bathroom door, Betsy lazed in the bath, a smile creeping over her sullen features. That'll teach them not to keep going on at me, she thought.

By the time Betsy returned downstairs, everybody was in the scullery, and they completely ignored her. She was no longer the centre of attention.

'The puppies are coming!' Ellie's blue eyes gleamed with excitement. 'She started soon after you went upstairs, and Ted says it's only a matter of minutes before they start arriving.'

'You should have called me!' Pushing her way through, Betsy saw how they had made Sunshine comfortable, laying her on a rug, with the window wide open to let in the fresh air.

Betsy made no attempt to comfort the dog. Instead she kept her distance. 'I hope she has six at least,' she said, rubbing her hands. 'That will start my savings off a treat.'

While Ellie soothed the animal with gentle talk, Peggy made sure there was plenty of water on hand. 'I expect she'll need lots to drink,' she remarked, seeing how the poor thing was panting and gasping. 'It must be a hard thing, bringing new life into the world.' Though she had no experience of it herself, more's the pity, she thought.

'I'd best get the bed ready,' Ted announced. 'I've finished the box so they'll not be able to get out and run all over. And there's plenty of room for Mammy and puppies both.' Proud as punch, he went to fetch it from the front room, where he'd been working on it for a fortnight.

'Look!' In a hushed voice, Ellie told them how she could see a little head peeping out. 'There . . . see?' And sure enough, the first baby was arriving.

Suddenly, without warning, the mother stood up and the puppy fell out, with Ellie catching it in the palms of her hands in case it should hurt itself dropping to the ground. 'Oh, Betsy!' Holding it up for her sister to see, she gasped in amazement. 'Isn't it wonderful?'

Betsy didn't think so. She saw the tiny thing, squirming in its own mess and secretions, and felt physically sick. 'I have to go back upstairs,' she muttered. 'I forgot something.' And was gone before they could turn round.

Peggy laughed. 'Some folk can't stand the sight of blood and such,' she said, 'but it's never bothered me.'

Nor Ellie, it seemed, because in rapid succession there arrived four more puppies; each one tended by Ellie, and laid carefully beside its mammy.

A short time later, Ted returned to tell them the dogs' bed was ready. While the women carried the puppies in a shawl, he gently lifted Sunshine, talking with her all the while, until he set her down inside the bed. One by one the puppies were laid alongside, and soon she was licking and fussing, and everything was fine.

'There you are.' Peggy was bursting with satisfaction. 'All's well that ends well.'

Ellie thought the bed was perfect. Set on plastic sheeting, the open wooden box and the long netted run was arranged beneath the window. 'So's you can open the window and freshen the room when it all gets too much,' Ted told his wife, who promptly protested that she would not allow it to 'get too much'.

'It's lovely,' Ellie told Ted, who grinned from ear to ear. 'And they're so happy and content.'

Long after the others had gone, Ellie stayed to watch and enjoy the new arrivals. After their fill of milk, the tiny brown puppies had snuggled up to their mammy and were sound and fast asleep.

Ellie stroked each one in turn. When she came to stroke Sunshine, she told her, 'You should be so proud. You've got five lovely babies.' And for the briefest moment the long, furry tail wagged excitedly, almost as if she understood what Ellie was saying.

That night, when Ellie lay in her bed, she thought about the events of the day. Then she thought about tomorrow, and all the new people she was about to meet. It was an exciting thing to start out in the big wide world.

When her thoughts turned to Mick, her excitement was tenfold.

———≫•◦•≪———

UP BRIGHT AND early, Ellie bathed and dressed. 'What's the rush?' Groaning, Betsy turned over in her bed. 'It's only seven o'clock!'

Throwing her towel on the bed, Ellie gave her a sisterly dig in the ribs. 'It's ten past,' she said, holding the clock in front of Betsy's face. 'We have to be at the factory by nine, so that means catching the eight-thirty train.'

'It's too early!'

Replacing the clock, Ellie reminded her, 'We're starting at nine o'clock today, because it's our first day. Tomorrow we'll have to be up and ready even earlier, so you might as well get used to it.'

'Go away!' Drawing the covers over her head, Betsy refused to listen.

'I thought you were all for earning your own money?'

'I never said that!'

'So, you're not getting out of bed?'

'I might, I might not.' Peering above the bedclothes she hissed, 'Just leave me alone!'

'Please yourself.' Leaving her to it, Ellie hurried down-stairs.

'You look smart, dear.' Peggy was waiting in the kitchen.

'Thank you.' In her clean blue blouse and her dark, calf-length skirt, Ellie looked every inch the new girl. Her long hair was shining and her eyes bright as the morning. 'I'm really excited,' she told Peggy, who had already seen that for herself.

'Breakfast is on the table. The toast is hot and the tea freshly brewed, and there's egg and bacon if you fancy it.' The warm, comforting smell permeated the air.

'I'm too excited to eat,' Ellie replied, 'but I could drink the sea dry.' Seating herself at the table, she poured a steaming hot cup of tea.

'You can't work on an empty stomach.' Peggy wagged a finger. 'At least try and eat some toast.'

With the brown, crispy toast staring her in the face, right next to a dish of rich, red strawberry jam, Ellie's appetite was beginning to rise. 'No egg or bacon though,' she said, and was already spreading her toast liberally with the succulent jam.

'Where's Betsy?' Peggy's anxious gaze went to the door.

'I've told her, but she won't get up.'

'And did you tell her what time it was?'

'Yes, but it made no difference.'

'Little devil!' Like a soldier on the march, Peggy went out of the room.

As Peggy went out, Ted came in. Dressed and ready for off, he had already had his breakfast. 'You look bright and cheerful,' he told Ellie. 'Aren't you nervous – first day an' all?' Shrugging on his jacket he stood at the door, ready to leave.

Ellie shook her head. 'No,' she told him. 'I'm really looking forward to it.'

He roved his eyes round the room. 'Other lass still abed, is she?'

'Peggy's gone to get her up,' Ellie said. 'I hope she has more luck than I did,' she remarked with a sigh, 'because Betsy wouldn't get up for *me*.'

Coming across the room, Ted gave her a fleeting kiss. 'So long as you're up, that's all you should worry about,' he declared. 'Don't make yourself late, waiting for her.' As he went out the door, he called back, 'Think on . . . I shall want to hear all about it when you get home tonight.'

It wasn't long before Peggy returned, with Betsy lagging behind. 'I'll hate the place, I know I will!' The girl was in one of her difficult moods.

'Nonsense! Sit yourself down, dear, and I'll make a fresh brew.' With that Peggy went into the kitchen, humming a tune, and pleased with herself.

Throwing herself into the chair, Betsy piled two eggs and a slice of bacon onto her plate. Before Peggy returned from the kitchen, that little lot had been devoured, and she was already into her second piece of toast and jam.

'That's the ticket,' Peggy encouraged. 'Set off on a full stomach and you'll sail through the day like a boat on the seas, that's what my mother used to say, God rest her.'

Ellie looked at her twin, bent and grumpy, with her tousled hair and bloodshot eyes, and she couldn't help but laugh. 'More like a barge down the canal,' she joked, and got a filthy look from Betsy for her troubles.

IT WAS TIME to leave. Betsy was ready, though she moaned and groaned the whole time. 'I won't like it, I know I won't!'

Proud and relieved, Peggy was there at the door to see them off. 'Now then, Betsy, you must be on your best behaviour,' she warned. 'It's your first day, remember, so you'll need to pay attention, or the boss might decide not to keep you on.'

The girl shrugged. 'He can please himself. I'm sure it won't bother *me* if he sends us packing.'

'Good morning. First day at work, is it?' Mrs Noonan lived in the end house; she was a nosy soul but well-meaning. 'Here's a word of advice: Keep your opinions to yourself and do as you're told – and you can't go wrong.'

Betsy opened her mouth to retort, but Ellie wisely intervened. 'Thank you, Mrs Noonan,' she replied. 'I'm sure we'll be all right.'

Peggy was still on the doorstep when they turned the corner. 'I meant what I said,' Betsy reiterated. 'I really *don't* care if we get shown the door.'

'Well, I do!' Ellie would not let her twin spoil this special day. 'You're beginning to get on my nerves with all your griping. Go back if you want to. But you'll be on your own, 'cause I'm off to earn a wage.' With that she quickened her steps.

When in that instance, the tram suddenly came into view at the end of Penny Street, she broke into a run. 'The tram's here, Betsy,' she cried. 'You'd best make up your mind now. If you don't get on it, you'll miss the train and then you won't have any choice.' Sprinting towards the tram with her arm up to alert the driver, she called out that they were on their way.

'Wait for me!' Betsy cried, and Ellie smiled to herself. She had already suspected that her sister would not go back to the house without her; however much she wanted to.

Puffing and panting, Betsy scrambled into the seat beside Ellie. 'I don't care what anybody says,' she gasped. 'If I don't like it, I won't stay.'

Ellie was past listening. Right now, as the tram rumbled towards the railway station, she was thinking of the day ahead. She wondered what kind of people she would be working with, and how they would treat her. From now on, every day would be different. Her whole *life* would be different. She was no longer a schoolgirl, she was a young woman; all grown-up and about to make her own way in the world. It was a wonderful feeling. And, more than anything, she was looking forward to seeing Mick again.

Betsy dug her in the ribs. 'Hey! I'm talking to you.'

'Sorry, Betsy. I didn't hear you,' Ellie apologised.

Her sister's face lifted in a crafty smile. 'You were thinking of *him*, weren't you?'

'Who?'

'You know who. Mick Fellowes.'

'Don't be daft.'

'Yes, you were! You like him, don't you?'

'I was just thinking, that's all,' Ellie said patiently.

'I know – you were thinking about *him*.' Betsy had no intention of letting the matter drop.

'I was thinking about what it might be like working at the factory, if you must know.'

'So why are you blushing all shades of crimson?' Betsy said triumphantly.

Knowing she could not answer without lying outright, Ellie turned her head away and stared out the window. It was true – she *was* blushing. And it was like that whenever she thought of Mick. It was like it now, as they got off the tram and ran all the way to the train. The nearer they got to Blackburn town, and Mick . . . the more excited she became.

The train ride was short but enjoyable. The train was like a real, live thing; singing as it went along, its wheels clanked against the iron rails, making that wonderful, rhythmic sound as it hurried on its way. All around them, great frothy balloons of steam whispered against the windows, before vanishing into thin air.

Inside the carriage, the early-morning folk chatted and

chuckled, and Ellie listened with interest. There was an elderly couple, busy making plans as to what they might buy at market. 'We need a new brush-head,' the woman said, and her husband mentioned how they never seemed to last five minutes these days.

In another pair of seats, two young women were discussing where to go on Saturday night; one wanted to go to the flicks, the other to the Palais. In the end, they agreed to go to the afternoon matinée, then on to the Palais afterwards.

A middle-aged couple were having a quiet argument, and just in front of Betsy and Ellie sat another, younger couple, staring into each other's eyes. They were obviously very much in love.

When the train arrived at Blackburn railway station, Ellie glanced at the clock. 'Oh no – we've only got five minutes to get there,' she said. 'Come on, sis. We'll have to run. We don't want to be late on our first day.'

Taking to their heels, the girls darted across the Boulevard, then down Ainsworth Street, up and over the bridge and they were there.

The shoe-factory was situated right at the end of a cobbled back street. 'It's not much of a place, is it?' Betsy never had a good word to say about anything or anybody.

They paused outside, looking up at the building and wishing they'd started the same time as everybody else because now, when they walked through those doors, everybody would look up and stare, and it would be awful.

The building was like any other warehouse; square and grey, with many small windows and two big doors, and outside, a great stack of boxes and sacks piled against the wall. There was a horse and cart, its wooden rim painted with the message in bold, white letters:

BRINDLE SHOES
A PLEASURE TO WEAR

There were also two newly purchased black vans painted with the same slogan; the vans now beginning to take their place in the scheme of things alongside the age-old means of horse and cart.

As they neared the entrance, they could hear the faint hum of machinery, and as the girls went through the doors and into their new world, the smell of leather and dye was overpowering.

Betsy made a face. 'Phew! I'm glad I'm not working down here!'

Ellie, though, thought it was a magical place. To the right and left of them were great vats of different-coloured dye. Above these, dripping from huge wooden racks, was layer upon layer of leather. It was obvious the leather had only just been dipped into the vats, because now the excess dye was raining back into the vats, making musical patterns as the drops fell one after the other into the liquid.

To the right of the vats, two men could be seen hauling away the dried leather; while further down the line, others were laying the pieces out on long tables, where they were trimmed and shaped before being stacked, in the different colours, on nearby trolleys. The trolleys were taken one at a time to a group of men, whose task was to cut the leather down to workable pieces. That done, the pieces were taken to yet another group of workers, mostly women.

Talking and laughing, and as yet unaware that they were being watched, the turbaned women sat up at the benches, their busy hands and minds turning the sheets of stiffened leather into shoes of every shape and size. When this highly skilled task was finished, the shoes were boxed and labelled, and stacked sky high onto yet more trolleys, which, when full, were wheeled away to be loaded into the various means of transport, ready for the shops.

'Well, well!' The man was short in stature, with a lovely smile and bright blue eyes that sparkled from a small, perfectly-shaped face. 'It's Ellie and Betsy Bolton, isn't it?' he recalled. 'Come to start work this very morning, am I right?'

'Good morning, Mr Brindle,' they replied, and though he was a charming man, they both felt a little in awe of him. After all, he was the boss here.

And being the boss, he was a very busy man. 'I'll hand you over to my foreman, if I may,' he announced, and even without being summoned, Mick Fellowes appeared from somewhere behind them. 'Ah! There you are, Mick.' Mr Brindle smiled on each in turn. 'You'll be well taken care of now,' he told them. Then off he went, and would not be seen again until Friday.

'He travels a lot,' Mick explained. 'He won't allow anybody else to buy the leather, see. It has to be the very best for his shoes. He reckons he's the only one who can tell a good skin from a bad one – and he's probably right.'

Smiling at Ellie, he made her heart turn over. 'Are you sure you've done the right thing in opting to work down here, instead of up in the office?'

Ellie looked around her. She heard the women laughing, and she saw how those ugly, misshapen portions of leather had been transformed into the most beautiful shoes. As she looked up, a little old man winked cheekily at her, then got a clip round the ear from his grinning female mate. It made her smile. Made her feel as if she belonged. 'I'm sure,' she told Mick.

'And so am I,' he said softly. So softly in fact, that Betsy looked at Ellie with a sly little grin. Her twin didn't even notice. She had eyes only for Mick.

As they walked along, Mick explained, 'You should know, lasses, the factory backs onto the canal. We have our fair share of rats in here, but it's all taken care of, so there's no need for you to be worried.'

But Ellie wasn't worried. Mick was here, and she would see him every working day. That was all she could think of.

As they turned the corner into the loading bay, Betsy was invited to look at the paperwork, parts of which she would be responsible for.

Meantime, Mick spoke to Ellie, his brown eyes shining down on her. 'I'm glad you're here,' he said simply.

And so was Ellie.

PART THREE

OCTOBER 1935
FINDING OUT

Chapter Eleven

D AISY HAD SEEN it coming, but now, when it was really happening, she felt afraid.

'He'll blame me, he allus does!' Shaking with fear she started crying. 'Don't go, miss,' she pleaded. 'Don't go without telling him, 'cause you know he'll only take it out on me.'

Listening, but not taking it in, Ruth continued to fill the portmanteau with clothes and belongings. 'Look, I'm not taking anything that doesn't belong to me. He can't say I've fleeced him – can he, eh? He's had his money's worth from me, and I've never once complained, not even when he . . . when he got that man to . . .'

'To what, miss?' Daisy had already heard enough whispers and innuendoes to know that something very bad had gone on, but she had never really been sure.

'Nothing, Daisy.' Realising how close she had come to branding her lover a murderer, Ruth Clegg took a deep breath and finished the sentence in a different direction. 'I was just thinking about how he manipulates things to his own advantage. Look at what he's done to his own mother – how cold and unloving he can be. And look how he's thrashed me at times! You must have seen and heard enough to know what a terrible bully Peter is.'

'That's what I mean, miss. When he comes home and finds you gone, it's *me* he'll get angry with.' She burst into tears.

Ruth shook her head. 'I've never refused him anything. So what's he got to be angry about, tell me that?'

Daisy couldn't stop shaking. 'But he will, miss! You know he will. When he gets in a temper he lashes out at the nearest thing, and with you gone, the nearest thing will be me, won't it?'

'Keep out of his way then, you daft devil!' Ruth didn't want the girl hurt. She was a nice enough little thing, when all was said and done. 'Look, Daisy, have you no mam or dad? Isn't there somewhere you can go, away from this place? Away from him?'

'No, miss.' Another thing that had made Daisy curious, was the manner in which Ruth was leaving, 'Are you really not taking any of them beautiful clothes, miss?'

'I want nothing from that bastard!' Ruth said bitterly. 'Besides, they weren't given out of love. They were payment for services rendered, that's all.' She sat on the bed and, looking up at Daisy, spoke from the heart. 'I'll admit that once upon a time I loved him – or was under his spell at any rate – and I stupidly thought there might be a chance I could end up being his wife. "Mrs Peter Williams".' She laughed harshly. 'What a sorry fool I was! Well, bugger him *and* his kind. I hope he rots in hell! As for the clothes, I never want to see them again. He can give them to his next floozie, that's what I say.' An idea struck her then. 'Daisy, why don't you take what you want, before he comes home. He won't know. He never took any real notice of what I was wearing anyway. Preferred me without me clothes on, I daresay.'

The younger girl was horrified. The very idea! 'Ooh, no, miss. I wouldn't dare.'

'Then yer a bloody fool, that's all I can say.' Gesturing to the drab clothes she had first worn on coming to this house, Ruth explained, 'These are mine, bought and paid for. I've left him a note. In it I wrote that it's over between us, and that I've told no one of my plans – not even you. So you see, Daisy, he has no reason to have a go at you, not if you don't know anything about it.'

Calling Daisy's attention to the ticking clock on the mantelpiece, she told her, 'I've a thirst on me like a raging bull.' It was fear, she knew – fear of him suddenly bursting in and seeing what she was up to. 'A nice hot brew wouldn't go amiss, with an extra dip of sugar into the bargain if you don't mind,' she told the hapless girl.

'Very well, miss.'

As she went away to put the kettle on, Daisy was not wholly convinced that she wouldn't be hung, drawn and quartered when the master got back.

While Daisy went to the kitchen, Ruth discreetly followed – along the landing and down the stairs, always a step or two behind Daisy, but soft enough for her not to know. At the bottom, she hurried across the hall to Peter's office.

Softly going inside she closed the door and standing with her back to it for a moment, realised the enormity of what she was about to do. 'Gawd, Ruth, if he ever finds out about this, you'll be cut into bite-size pieces and fed to the dogs in the street.' Closing her eyes, she caught her breath at her own foolhardiness.

In all the time she had lived in this house, she had never been invited into this room. Yet she knew it well, because hadn't she been bold enough to creep in here time and again, secretly checking on his hoard of money, and eavesdropping on his criminal dealings with men of shady repute. Peter Williams was an evil man. Little by little Ruth Clegg had come to learn that, and to be afraid for her own well-being.

Yet to her shame, she had stayed, enjoying what money could buy, getting used to being pampered with a maid, and eating from a table filled with food she had not cooked, wearing clothes that she would never have been able to afford, and sharing a bed lined with silken sheets. All of that had been good, and she might never have given it up, until he had made her with child, and threatened her life. Now, she had no choice. In leaving, she was doing what she should have done months ago.

She had no regrets about parting from him, only about having come so close to being as bad a person as he was. Damn his wicked soul!

Glittering with fear, her quick, sharp eyes glanced round the room. Well-lit and spacious, the room was lined with shelves and cupboards. In the centre stood a large oak desk, littered with piles of papers and grey boxes containing all manner of documents – records of his mother's properties, urgent repairs needed, numerous rental contracts and important details of property deals in the offing.

All that side of it was of small interest to Ruth. It was the amount of ready cash he kept in his hidey-hole that had drawn her to this room on this particular day. With this in mind, she went to the desk, opened the bottom drawer and, pulling out the little shelf that was secretly tucked under the lip, removed the small key that was lying there.

Next, she went to the far end of the room. Here she put her back to the tall filing cabinet and began easing it away from the wall; all the while her eyes darting to the door, her heart leaping at every sound and her movements so soft, the sharpest ears would not have detected them.

Built into the wall behind the cabinet was a heavy, grey metal safe. Sliding the key into the lock, she opened the door and caught her breath in amazement, for lying before her eyes was a great stack of notes and gold – more money than she had ever seen before. 'By! This isn't only the rent-money.' She gave a small whistle. 'That cunning bugger must have done some sort of a deal and not told me about it!' But then he hadn't told her about his work for some time now.

Quickly, before Daisy came looking for her with the tea, she took out the thick wad of notes and flipped them through her fingers. 'Cor! There must be *hundreds* here!' Not daring to take more, she counted out three and put the rest back, exactly as she had found them.

Next she took out the long, black box that contained the rent-money. A peep inside told her it was bulging with notes and coins alike. 'He can't have paid the money into the bank for ages,' she realised, 'but then the canny bugger won't use banks when he can hoard it away. The more of his mam's money he can hide from the accountant, the better.' That's what he had once told her. And that was obviously what he was doing here.

With shaking fingers, she dipped into the tin. Taking out two notes and a handful of coins, she slipped it all into her skirt pocket along with the rest. 'That should keep me going until after the bairn's born and I'm able to fend for myself.' She reckoned that Peter Williams owed her that much.

Having taken her dues, she then locked the safe and put the cabinet back where it was, being extra careful to set the feet in the same indentations on the carpet. She replaced the key and checked that all was well, and, as softly as she had entered, she left the same way. He'll never even know I was there, she thought triumphantly as she ran upstairs to her bedroom.

Quickly now, she took the money from her skirt pocket, with the exception of two silver coins, and tucked it all into the lining of her portmanteau. With the case in one hand she grabbed her coat from the arm of the chair and, taking one last look around, satisfied herself that she had left nothing behind. 'You can do what yer like now, Peter Williams. Yer can kill and steal and cheat and grow fat from your filthy doings, but you'll not put *me* in an early grave – not if I can help it, you won't!' With that she hurried downstairs.

Daisy was about to make her way up, tray in hand. 'Take it into the drawing room,' Ruth told her with a wink. 'It'll be a fitting end to my time in this house.'

Ever defiant, Ruth swept into the drawing room, with Daisy on her tail. She sat at the sofa, and allowed the girl to wait on her for the last time. 'You're a good lass, Daisy and, God forgive me, I've not treated you as well as I should.' Taking one of the silver coins out of her pocket, she pressed it into the young maid's hand. 'Here, I hope this tells you how truly sorry I am.'

'Oh, miss!' On seeing how much it was, Daisy began to cry. Even so, she wasted no time in dropping it into her pocket with a watery smile. 'Thank you, miss.'

'Don't forget now.' Ruth outlined what she must do. 'You're to say that as far as you know, I went out to do some shopping, and I won't be gone long.' While she spoke, she placed her leaving note on the mantelpiece.

'When he sees that, miss, he'll know I was lying.'

'No, he won't. He knows you do the drawing room early, before you go on to your other duties. So, you won't have seen

LET IT SHINE

the note. What's more, he'll not be able to prove otherwise, will he?'

'I hope not, miss.' Even with the silver coin warm and safe in her pocket, Daisy trembled at the very idea.

A few minutes later, Ruth was on her way, with the parting words: 'If he starts on you, Daisy, go and find another position with a decent family. You're a good worker, and honest with it.' Digging into her bag, she took out an envelope and handed it to her. 'Put this somewhere safe. It's a note from me as your housekeeper, saying how you have always been exemplary in character, and meticulous in your work.'

She laughed. 'It was the devil of a job, spelling them big words, and I'm not even sure I've got them right. But the letter says only good things, and I thought it just might help you in the future.'

'Thank you, miss. I'll put it away safe, like you said.'

''Bye then, Daisy. Take care of yourself, gal.'

'Bye, miss.' Daisy had lately changed her opinion about Ruth. 'I hope you get on all right, wherever you're going?' The latter was a half-hearted question.

Ruth smiled in return. 'It's best you don't know any more than what I've already told you,' she answered. 'For your own sake as well as mine.'

Daisy understood. 'All the same, mind how you go, miss.' And before Ruth had gone two steps down the street, she ran back inside and shut the door, leaning on it and wishing she, too, could make a bolt for it. At first she wept, feeling sorry for herself at being left behind at the mercy of that monster. But then a strange sort of calm came over her. She stood up tall and determined, a touch of defiance in her voice. 'If he so much as lays one hand on me, I'll be off to the police and tell them everything I know.'

Realising with a jolt just how much she *did* know, she then went at a run into the scullery, where she launched herself into a long and arduous series of tasks that would keep her mind off things. 'I'll try not to think about him,' she told herself. 'Not till he comes bursting through that door, demanding to know the whereabouts of his woman.'

Growing more fearful with every passing minute, she took to reciting Ruth's instructions until they were branded on her brain. '"She's gone out to do some shopping, sir, but she'll not be gone long. A letter, sir? What letter is that then? No, sir, I didn't know nothing about it . . . I did the drawing room early as allus. There weren't no letter in there, not that I seen. No sir, I ain't been back in the room since then".'

Over and over she repeated it, sounding like one of those broken fun-machines at the seaside, when you put a penny in the parrot cage and it chatted on and on, until you gave the machine a kick and put an end to it.

IT WAS HALF-PAST four by the time Ruth arrived at her mother's house.

'Yer ain't brought much, 'ave yer?' Freda still wasn't sure whether she'd made the right decision in having her there.

'I've brought all I need.' Knowing her from old, Ruth had no intention of confiding too much in her mother.

'You'd best come up, if you want to see where your bedroom is.' Without waiting for Ruth to catch her breath or even take off her coat, Freda went on up the stairs, her daughter keeping two steps behind.

At the second room on the left, Freda paused to fling open the door. 'There you go. I've cleaned it out and put new sheets and blankets on the bed. Mind you, I'll expect the amount back for what I've spent out, 'cause I ain't got money to throw about, even if *you* have.'

Ruth thought it wise to put her mother in the picture, right from the very start. 'I haven't got any money to throw about, any more than you have,' she answered. 'And if you think I'll be opening my purse every time you cry broke, you've got another think coming, because I won't!'

'So you'll see your mammy without a penny to her name, is that what yer saying, yer selfish little cow! After I've been good enough to take you in an' all. Shame on yer.'

Exasperated, Ruth laughed in her face. 'Don't come that one with me, Mam. It's *me*, Ruth, you're talking to – not this poor bloke you've got working his fingers to the bone to keep the roof over your ungrateful head.'

'Don't you talk about my Ernie like that. He's the best thing that ever happened to me.'

'I don't doubt that, 'cause you've not had one bloke that I recall who stayed with you for more than two minutes, and seeing as it's *his* house, I'm surprised he's not chucked you out on your ear long since.'

'Well, he ain't. And he ain't about to throw you out neither. That's the kind o' man he is.'

Ruth couldn't wait to meet this put-upon bloke. 'Look – I'm very grateful for his hospitality, which is probably more than you've ever been. But you can forget about wanting to steal away what bit of money I've managed to scrape together. Knowing you, I daresay he pays over a good part of his wage to you. So add to that the rent I'll be giving you, and you'll not be doing so bad.'

Freda, however, still hadn't given up hope. 'I've been thinking about that, and I reckon I undercharged you.'

'Oh you do, do you?' Ruth had half-suspected her mam wasn't yet done with her bargaining.

'Well, yeah. By my reckoning, I should really be getting . . . let me see now.' She paused to ponder, not daring to go over the top and frighten away a good source of income. 'Let's say we settle on another half-crown a week on top of what we agreed?'

Ruth was more amused than angry. 'Let's say we don't. Let's say I won't give you one farthing more. And if that isn't enough, then happen I should find lodgings where they'll be glad of renting out a spare room for ready cash, and no questions asked.'

Casting a critical gaze round the room she noticed how the old paint was peeling off the walls and the rug was threadbare beneath her feet. The tired curtains at the window were sagging to one side and there were two tiles missing off the fireplace surround. 'One look at this awful little room, and it should be me offering you a *reduction*.'

'Hmh!' Freda folded her arms, which was a sign that she was ready for a fight if there was one going. 'By! Yer an 'ard bugger, you are,' she grumbled. ''Ard as granite.'

Ruth kept hold of her portmanteau, just to show she was equally determined, though in fact she had no intention of leaving this house. It was her only sanctuary for the time being. 'Well, what's it to be?'

Giving her daughter a pathetic look, Freda told her, 'You'll rue the day yer talked to yer poor old mam like that. When I'm laid under the turf and you've nobody else to turn to, you'll be sorry, you'll see.'

'Aw, come on, Mam. You'll see us *all* off, and well you know it. You're too bloody wicked to die!' All the same, thinking about the prospect of losing her mam when she had only just found her again, was a sad thing. Her mam had been a thorn in her side for so long, it would be a strange old world without her.

'Look, Mam.' Placing her portmanteau on the bed, Ruth told her, 'Right now we need each other. Let's call a truce and see how we get on. What d'yer say?'

Surprised by the tenderness in her daughter's voice, Freda took a moment to turn it all over in her mind. 'I expect I've been a bit hard on you all at once,' she agreed. 'So we'll make it an extra tanner a week. All right?'

Ruth fell about laughing. 'You'll never change,' she said. And in a way, she was glad.

———◆◇◆———

TWO HOURS LATER, with the help of a scrubbing brush, hot water and a bar of Sunlight soap, a needle and thread, and a duster and polish, the room was bright as a new pin. The windows were shining after a going-over with the shammy leather, the rug was repaired, and the curtains had been pressed and now hung as they were meant to.

'My! You've worked wonders.' Freda entered with two mugs of tea, one of which she gave to Ruth. 'D'yer know, our kid, I reckon I were too generous asking for a tanner. I shoulda made it a shilling!'

The sudden sight of Ernie at the door made them almost leap out of their skin. 'I've been calling,' he told them, 'but the pair of youse were laughing so much you didn't hear me.' His gaze rested on Ruth. 'You must be Freda's daughter.' Making his way across the room, he held out his hand in greeting. 'Pleased to meet you, I'm sure.'

Ruth liked him straight off. What she saw was a big

bumbling fella, with kind, sad eyes and a soft, friendly voice. Still in his grubby work-clothes he looked worn out. 'The name's Ruth,' she said, and returned his smile without hesitation.

'Ah, that's it.' He looked embarrassed. 'Ruth, of course.'

Freda had a word or two to say to this. 'I *told* yer what her name was, you big dope. My God! Ruth's a common enough name: a child o'two could remember it.'

'Hey!' Ruth feigned indignation. 'Not so much of the "common" if you don't mind.'

While Ernie washed and changed, Freda ran off down the fish and chip shop, to buy three fish meals and dabs on each, with the money Ruth gave her. 'It's all we've got time for tonight,' she explained to Ernie when they all sat down to eat. 'I've been tidying up down here, while Ruth's made that little spare bedroom look really nice.'

Ernie turned to Ruth. 'I'm sorry you've had troubles. Freda didn't tell me exactly what they were, and neither should you, unless you've a mind.'

Ruth shook her head. 'I'm just grateful you've allowed me to stay here. It's only until I get myself sorted out, of course.'

His kind gaze roved the room. 'This is a nice little house. Warm and cosy of a wintertime, and cool enough in the summer. I hope you'll be happy here,' he said. Though it hadn't been happy for him. How could it be, when he was estranged from his son?

They ate their fish and chips and drank two whole pots of Freda's best tea. 'By! I can't recall when I've enjoyed a meal so much,' Ernie remarked. 'D'you know what, love, it must have been twelve month and more, since we had fish and chips.'

Freda agreed. 'Aye, well, now that our Ruth's here, happen she'll treat us more often, eh?'

'Oh, no.' Ernie had made up his mind. 'From now on, we'll have fish and chips every Friday, and the treat is on me.'

When the table was cleared, they sat and talked, and supped of the dandelion-wine Freda had been keeping for just such an occasion. They chatted about their lives, and how it was a pity they had been so long apart.

Inevitably the talk came round to Ernie's son. 'He's a good lad, is my Mick.' Ernie had tears in his eyes. 'Only we had a terrible falling-out after his mam passed on. Sometimes these things happen and it's a bit of a nightmare. Though I've every hope we'll find our way back . . . just like you and your mam did.'

'I'm sure you will.' Ruth knew only too well how easy it was for families to drift apart, before the young one matures, and the older one mellows, and somehow it all seems to come right in the end.

'He's a right old softie,' her mother said, 'but I do love him.' She glanced at Ernie and he was thrilled to see a spark of the old Freda he had wooed and won.

As the evening wore on, they laughed at each other's little stories and innuendos, and when Freda read out a list of dos and don'ts with regard to Ruth's staying with them, Ernie was amazed and delighted to see how she had come alive with the arrival of her daughter.

'I want the rent on time,' Freda began, 'and there'll be no fetching young men home at any time of the day and night – though of course me and Ernie won't object to the odd occasion. I mean, we were young ourselves once. I want my kitchen to be left as *you* find it – though if I've not had time to clean it behind me, I'll not be angry if you should feel the urge to take a cloth to it. But only as I say, if I've not had time to do it myself.'

'Which is usually most of the time,' Ernie chuckled.

To which Freda gave him one of her warning glances. 'Now then, Ernie love, don't let yer imagination run away with yer.'

To the growing amusement of the other two, she continued with her list.

'Being as Ernie hasn't yet got around to installing a bathroom in this house, you'll need to use the privy at the bottom of the yard. Now, I don't mind yer taking a jeremiah to bed, 'cause the Lord knows how cold it can be to yer bare arse out there in the middle of the night, but yer must make sure it gets emptied first thing of a morning. There's nothing worse than the pong o' dried piddle when you walk into a room.'

At this, Ruth and Ernie exchanged glances, and it was all they could do to keep a straight face.

'Right then!' Freda pressed on bossily. 'With regard to the privy, don't forget to leave the key so's me and Ernie can find it. Under the bucket in the back yard is a good place.'

Ruth could hardly contain herself by this time. 'You mean to say you actually *lock* the privy door?'

'Well, o' course we do! Some time back, the man next door had his privy *stolen*! The china bowl, wooden seat . . . everything! They even took the newspaper squares hanging on the wall. Two men were seen carrying it all away one dark night, but they were never caught. We'd be in a right mess if our privy went missing. Isn't that right, Ernie? *Ernie*?'

When she looked up, it was to see the big man red in the face from suppressing the laughter that threatened to engulf him. Ruth was in the same state. Suddenly, Freda began to see the funny side of what she'd been saying, and it wasn't long before the whole room echoed with the sound of their laughter.

And because of it, Ernie was happier than he had been in many a long time; though behind the laughter, his pain over the rift with Mick was like a clenched fist inside him.

———————————

WITH RUTH GONE, and Peter still not having shown his face, Daisy was like a cat on hot bricks. The afternoon had ticked away and now it was late, and she knew the tale she had to tell would not be good enough.

For the umpteenth time, she got out of her chair and began pacing the floor, wringing her hands together and moaning pitifully, 'What am I to tell him now? Oh, miss! What am I to tell him?'

From the hallway, she heard the grandfather clock striking all the way up to ten, like the countdown of doom. 'Stay calm,' she told herself firmly. 'Say she came back and went out again, and she'll be back at any minute.' Her face flickered into a nervous smile. 'That's it!' The smile settled. 'She went out shopping earlier, then she forgot summat and went out again.' She scratched her head. 'But where could she be going at this time of night?'

Again she took to pacing the floor, until an idea came to mind. 'The pub!' Clapping her hands together at her ingenuity, she laughed out loud. 'That's it! She's gone to the pub for some drink for the table, 'cause there ain't none left in the cellar. That's what I'll tell him. That's what I were told, and if it's a lie, then it ain't my fault, 'cause I only know what she told me, an' it ain't my place to ask questions.'

As she set about her late duties, she etched the instructions into her brain. 'Remember what you're to say,' she muttered as she set the table for his supper. 'You know nothing else but what you were told. Nothing whatsoever! You stick to that story, Daisy my gal, an' don't let him frighten yer.' Cheered by her own determination, she finished setting the table, and even managed a little song as she returned to the kitchen to fetch the condiments.

The sound of the key turning in the lock stopped her short. 'Oh, my Gawd, he's *here!*'

Merry from the drink, Peter came down the passage. 'Ruth? *Ruth!*' His voice reached all four corners of the house. 'Get your best frock on. We're going out celebrating. Do you hear me, woman? I've done the best deal of my life – bought a whole heap of properties cheap. In my own name too.' He chuckled. 'It might be my dear mother's money that paid for it, but the name on that contract is *mine!*'

There came the sound of doors opening and closing. 'Ruth! Where the hell are you?' He could be heard running up the stairs, then down again. 'Where the devil have you got to now?' Then he was at the kitchen door. 'Daisy, where is she?'

Her throat closing with fear, Daisy made herself stay calm. 'She went out shopping, sir. She told me she wouldn't be long, an' she weren't. Then she went out again – to the pub for some drink for the supper table. That's what she said.'

For what seemed an age he studied her face, seeming to look for the lies beneath. 'What time was that?' Suspicion sharpened his voice. 'What time was it when she went out again?'

Instinctively, Daisy glanced at the clock. 'About half an hour ago, sir.' Later she would have to visit the church and confess all her sins. 'She said she'd be back in no time.'

Following her gaze he looked up at the clock. 'A quarter past ten,' he noted. 'I'll give her ten more minutes, then I'd best go and find her.' The merriness he had come home with was now a sourness that glared at her from the door.

'I'll be in the drawing room,' he growled. 'Seeing as there seems to be no other drink worth having, you'd best fetch me a pot of tea.'

'Yes, sir.'

'And be quick about it!'

'Right away, sir.' When he'd gone, Daisy fell into the nearest chair, weak with relief. 'It's all right,' she whispered jubilantly. 'He believed you.'

Then, realising he would be after her if she didn't deliver the tea in sharp time, Daisy leaped up and began running about, boiling the kettle on the range, tipping the tea leaves into the big earthenware pot, setting the tray with cup, saucer and jug of milk . . . her hands trembling so much she twice spilled the milk and had to wipe the tray clean each time.

Taking the tray she went at a quickened pace along the passage and into the hall. She was about to open the door with one free hand, when suddenly there was a blood-curdling cry. The door flew open, the tray and its contents went hurtling across the carpet.

Startled out of her wits, Daisy was caught by the scruff of her neck and swung from her feet. 'WHAT THE HELL IS THIS, EH?'

When Ruth's letter was thrust before her eyes, she began to cry. 'I don't know, sir. I don't know nothing,' she wept.

'You're a bloody liar!' Shaking her as though she was a rag doll, he pinned her against the wall, his face so close to hers, she could see the small pink veins in his eyeballs. 'I don't like liars, so you'd best tell me the truth. WHERE IS SHE?'

'I don't know, sir.'

His fist came up and crashed against her temple. 'Does *that* help you remember?'

Daisy looked up at him, the blood teeming down her face. 'Don't hurt me,' she pleaded.

'I'll have to hurt you, Daisy – unless you tell me where she's gone.'

The girl shook her head. 'Honest to Gawd, I don't know.'

'Did she take anything of mine with her?'

'I never saw . . . she didn't tell me . . .'

He stopped her by putting his two hands round her neck and squeezing. 'Useless bitch! You're no good to me.' His hands were so tight round her throat she could feel her senses slipping away. Suddenly, mercifully, his hold slackened. 'The safe! My God, the safe!' He went at a run towards the office.

Loosened from his grip, Daisy slithered to the floor, where she lay, bloodied and half-senseless. In the back of her mind she could hear him crashing about, his voice raised to the roof. 'THE BITCH! THE DEVIOUS LITTLE BITCH!'

Out of the corner of one eye, Daisy saw him stride away. 'I'll have you, Ruth Clegg!' he muttered. 'There's no hiding place for *you*. I'll find you – and when I do . . . !'

His manic laughter lingered long after he was gone, out the door and into the night, his unforgiving heart set on revenge.

Chapter Twelve

UPSTAIRS IN THE office, the two men stood by the window, looking down on the workforce beneath. 'How's it all going?' the boss wanted to know. 'Will we have the order out as promised, do you think?'

Mick pointed to Ellie, who was examining the shoe she had just polished. 'If she has anything to do with it, we will.' He smiled, proud of the way his friend had fitted in.

Nodding in agreement, Mr Brindle stroked his face, his eyes intent on Ellie. 'She's a good girl,' he answered. 'A hard worker, that's for sure – *and* she takes a pride in what she's doing. Oh, I know we have plenty of good workers here, and I'm not saying anything different, but these days it's unusual to see a young lass actually enjoying what she does – taking such an interest, like. More often than not, they can't wait to get home and be off out with their mates.'

'I don't think Ellie *has* any mates,' Mick said quietly.

'Oh? Bit of a loner, is she?'

'Not so much a loner – just quiet, like.' Frowning, Mick moved away from the window. 'You know about her mam and dad, don't you, sir?'

'I've heard tell about it.' The older man shook his head. 'A shocking business.' Crossing the room, Mr Brindle sat himself behind the desk. Picking up a pencil he twiddled it round and round in the tips of his fingers. 'Burned alive in your own house. Dear God! It doesn't bear thinking about.'

'Aye, well, I'm sure Ellie thinks about it all the time.' Mick had often seen that faraway look on her face, and he guessed she was back there in Buncer Lane, on that Christmas night of horror. 'It's no wonder she pours her heart and soul into her work,' he mused. 'It must help put that dreadful business from her mind.'

'There was talk of some madman who got inside the house, so they say?'

'That's right.' Mick's heart lurched as he recalled the chaos. 'They thought Betsy was hysterical and who the devil wouldn't be, after what she'd been through? But Ellie backed her every inch of the way. According to Ellie, the man was intent on murdering the pair of them. Until the house was afire and he had to make good his escape.'

'And they'd never seen him before, isn't that what they said?'

'That's right. They never caught the bastard neither!' A look of hatred crossed his young face. 'Never mind hanging,' he muttered. 'If I ever got my hands on him, by hell I'd make him pay for what he did to that lovely family.'

'The young fella, your mate Larry – how's he doing these days?'

At this, Mick's face softened. 'He's doing fine. Last week he took four steps all on his own, without holding onto the bars or anything. His legs are getting stronger, and they reckon he'll be out of hospital in less than a month. O' course he won't be up and walking altogether, but it's only a matter of time. Mind you, it's been nearly three years.'

He sighed. 'Still, it's a bloody miracle the way he's come on.'

'Hmh.' Deep in thought, the little man nodded. 'If he's anything like that lass downstairs, he'll make it eventually, I'm sure.' Getting out from behind his desk, he strolled across the room, where he stood at the window again, watching Ellie, thinking what a grand little lass she was. 'Mick, lad?'

'Yes?' His foreman came to stand beside him, his eyes, too, drawn to Ellie.

'As you know, I like the new ones to work the full month before upping their wages. I like them to prove what they're made of.'

'I know that.'

'All the same, I've a mind to raise her wages now. What do you reckon to that?'

Mick smiled, his eyes on Ellie and his heart warmed by the sight of her. 'I reckon she's earned it.'

'And do you reckon she's earned a move along the bench?'

Mick had no hesitation. 'It doesn't matter where you put her, sir, she'll do well. I'd stake my life on it.'

'Hmh!' Folding his hands behind his back, Mr Brindle took to pacing the floor. A moment passed, before he stopped. 'Do you think she might cope with Quality Control? We had Alice leave last week. By! She was good at her work. I had thought to take on somebody with the same experience, but I believe young Ellie might train up well.'

Mick was bursting with pride. 'Quality Control, eh?' He knew how meticulous they had to be in that department. 'Give Ellie a chance, and she'll not let you down. She'll do a good job, you can have no fear of that.'

'Right!' George Brindle had done well in business, and had learned to trust his instinct. He trusted it now, as he trusted

Mick. 'You're right,' he said. 'The girl has the makings of something special. Send her up, Mick. I'll have a word.'

He glanced back at the main office. Betsy had just come through the door and was making her way down the steps to the factory floor, a sheaf of papers in her hand. 'Her twin, Betsy, she's a hard little devil. No doubt it's due to what happened – but someone needs to have a word with her on one or two little matters. I'd have her in when I've spoken to Ellie, but I must be off early. Things to do and all that.'

After a recent row between Betsy and one of the drivers, Mick had been expecting something of the kind. 'I've already had a word,' he admitted. 'I'm sure she'll have taken in what I said.' He had done his best to protect her from herself and her own bad temper, but he knew it was only a matter of time before the girl was summoned to the top office. And now, the time had come. 'Betsy's a good worker,' he said in her defence. 'It's just that she gets a bit above herself now and then.'

The other man gave a wry little smile. 'And we can't have *that* now, can we, eh?' His sharp eyes followed Betsy as she went along the factory floor and on towards the loading bay. 'No, Mick. You'll need to speak with her again before you leave for the evening. See to it, will you, lad.'

And, to his despair, Mick knew he had little option. 'I will,' he promised.

As he went down the steps to Ellie, he followed Betsy out the corner of his eye. You're a silly little bugger, he thought. You've got the chance to make it good here. Don't throw it away with your high and mighty manner!

Making a beeline for Ellie, he passed on the boss's instructions. 'Mr Brindle would like a word with you, Ellie. You're to make your way up to the office.'

'What does he want?' she asked fearfully. 'Have I done

summat wrong? Will I get the sack?' Looking up, she saw the boss staring down on her, and her heart missed a beat.

Mick immediately put her mind at rest. 'It's nothing like that,' he assured her. 'You've been here a month next week, and it's the normal procedure for the boss to see how you're fitting in.'

Ellie relaxed. 'For a minute I thought I might be about to get my marching orders.'

'Not a bit of it.' Mick gazed on her pretty face and those dark, sapphire eyes and he knew he could never love anyone else for as long as he lived.

'Am I to go now?'

'This very minute.'

'Can't I finish polishing this pair of shoes?' she asked. 'If I let this one dry, the other won't match up proper.'

'Go on then,' he agreed, because he knew she was right. 'Then it's up the steps and into the office with you.' Knowing that only good news awaited her, he was enjoying every minute.

While Ellie finished polishing the other shoe, Mick took a walk over to the loading bay, where Betsy was talking to the driver. He could hear the man protesting. 'I'm telling you that docket was signed and handed in along with the others. If you can't find it, then somebody else has lost it, not me!'

Betsy was equally adamant. 'Well, I've looked high and low. It couldn't have been handed in.'

'Look, miss! No offence, but I'll not argue with a snotty-nosed young lass. Let me have a word with somebody in authority.' The driver was clearly upset. Now, when he caught sight of Mick striding towards them, he stepped forward. 'Mick, will you tell her, for Chrissake! I handed the docket in last night, along with the others.'

'No, he didn't,' Betsy argued. 'He *couldn't* have.'

'God Almighty!' The driver rolled his eyes to heaven. 'She's calling me a liar. It's not the first bloody time neither!'

Mick took him aside. 'We can do without the language in front of the girl,' he reprimanded.

'Aye.' Fred was a family man and knew better. 'I'm sorry about that, but what right has she to tell me I didn't hand the damned thing in, when I know very well I did! I put *all* the dockets together, same as usual. I even put a band round them – that's the way I've allus done it. Now she's trying to say there's one missing. What's her game, that's what I'd like to know? Is she claiming I've done summat underhand with a load o' shoes, or what?'

'No, of course she isn't. She's learning the job and getting a bit carried away with it, that's all.'

'Well, she'd best learn a bit bloody quicker, 'cause if she comes at me again, I might just hand in me notice. I'll not be put on trial by no young lass, I can tell yer that!'

Mick did his best to defuse the situation. 'Look, Fred, you're one of our best drivers. You've been with us the longest and you're trusted by every one of us. You know that without me telling you, so calm down and let's see if I can get to the bottom of it.'

The driver took a deep breath. 'All right. But you'd best 'ave a word with her, 'cause if she's the one gonna be dealing with the dockets, she'd best find a better manner when talking to the drivers.' He looked at Mick and knew he could speak frankly to him. 'You've come up through the ranks yourself,' he recalled, 'but right from when you first started here as a scrawny kid, you've allus had the right manner, and the instinct for what is and what isn't.'

His glance shot to Betsy who was tapping her feet impatiently. 'Sort her out, Mick, else I'll be gone, and I mean it. I've worked here man and boy, and I had hoped to keep the job till I retired in ten years' time. But I'll not put up with being called a thief, you can be sure of that!'

Mick had never seen him so rattled. 'Come on now, Fred, she weren't calling you a thief.'

'As good as!'

'Look. Have a break, mate. Get yourself a cup of tea from the back office, and I'll see you later. I'll sort it. Don't you worry.'

The man nodded. 'Right. I'll leave it with you then.' And off he went.

While Fred was cooling his heels, and his temper, in the canteen, Mick took Betsy outside, where no one could hear what he was saying. 'Do you want to keep your job here, Betsy?' he asked outright.

When the girl stuck out her chin, as she did now, it was a sign that she was about to be difficult. 'He's lying. He said he turned in his docket, but he didn't. If he *had* turned it in, it would have been here with the rest of them, but it's nowhere to be seen. So where is it, tell me that?'

'I'll tell you *this*!' he answered steadily. 'You're wrong about Fred. And you're wrong about that loading-docket. Fred is no liar. He's a good, honest man. *And* he's worked here long enough to know the ropes. If he said he turned in that docket, *then he did*!'

Trying desperately to remember that she was Larry's and Ellie's sister, he kept calm, his voice sounding tolerant rather than reprimanding. But even so, she had no doubt but that he was angry. 'Now then, Betsy. I want you to go back and search that office from top to bottom. I want you to look in every corner, drawer and cupboard. Turn the waste-paper baskets inside out, if you have to.'

'I've already done that and it's not there!'

'Not good enough, Betsy,' he chided. 'Do it again . . . and again, until you find it. And when you do find it, I'll expect you to have the decency to apologise to Fred. Do you understand what I'm saying?'

'I won't find it, because it's not there.'

'Betsy!' Frustrated by her manner, he took a step closer.

'*It won't be there!* It wasn't there when me and Miss Turnbull searched before, and it won't be there now. Because it was never given in.'

Taking her by the shoulders, he held her there. 'Tell me something.'

'What?' She wriggled angrily away.

'Are you happy working here?'

'I expect so.'

'And do you "expect" to do well? Do you "expect" to take over some of the responsibility, when Miss Turnbull retires?'

'This month she's training me to take over the docket-filing, and next month I'm to be shown how to make the delivery routes. Miss Turnbull said she would gradually teach me all the office procedures, then I'll know as much as her. She said that when she retires in two years, I should be in charge of the office – if I keep my nose clean . . . that's what she said.'

'And she could be right. But remember this, Betsy. She is not the boss, and she is in no position to make that kind of decision. The best she can do is to train you up and, if you do well, she might put you up for promotion. But it won't be her who has the last word.' His wary glance went to the upper office, where the boss was looking down. 'It'll be Mr Brindle.'

'I know that.'

'Then you had better know *this*, too. You need to improve your manner with the drivers, or there will be no responsibilities for you, and no promotion.'

'What do you mean?' Unfortunately, Betsy could see no failings in herself.

'I mean that your attitude is all wrong. You're aggressive, and rude, and now Fred is convinced you're calling him a liar.'

'Well? He *is* a liar!'

Mick took a noisy intake of breath. 'See what I mean! Sorry, Betsy, but you're your own worst enemy. Look, just go and find that docket, and if the boss should ask to see you at some time in the future, for God's sake mind how you talk to him. Show him the respect he demands, or I can't answer for the consequences.'

As the girl strode off, he shook his head and blew out a long, gusty sigh. 'I've tried my best,' he groaned. 'If she chooses to pay no heed, there's little else I can do.' Returning to Ellie, he escorted her up to the office.

'I saw you just now,' Ellie remarked. 'Is Betsy in some kind of trouble?' If she was, it wouldn't be the first time.

'Just a misunderstanding.' Mick had no wish to cloud Ellie's big moment. 'Some docket or other went missing. It'll turn up, I'm sure.'

Ellie wasn't convinced. 'The drivers don't like her, do they?'

Mick forced a smile. 'I don't think you should worry too much about Betsy,' he said. 'She can take care of herself, if needs be.' Wishing Ellie had not seen him reprimanding her sister, Mick lapsed into silence.

The boss was waiting. 'Come in, young lady.' Ushering her to a chair before the desk, the little man asked Mick to close the door. When that was done, he lost no time in coming straight to the point. 'I've been watching you for some days now,' he told Ellie, 'and I am very impressed with the way you knuckle down to your work.'

'Thank you, sir.' Ellie went a deep shade of pink. 'I do enjoy working here.'

'That much is evident, my dear.' As was his manner when thinking things through, George Brindle began his pacing again, up and down, back and forth.

Suddenly he stopped right in front of her, his face beaming as he told her in a rush, 'I've a mind to put you in Quality Control, and raise your wages by one and sixpence a week. Do you think you could handle all that at once?'

Ellie was so shocked, she leaped to her feet. 'Oh, Mr Brindle, sir. Oh yes, thank you!' Quality Control. She could hardly believe it. 'That's just wonderful.'

'Good, then it's settled.' Taking hold of her hand he shook it vigorously. 'Start Monday morning.' Grabbing his coat, he put it smartly on as always, before addressing Mick, who was smiling at Ellie, and she at him. 'See to it, Mick, will you?'

'Yes, sir.' With the greatest of pleasure, he thought.

'And by the way, the landlord will be coming this afternoon for his money.' Pointing to the desk, Mr Brindle advised, 'The envelope is in there – top left-hand drawer. And mind you get a receipt, young man. Last time, the canny devil went off without signing it so this time I've put the receipt book in with the envelope. I can tell you, it's the dickens of a job getting a receipt once they've made off with the money in their pocket.'

'Don't worry, sir. I'll make sure he signs it.' Mick was acutely aware that Ellie was waiting beside him. 'I'd best get on.'

'Make sure you leave the place safe and sound, as usual,' the boss nagged.

'I will.'

'Right you are then, I'll be off. I'll see you bright and early Monday morning.' Having said his piece, he was out and away before Mick could reply.

Now, all of his attention was given to Ellie. 'After you, madam,' he grinned, showing her the door.

Ellie laughed. 'Don't be daft,' she said shyly. Just to be near him was wonderful.

In serious mood now, he took hold of her hand. 'I'm so proud of you,' he murmured, and she was so stirred by the tenderness in his eyes that she had to look away.

Seeing he had embarrassed her, he led her to the door. 'Right, young lady. We'd best get started.'

'Where are we going?'

'You'll see.'

The first thing he meant to do was introduce Ellie to the workers in the 'elite' Quality Control department. Mick felt slightly apprehensive on her behalf. Nice and pleasant though they were, they didn't usually take kindly to a new presence in their midst.

As it turned out, he need not have worried. 'You'll fit in 'ere a treat,' Jenny Brighton told Ellie. 'We've seen the way you work, and you're more than welcome alongside us.' And everyone without exception told her the very same.

As they made their way back to the polishing belt, Betsy came rushing up, docket in hand. 'It must have fallen out of the bundle,' she explained. 'Miss Turnbull found it at the back of the drawer.'

Mick was not impressed. 'And?'

Looking puzzled, she answered hesitantly, 'And – well,

here it is.' Holding out the docket she looked at him, wondering if he'd gone right out of his mind.

Mick realised he would have to spell it out. 'And now I assume you're on your way to see Fred, right?'

Betsy took a minute to realise what he was getting at. When the light finally dawned, her surly manner returned. 'Do I have to?'

'What do *you* think?' One raised eyebrow from Mick was enough to send her in search of the angry driver.

Putting two and two together, Ellie realised Betsy had got herself into some kind of trouble. 'She doesn't mean any harm,' she assured Mick. 'She just takes a bit longer to settle down, that's all.' All the same, it was a worry to Ellie. Somehow or other, as usual, Betsy seemed hellbent on destroying whatever opportunity came her way.

<hr />

FEELING SORRY FOR himself, Peter Williams made his way to the hospital. It was two o'clock and the shifts were just changing. 'Go straight through, Mr Williams,' the nurse told him.

Thankful that he had not engaged her in conversation, she took off her cap and pinnie and hung them on her allotted peg. There they would hang until Monday morning, and all her duties alongside.

'I'm off now,' she told her incoming colleague. Then she went out the door like any ordinary soul. First stop was the butcher's to get herself a juicy lamb chop, then home to a meal cooked by herself and enjoyed by herself. With no demanding man to tire her, and no offspring to tug at her skirts, she considered herself a fortunate woman.

Peter, however, was in no such buoyant mood. His mother had recently been moved to another, smaller ward, where she would not be disturbed by those around her.

The nurse passed him at the door to the ward. 'Your mother had a bad night last night,' she imparted. 'The doctor's been called to her twice this morning.' She spoke in a hushed voice, so Ada would not hear her.

'What did he have to say?'

The nurse smiled gently. 'A few weeks,' she told him compassionately. 'That's all I can tell you.'

'Is the doctor still here?'

The nurse shook her head. 'He's gone off-duty now. But Dr Marshall comes on duty within the hour.' With that she hurried away.

For a long time, Peter stood at the door, his gaze stretched to where his mother lay, long and still, her beautiful silver hair spilling over the pillow, and only her face peeping above those stark white sheets. Peter had often wished her gone, but now, after the events of the past few days, and seeing how frail and pathetic his mother had become, his feelings were in chaos.

He loved her, then he hated her. He needed her company, yet despised it. He wanted her dead, yet he had become used to visiting this awful place, until he had begun to wonder what he would do when she was gone and there was no more need.

Then there was that red-headed trollop, Ruth! There were times when he could easily have strangled her with his own two hands, yet he was lonely without her and he wanted her back, to have and to hold; to play like children and roll about the carpet, then to make love with that special fire only she had ever kindled in him. But she was somewhere he couldn't find her, and last night, like the many long nights since she had been gone, had been filled with loneliness, an unbearable torture inside him.

On hesitant footsteps, like a wicked boy who needed reassuring, he went to his mother's bedside. Here he sat quite still, his curious gaze on her sleeping face and his mind quickening with all manner of disturbing thoughts. Now was his chance. All he had to do was take the pillow and hold it ever so gently over her nose and mouth; just long enough to stop her breathing. Then she would be gone and he would have it all.

When the urge became a tide of fury inside him, he reached out with both hands. The softness of the pillow was like velvet beneath his touch. Gripping it tightly in his fists, he closed his eyes, trying to imagine how it would be. Just one swift moment and it would all be over.

As impetuously as he had gripped the pillow, he released it, his hands falling on the bed cover. If she was gone, he would have no one, and that was too sad for him to contemplate. Bending his head he began to sob.

When he looked up, it was to see Ada's eyes turned towards him. To his astonishment, they were moistened with tears, and so kind . . . so loving as they gazed on his tormented face.

Because she was unable to speak, he spoke to her, and he could hardly recognise his own voice. 'Mother?'

The eyes smiled on him. Then they closed, rested, then opened again.

Like the coward he was, he began to pour out his troubles onto the dying woman. He wanted sympathy. He needed her to know how utterly wretched his life was. 'She's gone, Mother,' he whined pitifully. 'She's gone, and she's nowhere to be found. I've searched high and low and it's no good. I'm so lonely, Mother. Oh, you can't know how lonely I am.'

While he cried on her shoulder, Ada never once took her eyes off him.

He told her how Ruth was the only woman he had ever

truly wanted. 'She's like me, you see,' he claimed. 'Outside, she's hard and ruthless, but inside, she's lonely. Nobody wants people like us, you see. Me and Ruth, we're labelled bad – wicked people. But no one understands. We're special, you see. *Different.*'

Devastated, Ada looked away.

'No! Look at me, Mother!' The tears and self-pity gave way to rage. Standing over her now, he stared into her face. 'MOTHER! LOOK AT ME.'

When she refused to open her eyes, he took hold of her hand, squeezing it until the blood drained away. She opened her eyes, but this time they weren't filled with warmth and forgiveness. This time they were hard and pained. Like those people he had mentioned before, she could not understand this man who was her own flesh and blood. Her only son.

He smiled, and was like someone she had never known. 'You hate me, don't you?' he hissed. 'I can see it in your eyes. You're like all the others, only worse, because *you* brought me into this cruel world. *You* made me what I am. Well, if you have hatred for me, then you can't even begin to know the hatred I feel for you. Don't forget – *I* put you in here, and I could finish you off right now if I wanted to. But I won't! You can rot away little by little instead. It's what you deserve.'

Unable to look at him any longer, she closed her eyes and this time she would not be made to open them again – not even when he held her nose between his fingers as he did now, making her gasp for air.

Confused by her courage, he snatched his hand away. 'All right then, bitch! Have it your way. I'm going now . . . things to do, money to collect.' He smiled. '*Your* money, Mother dear. Only now, it's mine. I've worked for it. It belongs to me. And so does Ruth. Oh, I'll find her – make no mistake about that. I'll find her, even if I have to turn this bastard town upside down.'

Unaware of what had gone on, the nurse returned. One look at Ada's grey face and she was concerned. 'I think you should let your mother get some rest now, Mr Williams,' she suggested. 'I've had a word with the doctor and he'll see you in an hour, if you can wait that long?'

Peter didn't answer. Instead he bent to kiss his mother on the cheek. 'I'll be back,' he whispered. 'We'll talk again.'

As he went out the door, Ada's eyes followed him, and this time, the nurse could see the fear there. 'It's all right,' she coaxed, misunderstanding. 'Your son will be back soon, I'm sure. Don't worry.' In her innocence, she didn't realise she had said the very thing Ada did not want to hear.

Half an hour later, Ada had another visitor – her old friend Jonas Carter the solicitor. 'How has she been?' he asked.

The nurse told him, 'I'm afraid she's worsening with every day that passes.'

Saddened by the news, he left Ada sleeping. 'Poor old dear,' he murmured. 'It must be a terrible thing, not being able to communicate.' He advised the nurse he would not call again. 'I'm sure she would want me to remember her the way she was.'

'I think she must have been very beautiful,' the nurse commented.

'Oh, she was,' he smiled. 'Fiery too. A real force to reckon with.' He took one last, long look at her. 'Such a pity,' he said huskily, and could not bear to be with her one moment longer.

———❦———

IT WAS FIFTEEN minutes to home-time.

From the upper office, Mick watched as Ellie tidied her

bench. First, she gathered all her belongings – lunch box, small hessian bag, brown earthenware mug and teaspoon, together with the half-emptied packet of tea, and paper-screw of sugar. When everything was packed neatly away into her bag, she went to the sink at the far end of the office and, wetting a dish-cloth, brought it back to wipe the bench clean from one end to the other. That done, she returned to the sink, where she washed out the cloth and draped it over the tap as it had been before.

By the time the siren went, like the other workers she was ready for off.

'See you Monday, Ellie lass,' they called. 'Mind you fetch enough biscuits to go round. Fond of a biscuit with our tea, we are.'

Joining the queue to clock out for the day, she kept a wary eye out for Betsy who, as yet, was nowhere to be seen.

She had clocked her card and was about to mount the stairs to the back office to seek out her sister when Mick caught up with her. 'Betsy's gone,' he said. 'I thought you knew?'

Ellie was astonished. 'Gone where?'

'I've no idea. All I know is, she clocked out five minutes ago.' Concerned that Ellie shouldn't worry, he told her to wait there and he'd see if he could catch up with her. And he went off at a run towards the main doors.

A few minutes later he was back. 'I'm sorry, love. There's no sign of her.'

Ellie was puzzled. 'Where can she have got to? Why didn't she tell me she was leaving early?'

Just then, Miss Turnbull went by and overheard. 'Your sister told me she had a dental appointment.' A look of suspicion came over her tiny features. 'She wasn't *lying*, I hope?'

'Oh, no!' Yet again, Ellie was called on to cover for her

twin. 'Come to think of it, she did tell me. Yes, I'm sure she did.'

'Hmh!' Giving her a curious glance, Miss Turnbull bade them both goodnight.

'*Did* Betsy tell you?' Mick asked. 'Really?'

Ellie shook her head. 'But then she doesn't tell me everything.'

Mick had a suggestion. 'It's getting dark outside. I don't like the idea of you walking to the tram-stop all on your own. Why don't you come back to the office while I finish up, then we can walk to it together.'

He couldn't know how his suggestion had set Ellie's heart pounding. 'I'd like that,' she replied, and was amazed at how calm her voice sounded, when inside she was all atremble.

When the last worker had left the premises, one person remained – a tall, well-dressed figure standing by the main doors. He seemed to be looking up, examining something above his head.

Mick thought he recognised the man, but couldn't be sure. 'Stay here a minute,' he told Ellie. 'I'll go and see who he is.'

Ellie watched as he went to the main doors and spoke with the gent. A moment later the two of them came halfway down the factory. 'It's Mr Williams, the landlord,' Mick explained. 'He's come to collect his rent.' Asking Ellie to wait on, he told her, 'It's all ready. I'll not be a minute. Don't you go away now.'

While Mick was gone, Ellie put on her coat, ready for the cold night outside.

For a moment, Peter Williams continued to examine the roof and walls. He could see signs of recent leaking, and in places the plaster had blown. But he took scant notice. He did not intend spending good money on this place. Oh no!

He had a mind to sell it, lock stock and barrel, once his mother had gone.

Seeing Ellie looking at him, he walked over to her. 'Work here, do you?' he asked abruptly. If that young foreman was bringing his bit of stuff under this roof for a spot of hanky panky, he would have something to say about it. Mind you, he thought, this was a pretty young thing. He wouldn't mind a bit of hanky panky with her himself. 'What's your name?'

'Ellie,' she answered politely, though for some reason she had taken an instant dislike to him. 'And yes, I do work here.'

'Hmh!' He looked her boldly up and down, before glancing to where Mick was closing the office door. 'That your boyfriend, is it? I saw you and him talking just now.'

Beneath his meaningful smile, Ellie blushed bright red. 'No, he's not my boyfriend.' Though she would have liked that more than anything else in the world.

Mesmerised by her dark blue eyes, he smiled in a way that put Ellie on her guard. 'Not your boyfriend, eh? Then all I can say is, more fool him.'

Just then Mick returned. 'There you are, Mr Williams.' He handed Peter the envelope. 'You'll find it's all there – in cash, as requested.'

Peter opened the envelope and, taking out the notes, counted them laboriously. 'Good!' Returning it all to the envelope, he signed the receipt book, turned on his heel and departed, without a backward glance, or a goodnight to either of them.

'Ignorant pig!' Mick muttered under his breath. 'I've never liked that bloke from day one.' He studied Ellie's face. 'What was he saying to you?'

'He was flirting with me.' She grinned. 'He asked if you were my boyfriend.'

'Oh, did he now?' Mick took both her hands in his. 'And what did you say to that, eh?'

'I said no, you weren't.'

Holding her hands he continued to gaze on her. He didn't say anything. He didn't want to spoil the moment. He had one question though. 'And what did you think to him flirting with you?'

Ellie glanced at Peter, who was about to go out the main doors. 'I didn't like him either.'

'You do right not to like him.' Releasing her hands, he followed her gaze to Peter Williams. 'They say he's a dark, secretive devil. Wealthy too. He's got money in the bank that would keep you and me in luxury for the rest of our lives – and our children behind us.'

Realising what he'd said, he fell silent for a moment, looking into Ellie's eyes and wanting to take her in his arms, but knowing it would be wrong. Unbeknown to him, Ellie was secretly wishing he would take hold of her. When, instead, he told her to hang on while he locked the back doors, her heart sank. When he strode away, her gaze followed him. 'Why didn't you kiss me?' she murmured. 'I know you wanted to. And I wouldn't have minded at all.' In truth, it would have been the most natural thing in the world.

<hr>

Outside, TILLY PARTRIDGE's great-nephew, John, was making his way to the factory doors. After learning from Tilly and Bertie that Ellie was now working at Brindle's shoe-factory, he had recalled how Mick had told him there might be work going here. So here he was, but not with any serious job-hunting motives. It was the thought of Ellie that had brought him here, and the chance of a good time.

With that in mind he came bounding round the corner, straight into Peter Williams. 'Hey! You bloody young idiot, what the hell do you think you're doing?'

After quickly collecting his belongings from the pavement, where the impact had sent them, Peter grabbed John by the coat lapels. 'What are you hanging around here for anyway? Up to mischief, are you, eh? Looking to get inside and see what you can make off with, is that it?' He shook him hard.

'I'm no thief!' Squirming from his grasp, John explained, 'I'm here looking for work. I know people who work here. The foreman told me there might be a job going.'

As he argued, John noticed the wallet lying on the ground. His quick mind deduced that here was a man of means and influence. If he kept the wallet he'd more than likely have the police on his back in no time at all, and he could well do without that. In the long run the best thing would be to hand it in. So, looking after his own scrawny neck, he pointed to the wallet. 'You'd best take that with you,' he told Peter, 'afore some real thief makes off with it.'

Seeing how his fat and full wallet was lying in the gutter behind him, Peter was astounded. He was also curious. 'What's your game, eh?' Putting the wallet in a safe place, he eyed the younger man with interest. 'You could have kept your mouth shut and made off with it. Why didn't you, eh? And don't tell me it never crossed your mind.'

Because he had nothing to lose, John came clean. 'Oh, it crossed my mind all right,' he admitted, 'only I can see what kind of influential gent you might be, an' you've also got a hell of a quick temper on you, too. If I were to have made off with that wallet, like as not there'd come one dark night when I'm walking down some alley – and I'd be left there with my head kicked in. Am I right?'

Peter nodded. 'Right *and* sensible,' he replied approvingly. 'Anyone who takes from me is sure to get their comeuppance. You do well to know it.'

John wanted rid of him. 'So, I can be on my way now, can I?' he asked cheekily. 'Much like yourself, I'm a busy man. I mean to find work before the end of the day.'

'What kind of work?'

'Anything that pays a good wage.'

Peter looked him up and down. He observed how John was built well, and possessed that certain street knowledge that would keep him out of trouble. More importantly, he knew how not to overstep the mark with his betters. 'I can give you work, if you've a mind for it.'

John didn't like this bloke much, but beggars couldn't be choosers. 'What sort o' work might that be then?'

Reaching into his pocket, Peter took out one of his business cards, which he handed over. 'Monday afternoon, round about four o'clock. And be sharp. I don't take kindly to time-wasters.' He pointed to the card. 'You'll find the address there.'

With that he strode away, leaving John staring after him. 'Hmh! He is a strange bugger an' no mistake!' He saw Peter turn the corner and wondered about him. Glancing down at the card, he read aloud, '*A and P Williams, Property Management*.' Smiling, he rammed it into his pocket. 'Can't lose nothing by going to see the bloke,' he mused. 'Come to think of it, I might even have done myself a favour. Monday afternoon, eh? Yes, why not?'

As he went away, all thoughts of seeing Ellie had vanished,

because now he was more interested in what this certain gent had to offer.

———⊷⊙⊶———

TEN MINUTES LATER, Ellie and Mick finally left the premises. As they walked along, the conversation went back to Betsy.

'I can't think where she could have gone,' Ellie fretted. 'She never said anything to you, did she, Mick?'

He shook his head. 'No, but I'm sure she'll be home when you get there.'

The talk turned to Larry. 'Will it be all right if I come back to Buncer Lane with you and see him?' Her brother had been lodging with Mick for some time now. The arrangement suited both young men very well.

Mick was thrilled. ''Course it's all right. But won't Peggy wonder where you've got to?'

Ellie had a confession to make. 'I know I should have checked with you first, but I did tell her that Betsy and I might be calling in on Larry before we went home tonight. I said not to make us any dinner, and that if we were to come straight home after all, we'd call in at the fish and chip shop on the way.'

Mick smiled down on her upturned face and as always when she looked at him out of those rich blue eyes, he felt a rush of something wonderful. 'You had it all worked out, then?'

Blushing beneath his intense gaze, Ellie looked away. 'So, I'll come and see our Larry on my own with you, if it's all right? I'm hoping Betsy will turn up there later. Maybe she went off to do some shopping first.'

''Course I'd like you to come!' It was just what he craved –

to spend a few more, precious hours in her company, especially on her own without her irritating twin.

On the tram they sat side by side, talking in earnest about this and that. 'I'm really proud of you,' he told Ellie. 'The boss puts great store in you.'

Ellie asked after Betsy's progress, but even though Mick tried his best to reassure her, she knew her sister was going the wrong way. 'Help her, Mick,' she pleaded. 'I know she'll come right in the end.'

'I'll do what I can,' he promised, 'but there's only so much I *can* do.' He didn't tell her the boss already had his eye on Betsy. He thought it better to wait and see how it all panned out. Wisely changing the subject, he told her, 'I know it's only been a week or so since you last saw Larry, but you'll be amazed at how he's come on in that short time.'

Impulsively, Ellie grabbed his hand. 'It's thanks to *you*,' she said excitedly. 'Oh Mick, you're the best mate in the world!'

Again, those wonderful blue eyes touched his soul, and he thought how . . . right then and there in front of all those people, he would have taken her in his arms and kissed her until she could hardly breathe.

But he couldn't. Not yet.

He didn't know how the very same emotions were taking hold of Ellie. In the dark outside, she could see his reflection in the window. He was looking down, his thoughts elsewhere. In that moment he seemed incredibly sad. Ellie sensed that he was thinking of his mother. And she loved him all the more for it.

Chapter Thirteen

As usual, Larry was delighted to see her. 'You stay there, sis,' he told her, and then, to her concern and delight, he got out of the wheelchair and very hesitantly began walking across the room towards her.

Halfway across, he made her gasp when his legs buckled beneath him and he fell, lopsided against the wall. When she made to go forward, he put up his hand. 'No, sis!' And so, her heart in her mouth, she waited until he righted himself and continued what to both of them seemed like a neverending journey.

When he fell into her arms, she held him for an age. 'I'm so proud of you, Larry,' she murmured, the tears rolling down her face. 'So very proud.'

All those agonising moments while Larry struggled to reach his sister, Mick had seen how Ellie was silently willing him on, desperate to help him yet knowing she must not. Knowing he had to make it alone.

In that moment, Mick's love for her had never been stronger, nor his determination to make her his wife. As he looked on at the pride and suffering she shared with her brother in her heart, taking every slow, difficult step with him,

Mick knew Ellie was a very special young woman. But then, hadn't he *always* known it?

Unaware of Mick's observance of her, Ellie held on to her brother, her heart swelled with love. After a moment, in case he should weary, she drew away. 'Let me help you back?'

He looked down on her, and she was humbled to see that he, too, was crying. 'I did it!' he said brokenly. 'I did it!'

Through misty eyes she smiled back at him. 'I always knew you would,' she whispered. 'I never doubted it. Not for one minute.'

He kissed her then on the forehead – a fond, brotherly kiss that said thank you for being here. Then he allowed himself to lean on her as she went with him to his wheelchair beside the fireplace.

When he was settled in the chair and Ellie was curled up on the rug beside him, Mick stepped forward to shake Larry's hand. 'You're a stubborn devil,' he said jokingly, 'but Ellie ain't the only one who's proud of you.'

'I've been practising all day, on and off,' Larry admitted. 'A few steps forward then back, until I felt I really could go right across the room.' Sighing happily, he told Mick, 'It's brought on a thirst though.' He glanced towards the kitchen which, after his lone trek, seemed a very short distance away. 'I'll mek us a brew.'

'Hey!' Seeing how that walk across the room had drained him, both Ellie and Mick offered to do the honours, but he wouldn't have it. '*I'll* mek the brew,' he insisted. 'One of youse nip down to the chip-shop.'

Mick knew his mate well enough to realise that neither he nor Ellie would change his mind once it was made up. 'I had a mind for a fish and chip tea anyroad,' he confessed. 'Right! What's the order then?'

Ellie said she wouldn't mind a packet of chips and a dab. 'I'll do the bread and butter while you're gone,' she offered, giving Larry a look that said, 'You're mashing the tea, Mick's going to the chip-shop, so doing the bread and butter is *my* contribution!'

And, rather than argue with her, he merely grinned and said, 'Don't forget – I like a plastering of butter on mine, and thick-cut bread, mind! None of your paper-thin rubbish.'

Ellie laughed. She hadn't forgotten.

'So, what do you want?' Mick was still waiting for his pal's order. 'It's Friday night, don't forget. There'll be a queue out the door if I don't get a move on.'

'Right. I'll have a large fish and chips with a dab,' Larry answered. 'Oh, an' a portion o' mushy peas. I reckon I've earned it.'

Mick cocked his head in admiration. 'I'm sure nobody's gonna argue with that, our kid,' he said. He grabbed his jacket and was gone in a minute, out the door and down towards the chippie at full run.

Larry took hold of his sister's hand. 'You can't know how good it is to see you.'

'It's good to be here,' she answered, 'Although I always hate to see our old house all boarded up. It makes me feel so sad. But to see you walk like that . . .' Lost for words, she shook her head. 'It's just wonderful, Larry.'

'Where's Betsy?'

'She'll be here.' Though Ellie couldn't be sure.

He grinned. 'I'm not sure I can do a re-run of going right across the room, but I can show her a few paces, or my name's not Larry Bolton.'

While Ellie prepared the bread and butter slices, Larry made the tea. 'I've got the hang of all this now,' he said, as he pushed himself from one end of the kitchen to the other. 'Mick's put everything within easy reach for me. Honest to God, Ellie, I don't know what I would have done without him. He's a great bloke.'

Ellie smiled to herself. She didn't need telling that, because she knew it already.

No sooner was the tea made and the bread and butter on the table, than Mick was back. 'No plates,' he instructed Ellie. 'Fish and chips are best straight out the paper.'

And that was how they enjoyed it. Fat, moist chunks of fish, thick chips with crispy edges, lots of salt and vinegar, all washed down with a steaming mug of tea. 'By! That were grand.' Full to bursting, Larry crumpled the chip paper on his knees. 'I don't mind telling yer, I were ready for that.'

Ellie cleared the rubbish away and Mick took it outside to the midden. 'It doesn't look like Betsy's coming.' Larry was obviously disappointed.

Inwardly angry, Ellie assured him, 'There'll be a good reason why she didn't come.' She was tired of making excuses for her sister, but what else could she do? 'I'm sure she'll make it tomorrow night.' Even if I have to drag her all the way, she thought.

'You'd best be off,' Larry reminded Ellie, 'or you'll have Peggy sending out the searchers.'

Before she left, Ellie told him again how thrilled she had been to see him walk across the room. 'But you mustn't overdo it,' she warned. And he promised he wouldn't.

'I'll see you as far as the tram-stop,' Mick suggested. Bringing her coat, he helped her on with it. 'You never know who's lurking about in the dark,' he said, then could have bitten his tongue.

Before she left, Ellie had one last hug for her brother.

'Take care of yourself,' she said. 'When I see Grandad, I'll tell him how well you're doing.'

She and Mick were on the outer step when Larry called Mick back.

'Hang on, love,' Mick said. 'I'll not be a minute.'

Rushing back inside, he found Larry standing by the table. 'I've overdone it.' He was grey in the face with pain. 'I think I need a hand back to the wheelchair.'

Taking him by the underarms, Mick eased him back; with every step they took, Larry gave a groan. When he was settled in the chair, Mick stood over him a moment, looking down on this friend of his, whose heart was as big as a lion's.

Stooping to his knees, he looked Larry straight in the eye. 'I might have known you'd overstretched yourself, walking all the way across the room like that. Jesus! I don't know how you did it, but what I do know is this – it was too far, too quickly. You have to be so careful. That's what the doc said, wasn't it? Be careful not to rush things. A few steps at a time, until your leg muscles begin to cope normally.'

For a moment, Larry gave no reply. Then, with a choked, angry voice he told Mick, 'I haven't got *time* to be careful! It's been three years, Mick, and I'm still a bloody cripple. And *he* did it to me. Every minute I'm locked in this wheelchair, every day that passes, the bastard who tore my family apart is out there, with two good legs. And a life to which he has no right.' He could say no more; emotion had overwhelmed him.

Mick's suspicions were right. 'I thought as much. It's all still eating away at you.' For the life of him, he could not blame his pal for that.

Tears of rage sped down Larry's face, as he admitted with passion, 'Yes, it's eating away at me. Yes, I'm driven by it. Not a minute passes when I don't long to take his neck in my hands and wring it, until that wicked life is snuffed out for good an' all! Just like he snuffed out my parents' life!' Emotionally and physically spent, he put his two hands over his face. 'I need to know why, Mick. I have to know. *Why were they killed?* Who would want to do a thing like that?'

After taking a moment to compose himself, he spoke to Mick in the softest of voices. 'You'd be the same, wouldn't you? If that evil devil had done that to *your* family . . . you would feel the same, wouldn't you?'

Mick had never seen Larry like this before. He was not a man easily given to tears of rage or emotion. Yet here he was, baring his deeper emotions for the first time; his face the face of a man crippled both outside and inside. It was plain to see that until the person responsible had been made to pay for the carnage he had caused in that delightful family, then Larry would have no peace of mind.

To Larry's question, Mick could give only one answer. 'Yes, you're right,' he said heavily. 'I would feel the very same.'

Larry leaned back in his chair, exhausted. 'I knew you'd understand, Mick. You of all people.'

Sensing that Larry had not yet finished, Mick waited a moment. When the question came, it shook him to his roots.

'You're fond of our Ellie, aren't you?'

Startled, Mick scrambled to his feet. 'In what way?'

'You know what way.'

'What meks you say that?'

'Because it's my *legs* that are damaged, not my eyes. I couldn't help but notice the way you were looking at her tonight.' When he saw that Mick was about to say something, he put up his hand. 'It's all right. I know all the arguments . . . she's not yet sixteen, and you're a few years older an' all that.

But you're not *that* much older, and you're a good man, Mick Fellowes. I know you'll do right by her.'

Mick gave a sigh of relief. 'I would never do anything to harm her, you know that.' Suddenly self-conscious, he lowered his gaze. 'I really love her, you know.'

'Aye. And she loves you.'

Mick looked up, his face wreathed in disbelief. 'No!' He shook his head. 'Oh, I had hoped that one day . . . but do you really reckon she loves me back?' He grinned like a happy schoolboy. 'No!'

Larry chuckled. 'Oh, aye. She's not a silly young lass. She's a young woman, with a woman's feelings. I saw it tonight. Our Ellie's as daft about you as you are about her.'

Just then, Ellie herself called out, 'Here, you two! It's getting right parky out here!' Her footsteps could be heard coming down the passage.

Larry nodded. 'Go on, lad. Don't keep my favourite sister waiting.'

'I'm on my way!' Mick called back, and the footsteps paused.

As Mick went out the door, Larry asked, 'Why don't you make it up with your dad? By! He'd welcome you with open arms.'

Mick remained with his back to him, his head bowed, and his voice bitter as he confessed, 'I don't know if I can ever forgive him.'

'*Try*, man!' Larry urged. 'I know how precious a family is, and when yer parents are gone, they're gone for good! There's no bringing 'em back. You know that as well as I do. Look, if your dad were to get run over tomorrow, God forbid, think how you'd feel.'

Unbeknown to anyone, Mick had already been thinking

along the same lines. Yet, he still couldn't find it in his heart to forgive the father who ran out when he was sorely needed. That was a cowardly thing, and Mick still had not come to terms with it. 'I'd best go,' he murmured. ''Bye, mate,' and hurried away to be with Ellie.

The tram was already half-filled with passengers and waiting at the terminal. 'We've got a minute or two,' Mick observed. 'The driver isn't ready for off yet.'

Ellie, too, had noticed how the driver seemed not to be in the slightest hurry. Lazily smoking his pipe, he leaned on the back end of the bus, laughing and chatting with a group of conductors. 'Are you sure it's him?'

Mick took another look. 'That's him all right,' he grinned. 'He's been on this run for three weeks now. He's not been known to leave a minute early nor arrive a minute later. You could set your watch by him.'

Ellie took his word for it. Unlike Mick, she was not all that familiar with the regular drivers. This one though, seemed to be a jovial fella. 'It's not often I'm waiting for the driver,' she chuckled. 'It's usually the other way round, with me running after the tram.'

Seeming not to have heard, he drew her into a shady corner, his voice trembling as he told her, 'Just now, Larry said something that made me wonder . . .'

When he hesitated, Ellie got the feeling that he was about to take her in his arms. Instead, he thrust his arms into his coat pocket and kicked at the ground with the toe of his boot.

Intrigued, she urged him to go on. 'Mick? What did my brother say?'

Mick looked up. 'He said that he saw how I was looking at you tonight.'

Ellie smiled. 'Did he now?' She, too, had seen the way he had looked at her, and it turned her heart over.

Mick nodded. 'He said . . . he knew how I felt about you.'

'And what did *you* say?'

There was a long moment before Mick drew the courage to admit, 'I told him I loved you . . . and that I would never do anything to harm you.'

'What did he say to that?' She was so close to him, it took her breath away.

Unsure, Mick gazed at her for a while, his heart leaping inside him. The shadows had fallen across her face, bathing the curve of her cheekbones, and outlining the fullness of her mouth. 'He said . . .' Pausing, he didn't know how to go on, and then the words came in a rush, ' . . . that you loved me too.'

'I do.' In the softest whisper she confided, 'I think I've loved you for ever.'

Like magic to his ears, her words lingered in the night air, and he could hardly believe it. 'You do?' His voice was incredulous. 'You *really* mean it?'

When she nodded, he grabbed her to him. 'Oh, Ellie!'

For as long as she lived, Ellie would remember that first real kiss; it would carry her through her youth and into old age, and when she was in her last days on this earth, the memory of it would still live on.

Afterwards, he held her for an age and she clung to him, not wanting to let him go. She half-expected him to say how he should not have done that, because she was too young and he should have known better. But he didn't say it, and she was glad.

Now, when she drew away, he opened his mouth to tell her something, and she laid a finger across his lips. 'No,' she murmured. 'Don't say anything.' In the background they heard the tram start up. 'I have to get back now,' she told him. 'Go home, Mick. We can talk later.'

He looked at her, his brown eyes melting into hers, and he knew that somehow, everything would be all right. 'Will I see you tomorrow?'

She shook her head. There was so much to think about. 'Monday,' she told him. 'I'll meet you after work.'

Realising how events had overtaken them, Mick knew they had to talk it through. 'Where?'

'By the lighthouse in Blackpool. Seven o'clock.' She pushed him away. 'Please, Mick. Go home now.'

Without further ado, she broke away and ran across to the tram, where she quickly climbed aboard. She saw him for a moment through the window. He waved, and then he was gone, out of sight, but not out of her life.

Too excited to think straight, Ellie deliberately concentrated on events going on around her. Two women were having a bawdy conversation, intermittently laughing out loud, an old man was having a nasty coughing fit, and another, younger fella was drinking a sneaky drop of whisky out of his flask, which he then slyly shoved back into his bag. Up ahead and standing on the running-board of his cab, the tram-driver was changing his destination roll. Over and over it went, until it showed the heading LYTHAM ST ANNES.

In a minute they were almost ready for off; the conductor was strapping his ticket-machine on, and now, his hand was poised ready to press the button that would let the driver know they were ready to leave.

Ellie looked out of the window, searching for Mick, but he was long gone. Suddenly, she saw a man coming out of a nearby alley. Following behind him was a girl. The man stopped, blocking Ellie's view, and made a gesture that seemed to suggest he was giving the girl money. Now he was moving away. My God! The girl wasn't much older than . . . Shocked to the core, Ellie gave a great gasp. Betsy! *It was her sister Betsy!*

Leaping out of her seat she ran down the aisle. ''Ere, miss! You can't get off now.' The conductor barred her way. 'We're on the move!'

'No! I have to get off!' Frantic, Ellie pushed her way through, and there was nothing he could do but press the stop button and hope it would bring the tram to a halt.

No matter, Ellie had jumped off the tram and was running across the boulevard. 'Betsy!' Soaring above the noise of engines and people, her voice went before her. 'Betsy, wait!'

Startled to see Ellie rushing towards her, Betsy did her best to tidy herself. Running her hands through her hair and pulling her jacket straight, she faced her twin head on. 'Where have *you* sprung from?'

Having run full pelt, dodging in and out of trams and queues, Ellie took a moment to catch her breath. Betsy, however, had a great deal to say. 'Have you been spying on me? Did Peggy send you out after me? Well, you can go back and tell her I'll do what I like and she can't stop me! I hate you all, so just go away and leave me alone.'

Indignant, Ellie drew herself up. 'Nobody sent me,' she replied breathlessly. 'I've been to Buncer Lane to see Larry, remember? I thought you were following on, and so did he. What have you been up to, Betsy? Who was that man?'

The girl stared at her wide-eyed and innocent. 'What man?'

Ellie drew her aside. 'Look, it's no good you denying it. I saw you from the tram. You came out of that alley with a man, and he gave you some money. I saw it with my own eyes!'

Knowing the game was up, Betsy made no further attempt to deny it. 'Look – I don't care what you think you saw,' she retorted, 'and I don't care what you say. I'm fed up with being told what to do and what not to do. I've had enough of working in that bloody factory, with people watching every move I make, and pulling me apart when I try to do my job. Miss Turnbull said it was only a matter of time before I get the sack anyway.' With that she folded her arms in that same, sullen manner Ellie had gotten used to. 'So you can bugger off, and leave me alone.'

But Ellie had no intention of going anywhere.

'Is that what all this is about?' she demanded incredulously. 'You, being abusive to that driver, blaming him for something that wasn't his fault, and now, because you didn't do your job properly, you go up some stinking alley with a stranger and sell yourself!' She spat the words out, as though they tasted bad on her tongue.

Betsy continued to glare at her. 'Stop going on at me! It's got nothing to do with you!'

In a spasm of rage, Ellie took hold of Betsy and drove her against the wall. 'Aren't you ashamed of yourself? Is that all you think you're worth – a few measly shillings! How long has it been going on, eh – tell me that! Because we're neither of us going *anywhere* until you've told me everything.'

Suddenly, Betsy was crying. 'I'm not going home.' Looking at Ellie with tearful eyes, she pleaded, 'Don't make me go back to Peggy, not yet. I can't face her. That man . . . I've never done it before. It was awful, Ellie! You won't tell Peggy, will you? Or Ted. Please promise you won't? I don't want them to throw me out.'

'They won't do that,' Ellie told her comfortingly. She

looked at her sister and felt she hardly knew her. 'Be honest with me. That man ... whatever made you do such a thing?'

'I was angry.'

'Who with?'

'You; them. Everybody!'

'Not yourself then?'

'Why should I be angry with myself?'

Betsy's answer was so typical, it made Ellie smile. Now, she needed to know only one thing. 'Do you mean to do it again?' she asked.

'Do what?'

'Do you mean to go down some dark alley and sell yourself to a stranger – and all because you're angry?'

It took a moment for Betsy to reply, as though she had to make it right in her own mind first. 'No,' she answered presently. 'I won't *ever* do it again.' And Ellie could tell by the tone of her voice that she was telling the truth.

In that moment, through her own sorry tears, Ellie looked at Betsy long and hard. She saw the dirt on her clothes and the way her hair was messed up; she saw how the lipstick on her mouth was all smudged and the mascara had run down her face with the tears, and her heart bled for this awkward girl who was her sister.

'Come on, our kid.' Reaching up, she put a comforting arm round her shoulder.

'Where are we going?'

Ellie looked about her. She knew from old that the lavvies on the boulevard were small and cramped and anyway, there was always a queue. 'We're going across there,' she answered, her gaze directed to the railway station adjacent.

'What for?'

'First we're going through into the lavvies so you can get washed and tidied up. While you're doing that, I'll ask the stationmaster if he can telephone Peggy and tell her we'll be late, 'cause we're going to see Grandad Bertie and Tilly before going home. It'll do us both a power of good to go and sit with them for a while, and have a bit of Tilly's home-made cake. You must be starving, Betsy. I've had fish and chips with Mick and Larry. We all wondered where on earth you'd got to.'

Betsy looked contrite. What a fool she'd made of herself. And yes, it would be very soothing to go and see the old 'uns. 'It's no good phoning Peggy,' she reminded Ellie. 'You know very well the phone's broken again. Ted says it's a useless contraption and he wishes he'd never had it put in, 'cause it's been nothing but trouble. "Neither use nor ornament", that's what he called it.'

'All the same, it's worth a try. He might have got the workmen out to it today.'

'All right, but I'll need to borrow a comb, and some lipstick.'

'Here, and don't flatten the end of it like you did before.' Taking the tube of lipstick from her work-bag, Ellie handed it to her. 'Put it on gently, then it won't look like you've been run over with a tin of red paint.'

In the lamplight, Betsy checked the colour and made a face. 'Why do you always use this shade?'

'Because I like it.'

'Well, I don't.'

'Hard luck – because it's all I've got.'

'I suppose it'll be all right . . . just for once. So, where's the comb?'

Fishing it out of her bag, Ellie handed it to her, together

with a hankie and two pieces of rice paper to powder her flushed cheeks. 'Go on then. Time's running away. I'll go and make the call, and meet you in the lavvies after.'

The station office was warm and cosy. There was no one there, except for the bearded stationmaster behind the desk, and some old female tramp warming her hands round the cheery fire in the grate in the waiting-room next door.

The stationmaster was very friendly. 'How can I help you, young lady?' he asked with a smile.

'I need to let someone know that my sister and I will be late home.' Ellie recalled the telephone number and wrote it down for him. 'Could you please contact her on this number, and tell me how much I owe you.'

Donning his tiny rimless spectacles, the man scrutinised the number. 'What's the person's name?'

'If a man answers, it's Ted – Mr Walters,' Ellie informed him. 'If it's a woman, her name is Mrs Peggy Walters.'

Taking the long black receiver off its hook, he dialled the given number and waited. 'Damned thing!' Apologising to Ellie for his language, he hung the receiver back on its hook and started again. This time he gave a broad grin as the telephone rang on the other end.

'Hello, is that Mrs Walters?' he asked. When Peggy affirmed it, he quickly handed the receiver to Ellie, though its stiffened cord required that Ellie should lean right over the counter to speak.

Peggy said that, although she knew the twins had gone to visit Larry, it was now past nine o'clock and she had been worried half out of her mind, wondering where the two of them were. And who was that man on the telephone? And why weren't they home, and where had they been? The nervous little woman sounded distraught.

After that, the line went all crackly and the stationmaster told Ellie to, 'Tap the voice end, it sometimes works.'

That was what she did, and though she realised Peggy could hear her voice, she could not hear her reply. 'It's all right, Peggy,' she said frantically. 'We're on the boulevard and we'll be home in no time.' Then she rehung the receiver with a grateful sigh. 'How much do I owe you?' she asked the station-master, taking out her purse, and handing him a few coins.

'It's all right, miss,' he said, 'you don't owe me nothing. You might owe it to the railways,' he gave a cheeky wink, 'but I won't tell them if you don't.'

So Ellie thanked him, dropped the coins into her pocket, and went out of the office.

Meantime, Betsy had made her way into the waiting-room where, keeping a discreet distance from the old woman tramp, she warmed herself by the fire. 'Hello, dearie.' Lonely and unloved, the old woman tried to draw her into conversation. All she got for her trouble was a hesitant smile and a few more inches between them.

Ellie was delighted with Betsy's appearance. 'You look altogether different now,' she said.

Betsy had plainly taken much trouble. Her face was clean and shining; the lipstick was carefully applied and her hair was combed through. Her clothes were straightened and neatly fastened, until there was little or no trace of the night's episode, save for a scratch down her ankle, which had bled and dried and was now hardly noticeable. Knowing that her sister truly regretted what she had done, Ellie decided to leave the subject alone.

Betsy did not receive the news that they were off home well. 'Why didn't you tell her we were going on to Grandad's!' she moaned. 'You *know* I didn't want to go home yet.'

'I had to tell her we were on our way back,' Ellie argued. 'She was going crazy. She cried down the telephone and everything. Then I couldn't hear what she was saying, and so I told her we'd be home in no time, and we will. Besides, what if she sends Ted out looking for us? It wouldn't be right, Betsy. Anyway, you look fine. We've been to see Larry, that's what I let her think. May God forgive me for lying, although it was really only half a lie.' She hadn't even had a chance yet to tell Betsy about their brother's amazing walk across the room. Nor had she had any time to mull over the equally amazing developments in her own love-life!

When Betsy began to sulk, Ellie promised it would be all right. 'Look,' she told her, 'we can go and see Grandad another day.' Although she suspected Betsy wasn't too concerned about Bertie. She was more worried about Peggy seeing some change in her.

'You look absolutely fine,' Ellie told her again. 'No different than always.'

'That's right, dearie.' The old woman's voice cut through their conversation. Looking first at Betsy, then Ellie, she said softly, 'This your sister, is it?'

Surprised, Ellie told her yes, it was. Although the girls were twins, they were not identical, and each had a different build and colouring.

'She's an 'ansom gal, ain't she? And you . . . such a pretty little thing an' all.' Taking a deep, withering sigh, she confided, 'I had four grandchildren – three lads and a lass, but I don't know where they are now. Me son took 'em away with his new wife, and I haven't seen 'em for months.'

Tears glistened in her old eyes. 'Yer mustn't forget to go and see yer grandad, like you said.' She wagged a finger at Betsy. 'And yer to go straight home, like yer sister wants yer to. 'Cause yer mam will be that worried, an' yer don't want yer dad traipsing the streets of a night, looking everywhere for yer. Not like me. I ain't never found 'em, see. Not yet I ain't.'

She smiled, the saddest smile Ellie had ever seen. 'But I will!' Her voice and her concentration faded. 'One o' these fine days, I'll be walking down the street and there they'll be.'

Betsy looked at Ellie in astonishment. 'She's been listening, the whole time.'

Ellie nodded. 'I expect she's lonely.' Going across to the old woman, she reached into her pocket and found the coins returned to her by the stationmaster. Discreetly dropping them into the old lady's hand, she told her softly, 'I hope you find your son, and grandchildren.'

The tramp clutched the coins in her fist. 'God bless yer, dearie.' Looking up at Betsy, she added, 'You look lovely. Go on home now, eh?' Then she ambled out into the night, across to the pub where she would partake of a drop o' the warming stuff. After that, she would set off again, searching for her long-lost family.

Chapter Fourteen

A T FOUR O'CLOCK the following Monday, Tilly's great-nephew John arrived at Summerfield House, the Williamses imposing home in West Gardens, Lytham St Anne's.

From the dining-room window, Daisy noticed him arrive. She saw him pause at the gate and look up at the house in awe, and she wondered who he might be. Looks like a smart Alec to me, she thought, observing his clean-cut jacket and dark tie which she thought did not hide the rascal underneath.

Greatly impressed with the size and quality of the house, John could not help but wonder what he was getting himself into. 'Best foot forward, lad,' he said. 'The man was good enough to offer you a job, so you should be grateful. All the same, you would do well to find out what's expected of you, afore you say yes to anything.'

With this in mind, he lingered a second or two longer before coming up the path to the front door, where he straightened his tie, rubbed his shoes against each trouser leg and, raising his hand, took up the knocker and let it fall twice against the brass plate.

After tripping over the table-leg, Daisy went at a run to

the front door. Guardedly inching open the door, she peered at him. 'Yes?'

John thought her strange. 'Is this the house of Mr Peter Williams?'

Opening the door wider, she gave a little cough. 'Yes, sir, can I help you?'

'I've come to see Mr Williams,' he said, holding out the card he was given that day outside Brindle's shoe-factory. 'I've got an appointment.'

'I see.' Yet she couldn't 'see' at all, because Daisy had never learned to read nor write. 'You'd best come in then. I'll see if he's in his office.'

Stepping aside, she allowed him to walk by her. 'I say!' Taken aback by the luxury of his surroundings, John gave a whistle. 'He's not short of a bob or two, I can see that.'

Hurriedly closing the door she saw him loitering too close to the dining room, where she had been polishing the silver. 'If you'll just wait here, sir?' Gesturing to a high-backed chair, she waited until he was seated before scurrying away to find the master.

The moment she'd gone, John took the opportunity to wander a little. He peeped into the drawing room and was amazed at the wonderful pictures adorning all four walls. 'All right for some!' he marvelled.

The dining room was the same, except there were all manner of beautiful silver artefacts, set out on a cloth over the table, obviously in the process of being cleaned. 'Bloody 'ell!' Stepping inside, he touched them with reverence; the silver candlestick, the fruit bowl, and the dainty figurines. 'Beautiful!' The fact that he had never owned such things didn't mean he couldn't appreciate them. He fingered the smaller pieces – the Georgian snuff-tin and matching miniature clocks. 'Hmh! I could make off with these and no one would be any the wiser.'

'Don't even think about it.' Peter Williams was right behind him. 'Unless you want your fingers chopped off one by one?'

Badly shaken, John dropped the ornaments and swung round, his eyes wide as midden-lids. 'Mr Williams! I didn't see you there. I didn't mean nothing – just idle talk, that's all it was.'

Daisy backed away, waiting for the explosion she was certain would come. She was wrong.

'Down the corridor, first on the left, and keep your eyes forward.' Indicating the way, Peter Williams waited until John had started the short journey, then he followed at a discreet distance behind. 'Inside!' he barked when John paused outside the doorway. 'And don't sit until I tell you to.'

As the two of them disappeared one behind the other into the office, Daisy peeped from the dining-room doorway. 'I wouldn't like to be in that young man's shoes, no, I would not!' Before the master might look out and see her there she fled back into the dining room, where she examined the small silver pieces he had held, crossly polishing off his fingermarks. 'Still, it would serve that devil right, if somebody *did* make off with his precious silver,' she mused.

Just then she almost leaped out of her skin, when the grandfather clock in the corner struck the quarter hour. White-faced and shaken, she grabbed up the rest of the pieces and began polishing like a fiend out of hell.

In the office, Peter faced the younger man across the desk. 'I suppose you've come about the job?' He smiled, but it was an odd, lopsided kind of smile – more like a nervous twitch, John thought.

'Yes, sir. I was worried you might have forgotten.' His weary eyes shifted to the deep leather armchair beside him. He had walked a long way to this house, and now he ached to sit down. Besides, standing to attention was not something he was used to.

'I never forget anything.' Getting out of the chair, Peter walked round the desk.

Feeling bolder, John grinned widely. 'That's good, 'cause I need a job, and I'm ready to start whenever—' The word lodged in his throat when, without warning, the other man drew back his fist and punched him hard on the face.

'Jesus!' Looking up from the chair where he had landed, John wiped blood from his nose with a trembling hand. 'What was that for?'

Peter stared down on him. 'That was just a small reminder that you are *never again* to touch anything that belongs to me.' Giving him a kick he growled, 'Do you understand my meaning?'

Realising he had stepped out of his depth, John feverishly nodded his head. 'Yes, sir, I understand.'

'Get up!'

When John scrambled out of the chair and stood before him, Peter leaned forward, his eyes staring into the younger man's. 'Do you still want the job?'

'Yes, sir.' After what had happened, he was almost afraid to refuse. His whole head throbbed with pain and he felt in a state of shock. He just hoped none of his teeth were loose.

'Can I trust you?'

'Yes, sir.'

'It didn't seem like it back there.'

'That was just a slip. I would never steal from you.'

'Ah! Then you *would* steal? If not from me?'

'No, sir.'

'Liar!' Peter banged his fist on the table.

John had to admit, 'Well, if my life depended on it, I suppose I might.'

'Ah, the truth at last. I suppose that's something.'

'I would never steal from *you*,' John assured him. 'As God's my judge, I wouldn't.'

Peter laughed out loud. 'I should hope not.' The laugh was abruptly silenced as he glanced at John with menace. 'Take anything of mine, and you sign your own death warrant.'

'I wouldn't! You have my word.'

'Your word?'

'Yes, sir.'

'Tell me the truth now. Are you afraid of me?'

John hesitated. In all his life he had never been afraid of anyone. But this fella was something different. To John, Peter Williams seemed quite mad.

'Well?'

'Yes, sir, I think I am.'

Delighted, Peter laughed out loud again. 'Good! *Good!* It means you've learnt a lesson.' Quite matter-of-fact now, he threw a piece of paper across the desk. 'Read it. Aloud, so I know you've got it right.'

Taking the paper between his hands, John first scanned it.

'I said *read* it. Or can't you read? If you can't follow a simple instruction you might as well go now, because you're no good to me.'

Inwardly angry, John began to read, and while he read, Peter leaned back in his chair and listened intently. When the reading was over, he praised the young man. 'You read well. Now tell me what it all meant.'

Feeling like a kid at school, John interpreted the instructions as he understood them. 'I'm to collect rent from these addresses; the money collected will be kept safe in a bag, supplied by you, and I must bring the same bag to you at the end of each day . . .'

'Without fail,' Peter prompted.

'Yes, without fail.' Swallowing hard, he continued, 'I'm to write down anyone who has not paid, or will not pay, and hand the names to you at the end of each day. The tenants should have the rent money in the correct coinage. I'm not to give out any change.'

'So?' Impatient, Peter began tapping his pencil. 'For pity's sake, get a move on, man!'

'So . . . whatever they offer over and above the rent for that week, will be carried over and taken off the following week. There will be no change given, no matter how much they might argue.'

'And?'

'If anyone should miss paying the rent for two weeks on the trot, I'm to throw them out and change the locks, so they can't ever get back in again.'

'That's it. And now for the best bit?'

'I'm to be paid a regular wage of two shillings a week, and an extra sixpence for every rent I collect.' He took a deep breath. 'I'm to be paid on a Friday, but my money will be reckoned from Thursday to Thursday, since you won't have time to check the Friday collection until the Monday.'

Peter finished it for him. 'And if the Friday collection doesn't add up, you will be the loser when I next pay you.'

'That's about it, sir.'

'And are you still interested?'

'Yes, sir. Like I said, I need the work and I need the money.'

'I have one more instruction which I would rather not have written down for any nosy parker to see.' Coming to sit on the edge of the desk, he asked meaningfully, 'Have you ever had a woman, young sir?'

Shifting uncomfortably from one foot to the other, John was acutely embarrassed. 'Not lately. But yes, I've had a woman, o' course I have.' And even if he hadn't, he wouldn't be stupid enough to admit it.

'Cast your mind back, man. What *kind* of woman was she?'

'OK, I suppose.'

'Warm?'

'I expect so.'

'Squirming like a puppy in your arms?'

'Not that I recall, sir, no.'

'Did she have a mass of hair, red as fire and shining like gold? Did she purr like a kitten whenever you kissed her? When you made love, was it the most exciting, most wonderful experience of your life? And when it was over, did she lie in your arms, moulded to your body, your two hearts beating as one? And did you long to make love all over again?'

John licked his lips. 'No, sir. It was never like that.'

'Then you lied!'

'Beg pardon, sir?'

'You've *never* had a woman!' Peter's voice softened. 'But I have. She was the only woman who ever made me feel like that. She made me love her like I have never loved anyone in the whole of my life before. I adored her! Spent a fortune on her, and then she ran out on me.'

'I'm sorry, sir. That's terrible.' In truth John couldn't blame her for running from this madman, whoever she was.

'I want you to find her. *Find her and bring her back. Promise her the world if you have to.*'

Horrified, John shook his head. 'I'm sorry, sir. Happen it might be best if I didn't take the job, after all. I thought it were just collecting rent. I didn't know you wanted me to go people-searching. I'm not a detective, sir. No, sir. I can't do it, thank you all the same.'

'You don't understand, you fool!' Gripping him by the collar he lifted the young man off his feet. 'I'm not asking you to kidnap her, or drag her here against her will, nor am I asking you to go out in search of her.' He dropped him to his feet with a bump. 'I'm not so foolish to imagine you're capable of such a delicate job. No! I'm saying when you go about your work, collecting the rent and peering into people's parlours, keep a wary eye out for her. If by chance you should happen to see her, or hear of her whereabouts, come back and tell me, and I'll do the rest. Can you do that?'

'I reckon so. What's her name, sir?'

'Ruth. Ruth Clegg. She's young, shapely, with such a mass of flame-red hair and green eyes – green like the ocean.' He grew excited. 'If you saw her, you'd know her straight off.'

'I'll keep her in mind, sir. If I happen to catch sight of her, or hear of anything, like you said, I'll let you know right away.'

'That's it!' Peter had a feeling that at long last, with two pairs of eyes searching, his Ruth would be found.

'When am I to start, sir?'

'Right away, this very evening.' Going to his desk, Peter took out a small leather pouch from which he drew a single silver florin, which he laid on the desk. 'One week in hand,' he explained. 'Take it.'

Before the other man could change his mind, John snatched it up. 'Thank you, sir.'

'You will need this.' Pushing a narrow briefcase across the desk, Peter told John, 'In there you'll find a ledger, each page written with names and addresses. When they pay you, you must sign their rent-book and enter the payment against their name in this ledger.'

'It sounds simple enough.'

'It is. There is also a leather bag in the back cover, for putting the money in.' He handed him another list. 'These are new properties I've recently acquired. As yet I've not had time to enter the names into the ledger. I shall expect that to be done before you come back with your first day's collection.'

He pointed to the door. 'Now be off with you. And mind you hide the bag well on your person, or you'll be set on by villains before you know it.'

'Right, sir.'

'You won't forget what I said, will you? About the stealing?'

'No, sir, I won't forget.' Not in a month of Sundays, he wouldn't.

Once outside, John took a deep, invigorating breath of air. '"Red hair shining like gold,"' he quoted. 'Makes a man want to love her all over again.' Clicking his tongue, he sauntered away. 'Too good for that bastard, I shouldn't wonder!' He felt the coin lying in the bottom of his trouser pocket. 'First stop the pub,' he decided. 'By! I've a thirst like a bull elephant.'

Daisy watched him go. 'You'll regret it,' she said sagely. 'One way or another he's ruined everything he's touched. He'll ruin you too. You just mark my words, Mr Smart Alec.'

Chapter Fifteen

I T WAS ELLIE'S turn to make the tea.

'I want an extra spoon of sugar in mine.' The big, jolly-faced woman had worked at the factory ever since it opened; next week she would retire with honours. Outspoken and amiable, there was no doubt she would be sadly missed.

'Well, bugger me, Bertha!' The woman on the second but one chair to her left couldn't believe it. 'I've never known you to have sugar in your tea,' she said. 'Not in all the years I've known yer!'

'Aye, well, I had a fella for the first time in two years last night.' Her raucous laughter echoed all over that big warehouse. 'I need me energy.' Winking at Ellie she asked, 'Best mek it *two* spoons, lass. I've an idea I might bed him again tonight . . . if I'm lucky.'

Past being embarrassed by anything these lovely ladies said, Ellie went away chuckling. In the little scullery at the back of the factory, she sang softly as she busied herself making the eight mugs of tea. She had so much to sing about, she thought. She and Mick had spoken of their love for each other, and now she couldn't wait to get up of a morning to be with him. They had their nights out together, and everything was right and above board. Just as Mick had promised, he had never done, nor would ever do, anything to harm her.

Also, things were better at home since that awful incident with Betsy. It was as if she had come through a storm and now she was more settled in herself. She had even knuckled down at work.

Ellie herself had never been happier. In love for the first and last time in her life, she couldn't wait for the months to pass, so she and Mick could announce their love to the world. For now though, she had to settle for a stolen kiss and holding hands, and a night at the pictures where they kissed and cuddled in the back seat. Even here, at work, when no one was looking, he would take her in his arms and hold her. It was the most wonderful feeling. Her family – Grandad and Larry and Betsy – meant the world to her and always would. But Mick was her reason for living.

And so now, she sang and boiled the kettle, spooned the tea into the pot, and almost fainted when she turned about to see Mick standing at the door, a smile on his face as he enjoyed her singing. 'Someone's happy,' he said, and came in to be with her.

Embarrassed to be caught offguard, Ellie blushed pink. 'I didn't know you were standing there,' she chided. 'Sneaking up on me like that.'

He slid his arm round her. 'It's lovely hearing you sing,' he murmured. 'Since you've been here, this place has been so much brighter. You've brought everybody together, and they all love you.' He stroked her hair and smiled into her pretty eyes. 'You're like a ray of sunshine on a dull day.'

Ellie snuggled up to him, her eyes shining with mischief. 'Kiss me then.'

He laughed at her boldness. 'You little hussy!'

'Go on. Kiss me!' She glanced at the door. 'There's nobody about, and anyway, I'll be sixteen soon and we can tell them all.'

He, too, glanced at the door and it was true; there was no one there but them. Sliding his arms round her waist he drew her to him, for a moment gazing down on her and thinking how fortunate a man he was, to have the love of this delightful creature. Bending his head, he put his mouth ever so gently over hers; he felt the softness of her lips and the moistness of her mouth, and his senses were deeply stirred.

Ellie closed her eyes, immersing herself in that wonderful kiss; a gentle kiss at first, then stronger and more passionate. When at last she opened her eyes, it was to see him looking down on her. 'I love you, Ellie Bolton,' he murmured, and she kissed him again, briefly this time. 'You'd best go,' she suggested with a smile, 'before they come looking for me.'

When he'd gone, she commenced singing again. With the scullery being close to the main doors, her voice carried to the street; to the ears of the new rent-collector. About to enter the premises, John paused, cocking an ear to her voice and smiling when he recognised it as belonging to Ellie Bolton, the girl to whom he had long since taken a fancy.

Unaware of his approach, she was still singing when John found his way to her. 'Well now, if it isn't our Ellie!'

Ellie had been surprised when she discovered he was working for Peter Williams, and she was even more surprised to see him here, in the scullery. 'You've just missed Mick,' she said. 'He's up in the office if you're after the rent.'

He glanced at the row of mugs, all steaming with freshly brewed tea. 'I wouldn't mind one of them,' he said. 'It's bloody freezing outside.' He rubbed his hands together and blew in them, and though she had never really taken a liking to him, Ellie took pity.

Removing her own mug from the row, she handed it to him. 'There you are. Look, I've got to go, or the tea will be cold. But don't hang about in here. It's out of bounds for visitors.'

As she turned to put the mugs on the tray, he put his tea on the table, and grabbed her so hard round the waist that she let out a cry. 'This is nice,' he whispered suggestively, his mouth against her ear. 'You and me all alone in here.'

Unfortunately for Ellie, the machines outside were now in full flow, drowning out her cry. However, Mick had seen John come in, and then, when he had the rent-money to hand, and was about to run down the steps, he noticed John making his way into the scullery.

In a minute he was on him.

Dragging him along by the scruff of his collar, he took him all the way to the exit door, throwing him out with such force that he rolled over and over on the ground – unhurt but with his pride deeply wounded. 'There's your rent-money!' Mick flung the envelope across the ground after him. 'Now be off with you.'

'What about the book?' John stood up shakily, retrieved his briefcase from the ground. He had Peter's instructions in mind. 'You have to sign the book!'

'To hell with the book!' Mick retorted. 'Tell your boss why it's not signed, and tell him this an' all: if you ever come inside this factory and lay a hand on any of these women again, I'll make sure you never get through that door again. You tell him that, and see what he has to say.'

'It was just a friendly gesture,' John shouted. 'I didn't mean no harm. There was no need for you to go bloody mad!'

When Mick took a step forward, John grabbed up his envelope and made a hasty retreat. 'I'll be back next week,' he called while on the run. 'You can sign the book then.'

As Mick watched him go hell-for-leather down the street, he couldn't help but laugh. 'Silly young bugger,' he chuckled. 'He's got a lot to learn. Still, I'll not see him in trouble. I'll sign his precious book next week, and we'll say no more about the matter.'

When Mick returned to the factory, he was still chuckling. 'I don't think he'll bother you again,' he told Ellie, and it turned out that John had made approaches to several other women at different times, since he took over the collection from Peter Williams.

'Were he the one you had last night?' Tilly asked Bertha slyly.

'Were he heckaslike!' The big woman laughed. 'That little runt ain't got enough to keep me going for two *minutes*, never mind two hours,' she boasted.

And the factory rocked with laughter.

———⟫•⟪———

JOHN'S NEXT PORT of call was the top end of Blackburn. Pausing to brush the dust off his clothes, he took out his book and consulted it. 'Freda and Ernie Fellowes.'

Having entrusted the address to mind, he then thrust the book into his briefcase. 'Freda Fellowes.' He groaned. 'That's the woman who hides every time she sees me coming.' With his pride sorely bruised at Mick's treatment of him, he squared his shoulders and strode ahead with purpose. 'She'll not bloody well hide from me this time,' he vowed. 'I've had enough aggravation to last me a lifetime!'

He muttered all the way down the street. 'I'm already going back with the factory book not signed. I'm damned if I'll go back for the third week running without rent from that harpy!'

FREDA WAS READY for off. 'I'll not be long,' she told Ruth. 'If the rent man comes, tell him I'll see him next week.'

'You can't do that, our Mam!' Much as she had come to love her mam all over again, Ruth was exasperated by her cavalier attitude to paying the rent. 'You've already missed him twice.'

'Aye, well, I'm a bit short this week. Tell him I'll catch up next time.' Pausing on the doorstep, Freda took a tube of lipstick from her bag. Impatiently removing the top, she pushed the crimson stick until it was half-exposed, then traced it over her mouth. 'Tastes like peppermint,' she said, smacking her lips together. Replacing the lipstick, she took out a comb and fluffed up her hair, until it looked like she'd had a fright. 'Right, lass.' Turning round for inspection, she asked, 'How do I look?'

Dropping the shammy-leather back into the bucket, Ruth looked at her mam, and couldn't help but smile. She saw the new black coat, fitting at the waist, and open at the neck; she observed the tight-fitting jumper beneath and the high-heeled shoes that showed off her slim ankles, and the made-up face, and she wondered, 'Are you off to a party or summat?'

'Don't be daft! You know very well I'm joining Ernie for a pint at the pub.'

'Well, *you're* overdressed, if you ask me.'

Freda didn't care. 'I'm *not* asking you, then, and anyway,

yer never know who yer might meet down the pub. I mean, I might come across some wealthy old fool who could whisk me away to foreign parts.' As she spoke, she went all dreamy. 'This time next week I could be swanning about in New York, or lying on a beach in some exotic land.'

'So, you'd leave Ernie behind then, would you?'

Her mother thought a moment. 'Well no, happen not,' she admitted with a warm smile. 'I've kinda got used to my Ernie. To tell you the truth, I wouldn't know what to do without him now.' All the same, as she tottered off down the street on those magnificent high heels, she laughed out loud. 'Happen I could keep Ernie, and the wealthy old fool an' all,' she cackled. 'Then I could tell the rent man to take a running jump.'

'Be sure and tell Ernie you've not left the money for the rent again – for the third week running,' Ruth called out. 'Happen he'll not be so fond of you when he finds out you've been risking him losing the roof from over his head.'

Unconcerned, Freda waved a hand. 'I've told yer – I'll catch up.'

'So you keep saying!'

All she got for her trouble was a rude gesture and a smile. 'See yer later, our kid,' she warbled. In a minute she was gone, out of sight, but not out of mind.

'You'll be the death of me,' Ruth groaned. And went back to her window-cleaning before it got too cold. She had finished the downstairs windows and was started on the upstairs, when John came into sight.

Seeing this woman up the ladder, donned in long skirt and brightly coloured turban that hid her hair, he thought at first it must be the lady of the house. 'Gotcha!' Quickening his steps, he hurried towards her. On reaching the bottom of the ladder, he realised that she was so intent on her task, she had no idea he was there. So, having been cheated of a private minute or two with Ellie, he decided to take stock of this woman before making his presence known.

Almost directly beneath the ladder, he took a moment or two to enjoy the view. Polishing the window meant Ruth reaching up and down, then backwards and forwards, and as she did so, her skirt stretched higher and higher. He could see right up to her bare thighs, the shape of which sent a thrill through him.

'Them's a smashing pair o' legs you've got there, missus!' he called up cheekily, and now, as she looked down on him with astonishment, he thought her a most attractive woman.

'What the devil d'you think you're doing?' Throwing the cloth down before her, Ruth almost slapped him in the face with it. 'What gives you the bloody right to stand there and look up my skirt, you dirty little ponce. Get away!' Now on his level, she gave him a push. 'Go on! Clear off, before I call the police!'

Protecting himself when she began smacking him, he cried out with a laugh. 'Hey! Leave off! I'm here for the rent. It ain't my fault if you were up the ladder showing yer fanny to all and sundry!'

'The *rent*?' Her temper melted away and now she was looking at him in a different light.

'That's right.'

'You're not the usual man. He's short and round with a bald head – Mr Collins, he's called.'

'Aye, well, Mr Collins sold his entire properties to my boss, and now I'm your new rent-collector.'

He saw how she was with child and he was puzzled. According to his notes, the woman who lived here was older. 'A right scrawny bitch who doesn't pay her rent from one week's end to the next and was twice threatened with eviction.'

This woman must be what . . . in her early twenties, not much older than himself. And she could never be described as 'scrawny'. Even with her swollen belly, she was very attractive. 'Three weeks,' he repeated, tapping the book under his arm. 'It's all in here.'

'Would you settle for this week's, and another week off the arrears?' Ruth thought it worth a try, but wasn't surprised by his answer.

'Nope. I'm under strict instructions to collect for all three weeks.' He looked her in the eye and thought she had the loveliest face, even if it *was* smudged and dirty. 'There's three weeks owing, and I'm not leaving without it.'

Now it was Ruth's turn to observe *him*, and even though he was here making threats after her money, she had taken a liking to him. She wondered if it was because she hadn't had a man's arms round her in so long, she was prepared to consider anything in trousers. But no, she decided, it wasn't that. It was the bold manner in which he had lingered under the ladder to see up her skirt, and the twinkle in his eye when she faced him about it. 'Rent aside, you're a cheeky devil,' she said, and couldn't help the little smile twitching at her mouth.

'That's me,' he said, having taken a liking to her also. 'Cheeky Charlie, that's what they call me.'

'Well, Cheeky Charlie, you'd best get yourself inside. I'll see if me mam's left a bob or two for you.' But she held out little hope of that. Instead, she suspected she would have to raid her own store of money, and not for the first time neither. She smiled, and for a minute he was lost. She really was the loveliest thing.

'Go on,' she urged. 'Inside with you, while I empty this bucket.'

When she went to pick up the bucket he stopped her.

'That's too heavy for a woman in your condition,' he said. 'Give it here.' Taking the bucket from her, he tipped the grimy water into the gutter. Keeping hold of the bucket, he walked before her down the passage to the parlour. 'I meant what I said,' he flattered her. 'You've got a lovely pair of shapely legs, if you don't mind me saying?'

Ruth looked him up and down as they came into the parlour; not a big-built fella, she thought, but not bad. Not bad at all. 'If you don't mind *me* saying, you've got a great pair of bow legs. By! You could run a tram through them and still have room for a wagon.'

'What!' He looked shocked, until he saw her grinning and knew she was only getting her own back. 'OK,' he laughed. 'I asked for that.'

Ruth paid him the rent and signed the book and would have sent him on his merry way, only she had not laughed like this in ages. 'You can stay for a brew if you like,' she said, hoping he would say yes.

When he accepted, she told him to settle himself. 'I'll not be long. Oh, and would you like a biscuit?'

'I'd love one – two, if they're going.'

'I'll fetch a plateful,' she promised. 'We'll share 'em.' Taking off her coat, she went into the kitchen, while John eased himself into the armchair beside the fire.

'I bet you were cold up that ladder,' he remarked. He chatted across the room, making pleasant conversation and feeling easier with her than he could ever have imagined. After all, she was a complete stranger to him, wasn't she?

'I don't feel the cold,' she replied, and he didn't wonder at it. A capable woman, this one, he thought.

'I expect your husband normally cleans the windows, does he?' he probed.

Returning with tea and biscuits, she told him, 'I haven't got a husband. There was a man I might have wed. Instead, I ran off and left him.'

Shocked and delighted, he asked, 'Can I ask why you did that . . . seeing as you're . . .' He glanced at her swollen belly. 'I mean, it can't have been an easy decision.'

Setting the tray on the table, she told him plainly, 'I left him because he was the worst bastard. He doesn't know I'm carrying his child, and if I have my way, he never will.'

'Were you frightened of him?'

She handed him his tea. 'Not at first. Not until I found out what terrible things he was capable of.' Sitting in the armchair opposite, she rolled the warm cup between her cold hands and took a sip of tea. After a moment, she placed the cup in the hearth and suddenly whisked off her turban. 'By! It's good to get that off. I'm not used to wearing turbans. It's me mam's.'

Looking up on her comment, he couldn't believe his eyes. 'My God! You're beautiful!' It was like he'd suddenly been frozen; with his cup halfway to his mouth he stared at her, eyes wide open, disbelieving. In that moment when she had whipped away the turban, he didn't know why, but he had the strongest sensation; almost as though he'd been kicked in the stomach by a navvy.

Now, as she shook her hair, he was half-blinded by the dazzling reds and gold in that mass of glory; lit by the firelight and framing her face, it was a splendid sight.

'I don't know about beautiful,' she laughed, running her two hands through her hair, before collecting her cup. 'Lately, when I look in the mirror, I see "fat and ugly", and it feels like it will never end. I've no husband, no home, and when this comes along,' she patted her bulging stomach, 'things can only get worse.'

'So, when you ran off from this bloke, your mam took you in? That was good of her.' Deep down, something about her worried him, but John didn't yet know what it was.

Ruth laughed. 'Years ago, I ran off from her an' all,' she admitted. 'You can't know what she was like. She's got a filthy temper, and a mouth that could shame a truck-driver. My mam can be a right sod . . . come to think of it, I were no different. We fought like cat and dog, and in the end, I couldn't live with her. We hadn't seen each other in years, until this.' Again, she patted her bulge. 'But she's been good to me. She's changed in her old age. I think we both have.'

'I envy you,' he said. 'My parents are miles away down South, and I've allus been a bit of a loner.' He held out his hand. 'The name's John.'

Shaking his hand, she felt as if she'd known him all her life. 'I'm Ruth,' she said, 'Ruth Clegg,' and when she smiled, her eyes lighting with pleasure, it hit him like a ton of bricks. 'Jesus! *You're Peter Williams's woman, aren't you?*'

For what seemed an eternity, she stared at him, her eyes widening with terror. Then she was on her feet, screaming at him. '*He* sent you here, didn't he? *He* sent you here to root me out! Oh dear God! What shall I do? What shall I do?' She was screaming and sobbing, and John was shocked and helpless. 'You can tell him I'll be gone when he comes here,' she gabbled. 'I'll be gone, to somewhere he'll never find me. Tell him that. GO ON!' Beating his chest with her two fists, she gave a cry and seemed to collapse in his arms, but he held her there, whispering softly to calm her.

'No, he didn't send me. He has no idea where you are, and he won't learn it from me. I know I'm a bit of a bugger, and there are some things I might do for money, but shopping you to that bastard isn't one of them.' John led her to the chair and this time it was his turn to make the tea. While she sat and contemplated the consequences of being found out, he searched the cupboards and located a half-filled bottle of brandy. 'That's our mam's,' she warned. 'Leave it be.'

'From what you tell me, she wouldn't mind – not after the shock I gave you just now.'

A few moments later, he returned from the kitchen with a freshly brewed mug of tea, and in it a sizeable measure of brandy.

Ruth took one sip and made a face. 'Ohh! It tastes awful!' Inside her the baby gave a tiny leap. But she drank it all down, and afterwards felt a great deal calmer; it was an odd thing, but she felt as if she could trust this man. 'Please, John. You won't tell him you've found me, will you?' she pleaded. 'I've nowhere else to run, and very little money. When I came here I did have a bit put by, but it's nearly all gone now.'

John looked at her tear-stained face and for the first time in his life he was about to put someone else before himself. He recalled Peter Williams's earlier threats about stealing what belonged to him; he knew he was supposed to report the finding of Ruth Clegg, or face the consequences.

Knowing that man's reputation, he was confused and afraid, but most of all, he was in love. *For the first time in his miserable life, he was really in love.* If someone had told him it could happen as quickly as that, he would have laughed in their face. But it was true, and he was the proof.

In answer to her question, he told her, 'I won't breathe a word to a soul. Peter Williams won't learn anything from me, and nor will anyone else for that matter.'

Afraid to believe him; afraid not to, Ruth looked into his eyes, trying to find a semblance of his true nature. She didn't know him from Adam, and yet she knew him like he knew himself. 'I want to believe you,' she said.

'You can.' He took her hand in both of his, shivering with delight when he felt her skin, warm and soft to the touch. 'You have to take me at my word,' he murmured.

'I want to,' she said again. 'It's Peter I'm afraid of, not you. You've been so kind, and to tell you the truth, I've never chatted with anyone like I've chatted with you. I could never talk to Peter; more often than not, he talked with his fist.'

'Did you love him?' It felt so natural to ask such a personal question.

Her face contorted with bitterness. 'I did at first. Then I *hated* him!'

'It was a brave thing to do ... running out on that bastard.'

She gave a small wry laugh. 'It was either that or be beaten black and blue when he found out I was pregnant.' She gave a long, weary sigh. 'I wasn't happy,' she confessed. 'I hadn't been happy in a long time. You see, I'd forgotten the normal things in life. I'd forgotten family and freedom.'

'And now?'

She smiled. 'You're the first person to make me laugh in a very long time. Look around you,' she urged. 'There are no expensive pictures or silver to polish. In my wardrobe you won't find classy dresses or fur stoles. There are no maids, or fancy meals on the table. It's just a modest little house, and we're just ordinary people. And shall I tell you something, John?' She smiled, a warm, satisfied smile. 'I've never been happier. Me and Mam are getting on like we used to, and she's even having a go at knitting for her first grandchild.' She chuckled. 'If you knew her like I do, you'd realise how unnatural that is.'

'Then along comes John to turn your world upside down?'

The fear returned. 'You're the first person I've told about my situation, except for Mam and Ernie, of course. But yes, I'm frightened now. Frightened to stay here, in case he finds out.' A kind of terror filled her heart. 'If he tracks me down, he'll kill me and the child – I know he will.'

'To hear *him* talk, he adores the ground you walk on,' John said gruffly. 'Why should he want to kill you?'

Hesitating, she muttered, 'Because I was his possession. He owned me, body and soul, and he never parts with any of his possessions. Also,' she shuddered, '*I know what he did.*'

John thought for a moment. 'Well, I know he's the worst kind of monster – I've seen that for myself in the way he treats that little maid of his and in his dealings with me. The man is unbalanced. But what could he have done that was so terrible he might want to *kill* you?'

Ruth studied his face a moment. She really liked him, and yes, she thought she might even be able to trust him. For one desperate minute she almost blurted out about how, three years ago, Peter Williams had sent a villain to kill Sylvia Bolton, his half-sister who he was afraid would inherit his mother's money, and how it all went wrong, and because of that, both Sylvia and her husband were killed, and her son badly injured. The house had burnt down and the twin girls, Ellie and Betsy Bolton, had been orphaned and sent to live with strangers.

She had made it her business to find out all these things, and now she wished to God she hadn't! Especially when the man he sent to murder that poor woman was himself murdered by Peter's own hand. Now, the same fate awaited her.

John could see the fear on her face. 'It might be good to get it off your chest,' he suggested.

'No!' She shook her head. 'Later maybe. If we get to know each other better.'

'And is that a possibility?'

'Who knows?' Drawing away her hand, she told him, 'You'd best go. I know what he's like if the rent money is delivered late.'

'I won't tell, you know,' he assured her. 'You have to believe me.'

'I'll see you to the door.' Ruth almost fell over when she tried to stand up. 'That's Mam's brandy,' she chuckled. 'I think I'm a bit worse for wear. Since I've been here, I've hardly touched the stuff.' At the door, she laid bare her feelings. 'I wonder if I should go away from here?' she mused.

'Why do that?' His heart sank at the idea.

'Because I still don't know if I should trust you.'

'I've an idea.'

'Oh, and what might that be?'

'You say you're not sure if you can trust me?'

'Can you blame me?'

'No. But think about *this*.' Stepping closer in case a passing neighbour might hear, he said, 'Peter Williams instructed me to watch out for you. I said I would, because at that time I didn't know you. I didn't know how you'd creep up on me, and turn me inside out like you have.'

She smiled. 'You're a charmer, I'll say that for you.'

'I'm also a bloody fool!' Sighing he blew it out in a noisy rush. 'If I go against Peter Williams, which I intend doing, it won't only be your neck that's stuck out, it'll be mine as well.'

'So why are you doing it? Why don't you tell him you've found me?'

'Because for once in my life, I intend doing summat right

for a change.' He gave a cheeky wink. 'And because I've taken a fancy to you.' He paused, making sure he had her full attention. 'And because you've agreed to let me take yer to the flicks on Saturday.'

It took a moment for her to realise what he was saying, and another moment for her to decide if it was wise or not. The idea of going out again, arm-in-arm with a man who treated her like she was somebody, was irresistible.

'I'd like that,' she said happily.

It was to be the first of many enjoyable outings together.

Chapter Sixteen

CURIOUS TO KNOW what was going on, Daisy pressed her ear to the door and listened. She had seen the man arrive and noted how the master had beaten her to answering the door, and when the man was admitted, he had been taken almost at a run into the office.

Through the keyhole she could see Peter Williams pacing the floor, up and down, up and down, jaw set hard and fists clenched, as if about to smack somebody down. She could hear every word he was saying. 'I knew it!' she nodded. 'It's to do with Ruth Clegg.'

His voice came to her clear and strong. 'I want her found, do you hear? I've spent a small fortune on private detectives and it's all been for nothing. *Nothing!*'

'It's not private detectives you want, if you don't mind me saying, sir.'

'Oh, so you think you can do better, do you? Well, you'd best tell me just how you mean to go about finding her. I want value for my money, do you hear? *I want results!*' Punching one fist into the other, he began to yell dementedly, '*I want Ruth Clegg brought back here, where she belongs!*'

'I know what you want, sir.' The other man was beginning

JOSEPHINE COX

to wonder if he'd bitten off more than he could chew with this one. 'Isn't that why I'm here?'

'So how will *you* find her, when others couldn't?' Exhausted by his own temper, Peter Williams leaned against his desk and stared the fellow down. 'Well? I'm waiting,' he said nastily.

The other man took a moment to gather his wits. If he was to make his money, he would have to come up with the goods, he knew that.

'First of all, we're not like private detectives. We don't pussy-foot around, and we're not too particular how we get the job done, so long as we get it done, if you follow my meaning. If someone gets in the way, we know how to deal with them. We're a team, you see – unlike your ordinary private detective. We're part of a network all over the country. We know our job, and we do it well.' He was always amazed at what a brilliant liar he was.

'Sounds convincing,' Peter grunted. Maybe this fellow could do something, after all.

'And so it should, because if this young woman is anywhere in the country, we'll root her out. You've got my word on it.'

'I don't want your word. I want her back here. The sooner the better!'

When she heard them winding up the details, Daisy ran into the scullery and closed the door. 'Blimey!' Her eyes stuck out like hat-pegs as she recalled the conversation. 'Gawd help her, he's hired a bunch o' thugs to track 'er down!'

Breathing in, she waited until they had passed. She could hear them talking just outside the door. A moment later they walked away; the front door opened and closed and then she heard the master's footsteps taking him back to the study.

Softly, she crept away, upstairs to her attic room, to think through these latest developments. One thing was for certain: 'I wouldn't like to be Ruth Clegg, not in any shape nor form. Not for all the money in the world, I wouldn't.'

━━━━▶•◀━━━━

O N THE FOLLOWING Friday evening, after following a series of false trails and coming to nothing, the same man who had visited Peter Williams at his house, found his way into a bar in Mill Hill. 'Beer and a chaser,' he told the barman. When they came he drank them down and ordered two more.

'Knocking 'em back a bit, ain't yer, matey?' The big fella at the next table was the friendly type who liked to chat.

'Bugger off!'

'Been let down, 'ave yer?' He was a persistent sort. 'Some woman been running rings round yer, has she?' When he laughed, as he did now, he displayed a perfect set of white teeth, which seemed all the more odd in that roughened face strewn with greying whiskers.

'Look, piss off, will you!'

'See that young fella over there?' the bloke went on, ignoring him.

Curious despite himself, the other man looked up. 'What about him?'

At that very moment, the young man in question finished his pint. 'Night, Jack,' he called to the barman. 'See you next week.'

The whiskered man continued his badgering. 'Yer should tek a few lessons from him,' he sniggered. 'He knows how to get and keep a woman.'

'Is that so?' Christ, would this fat idiot never leave him in peace!

'No doubt about it. To look at him, you wouldn't think he'd got it in him, but I'm telling you, he's got this woman . . .' Rolling his eyes he made a shapely figure with the flat of his hands. 'Bee-*you*-tiful creature, she is.'

'You don't say.'

'Redhead . . . green eyes. A man's dream, she is. That young fella is either summat special or just downright lucky. What she sees in *him*, the Lord only knows—'

'What did you say?' Now he was really paying attention. 'Did you say she were a redhead? Attractive, is she?'

'That's right, matey. Like I said, yer should take a leaf out of that young man's book.' When the other man grabbed him by the shirt, he was taken by surprise. 'Hey! There's no need to get nasty, dammit!'

'What was she called – the redhead? *What was her name?*'

'Don't know. But it ain't no use you going after her, 'cause she ain't got eyes for nobody except for that young fella-me-lad.'

'What name does he go by then?'

'Don't know that neither. Ask the barman. Old Jack here knows everybody.'

A moment later, the whiskered man was proved to be right.

'His name's John,' the barman revealed. 'I can't recall his second name. Don't know as I've ever heard it said.'

'The woman, the redhead. What's her name?'

This time the barman was not so communicative. 'Well now, I'm not sure I can remember that.' His eyes looked shifty. 'Me memory ain't so good as what it was – if you know what I mean.'

A half-crown brightened his memory no end. 'Ruth,' he said. 'Her name is Ruth. By! She's a beauty an' no mistake. Pity she's got a belly like a barge though. But it don't hide the shape beneath, I can tell you that.'

The other man gave a long sigh of relief. 'Where can I find her?'

'I've no idea.' Even the showing of another half-crown didn't help, though he earned it another way. 'The young fella's a rent-collector. He works the factories and the top end of Blackburn – Mill Hill, all round here.' And that was as much as he knew.

Without so much as a thank you, the other man rushed outside, but there was no sign of the young fella. He was already long gone.

No matter. He smiled, a secretive little smile. He had more than enough to be going on with.

Losing no time, he set off to find his men.

——◆——

PETER WILLIAMS WAS as restless as a cat on hot bricks. He hadn't slept all night, thinking about Ruth. Looking out the bedroom window, he stared across the early morning skies. 'Where are you? If he doesn't find you, I don't know what I'll do. It's not just the fact that you took some of my money – though I'll have to punish you for that. I miss you, Ruth.'

He laughed quietly. 'They say you never know what you've got until it's gone, and it's true. I need you, Ruth. I'll turn every last stone upside down, until I find you.'

It was five o' clock and still pitch black outside when he came down the stairs, almost frightening Daisy out of her life. Standing at the kitchen sink, glass of water in hand, she swung round, dropping the glass to the floor, where it smashed into a million fragments. 'Oh sir, you scared me!'

'What the devil are you doing down here this time of a morning!'

'I couldn't sleep, sir. I were thirsty.'

'I'm going out,' he informed her.

'What time will you be back, sir? So's I know when to get the breakfast going, like.'

'I don't expect I'll be back for breakfast.' He pointed to the shattered glass. 'Clean that up and be quick about it!' But he didn't seem his usual self. The anger had no force in it.

By the time Daisy turned to go into the pantry for the brush, he was gone. 'Going out this time of a morning . . . to look for his woman, I daresay,' she muttered as she searched for the dustpan. 'Bursting in on me like that, scaring me half to death. Mad, that's what he is. Stark, staring mad! He gets worse every day, I'd swear to it. God knows where it's all going to end.'

As she came out of the kitchen, the phone in the hallway rang and gave her another scare. This time the dustpan went flying, and the brush with it. 'Oh, my dear Gawd, whatever next?' Clutching her heart, she quickened her steps into the hallway, where she stared down at the telephone on the little table.

As it rang she continued to stare; time and again she reached out to take up the receiver, and each time she quickly drew her hand away. 'Blessed thing!' she said nervously. 'Why did he want to go and have a contraption like that fitted, eh? Noisy damned article!'

Unable to stand its shrieking any longer, she snatched up the receiver and put it to her ear. 'There's nothing there,' she grumbled, and was about to put it back down again, when she heard a muffled voice at the other end. 'Hello?' She put it back to her ear, and the voice seemed to go away again.

She looked at the receiver and, realising she might have it the wrong way round, put the other end to her ear. 'Hello, who's that?' She glanced at the clock. 'It's only ten past five,' she burst out. 'Who's that? Who's there?' She began to wonder how much more she could take.

'It's Queen Park Hospital,' the voice explained. 'I'd like to speak with Mr Peter Williams, please.'

'He ain't 'ere!' Shouting down the phone in case the other person couldn't hear her, Daisy bellowed: 'He's gone out and says he won't be back for breakfast.'

'I see. Could you give him a message when he gets back, please. Could you tell him his mother's taken a turn for the worse, and he should get to the hospital straight away.'

'Yes, ma'am. Thank you.'

'That's the message. His mother's taken a turn for the worse, and he's to come to the hospital. Now, you won't forget that, will you?'

'No, ma'am.' And she twice repeated the message just in case.

Carefully, Daisy returned the receiver to its hook. 'My! It's one thing after another,' she groaned. 'That poor old woman. All this time she's hung on, like she's been waiting for summat. That's a strange thing, that is. Ruth Clegg's gone, and it looks like his mam's about to pop her clogs an' all.'

Sauntering into the kitchen she seated herself at the table, her mind filled with all things nasty. 'Poor old thing. He didn't give her much of a life, did he, eh? Allus shouting and arguing – wanting her dead. I saw it all. That day, when she fell down, he wanted her dead. But she showed him, didn't she, eh? Got the heart of a lion she has. "I'll go when I'm good an' ready", that's what she said to herself, and by Gawd, she's hung on like a good 'un.'

Mentally shaking herself, she stood up. 'He's a bad man. His mam knew it, and I know it. Ruth Clegg knew it too. If she's got any sense, she'll stay hidden.' Glancing nervously at the door, she picked up her brush and dustpan and set about tidying the floor.

JONAS CARTER WAS woken from a deep sleep by the sound of his telephone ringing. Grabbing his robe he threw it on and hurried down the stairs, where he did not hesitate in snatching up the receiver. 'Hello?'

He listened to what the caller had to say. 'I'm sorry, Mr Carter. I have tried to reach her son, but he's not at home.'

'I understand. Thank you, Sister. I'll be along as fast as I can.'

Chapter Seventeen

BETSY WAS SET to hurry away after the tram. 'I'll walk back with Mick,' Ellie had told her. 'You go on if you like, I'll only be ten minutes or so behind you.'

Betsy had long realised how it was between her sister and Mick; there once was a time when she would have derided her for it, but since that night at the boulevard, when she had fallen as low as could be, Betsy had brought about a change in herself. She was so grateful that no terrible consequences had befallen her after selling her virginity to that squalid stranger. Her view of life would never be the same again.

'You really love him, don't you?' she asked now.

Ellie looked to where Mick was walking across the floor, and her heart turned over as it always did. 'Yes,' she answered shyly. 'I love him so much.'

Her twin didn't envy her. It wasn't her kind of love and never would be. 'I'll go ahead then, shall I? Let you and Mick walk back together.'

'Only if you want to.' Ellie valued her every minute with Mick, but it was dark and a sense of dread rippled through her. She had never felt truly safe at night since the attack on their house in Buncer Lane. 'No, come to think of it, we'd best all walk back together.'

But Betsy wouldn't hear of it. 'I'll see you at the tram-stop,' she said, and hurried away before Ellie could stop her.

Mick was just locking the office door, when John arrived. 'Sorry I'm late,' he told Mick. 'I've had a few difficult collections to make. It's put me all back.'

'You've only just caught me,' Mick told him. They had long ago patched up their quarrel.

When he was paid and the book duly signed, John took a minute to pass the time of evening with Ellie, only this time he didn't flirt or make suggestive remarks because now he had the love of his life, and he was in a hurry to get to her.

'Take care now,' he told them both, and went away at the dash. The thought of Ruth waiting for him was like wings to his feet.

As he turned away from locking the main doors, Mick thought he saw someone loitering in the shadows. 'Who's there?' He went forward, but couldn't see anyone.

'Who was it?' Ellie had been afraid for him. For some reason her nerves were all on edge tonight. She was afraid for Betsy, too. 'We'd best get a shift on, Mick,' she suggested. 'Betsy went ahead all on her own.'

With his arm round her, he took her at a quicker pace, along the alley and down towards the canal. 'There's not a soul about,' he told her. 'I must have been imagining things.' The reassuring remark was merely to pacify her, because he knew he *had* seen something, though he wasn't sure what.

'Hey, you two. Hang on a minute. I can't keep up!'

The familiar voice caused them to stop and stare. It was Larry, and he was walking better than ever, albeit with a slow, cumbersome gait.

'Larry!' Ellie laughed out loud. Running to him, she threw her arms about his waist. 'What are you doing here in the dark? How did you get here?'

Mick was relieved. 'It must have been you I saw out of the corner of my eye,' he deduced. 'It's good to see you walking so well, but, like Ellie said, what in God's name are you doing here?'

Larry's eyes shone with pride. 'My legs have been getting stronger and stronger. I had to find out what I was capable of, so I thought I'd come and give you both a surprise,' he grinned.

'You certainly did that,' Mick said, giving Larry a hearty slap on the back. 'You did well, mate, but you mustn't overdo it and put yourself back again.' Like Ellie, Mick was thrilled to see Larry so steady on his legs, and he knew just how much effort and determination had gone into bringing him this far.

Ellie too, had a warning. 'Another few minutes and we'd have been out of sight.'

Larry realised that. 'I didn't know it would take me so long,' he admitted. 'But I got here, and I feel better for having done it.'

'And how do you feel about walking back to the tram-stop?'

Cuddling her tight, he ordered mischievously, 'Lead on! And mind I don't overtake the pair of youse.'

❖

S OME WAY IN front, John went his usual route down to Penny Street and the canal, then on towards the tram-stop, where he would catch a tram to Ruth's street. He had a couple of collections to make there, then he'd go on to Ruth's house, where he would have his tea with her and the family. By now this had become a regular arrangement, and one which he really looked forward to. He would meet up with Ruth later tonight and take her out after he'd dropped the rent-money off at Summerfield House.

He was so engrossed in his thoughts that he didn't hear the two men sidle up behind him. By the time he noticed them and felt a first prickle of fear, they were already on him, fighting him to the wall and holding him there. 'Where is she?' The bigger of the two men held him in a stranglehold by the neck of his shirt.

'I don't know what you mean,' he gurgled. At first he feared they had grabbed him to steal the money in his bag. Now though, he knew different. It was far worse than that. *They were after Ruth.* Peter Williams was behind it, he was sure. Somehow or another, that madman had found out he was seeing her.

'Oh, you know what we mean right enough,' the big fella snapped. 'And if you don't feel like talking, there's ways and means to make you talk, and we know every single one of 'em.' Sniggering, he turned to his colleague. 'Ain't that right?'

The other fella nodded. 'That's right enough, yeah.'

But John would not talk. He would not put Ruth in danger, even if his own life was at stake. So they set about him, and showed no mercy.

As Ellie and Mick turned the corner on to Penny Street, Mick caught sight of them; they had the smaller man on the ground and were taking it in turns to kick seven bells out of him. 'Hey! What the devil d'you think you're doing! Leave him be!'

Without thought for himself, Mick ran forward, at the

same time giving instructions to Larry. 'Keep away,' he cried. 'Take Ellie and get away home.'

But they had no intention of leaving him there.

As Mick ran forward, with Ellie and Larry close behind, the two thugs ran in the other direction, leaving their victim seemingly lifeless on the ground. Falling to his knees, Mick was appalled by the injuries that met his eye. 'John!' Behind the blood and torn skin, he could only just recognise who it was. 'Jesus, Mary and Joseph! What have they done to you?' Cradling the young man in his arms, he thought he was holding a corpse.

'Good God!' Like Mick, Larry was incensed by the violence of the attack. Ellie, too, was so shocked she couldn't take it in. All she could do was kneel down and talk to John, much the same as Mick had, to reassure him, and to tell him she was going for help.

Leaving Mick and Larry there, that was just what she did. She ran to the nearest pub and told them what had happened. While help was being summoned, she dashed back, and as she ran, she prayed John would be all right.

Realising that his Ruth was in terrible danger, John struggled to speak. 'It's all right, mate,' Mick said comfortingly. 'Ellie's gone for help. The ambulance will be here soon.'

'No . . . o . . .' Straining towards Mick, John whispered, 'Ru . . . th . . .'

Realising he had something desperate to tell him, Mick bent his head and listened. In a series of gasps, the wounded man told him how his attackers meant to get Ruth. He begged Mick to go and save her. And when he heard the address, Mick could hardly believe his ears. *That was where his father lived!*

He exchanged a worried look with Larry.

'I'll get the police, and you warn Ruth,' said Larry,

knowing he wouldn't be able to keep up with Mick, and he began to walk away as Ellie returned. She was too frightened for John to ask where her brother had gone.

A few minutes later, the ambulance arrived, its bell tinkling, to take John away. 'I'll see to it,' Mick promised when John's stricken eyes sought him out. 'Don't worry.'

As quickly as he could, without seeming too frantic, he took Ellie to the tram-stop. The usual tram had already gone, with Betsy on it. 'Try not to think too much about it,' Mick told her, but it would be a long time before Ellie got the terrible scene out of her mind.

Having seen her safely on the tram, Mick lost no time in making his way to his father's house. Answering the knock on the door, Ernie Fellowes was amazed to see his son standing there. 'Mick!' His face creased in an astonished smile. 'Oh, Mick . . .' Then his gaze fell on Mick's coat, which was stained with blood. 'What's happened? Are you hurt?' The smile fell away. 'Come inside, lad, quick!'

Ernie could see now that Mick wasn't hurt as he'd first thought. Yet he didn't know what to think as he let Mick through the door. His son was here, at his home, after all this time. It was a miracle.

'I need to talk with Ruth.' Mick had no time to explain, only to come straight to the point.

Opening the parlour door, Ernie ushered him in. As Mick brushed by, there was a tear in the older man's eye. 'I can't believe it,' he kept saying. 'You're in my house. I can't believe it.' In his heart, he prayed it might be a new beginning.

Ruth and her mam looked up as Mick walked in. 'I've come with a message from John,' he said urgently, and to their horror, began to relate what the wounded man had told him. The two women, one pregnant and nearly at her time, clung together in fear.

Outside, in the lonely dark street, Ellie lingered on the pavement. Mick had been so frantic to get her on the tram home that she had sensed there was something he wasn't telling her. Convinced that something had gone on between him, Larry and John when she was away summoning help, it occurred to her that he might be in some kind of danger and didn't want her involved. With this in mind, the minute his back was turned, she had sneaked off the tram to follow him on foot.

'Something's not right,' she murmured fretfully. 'I'm not leaving here without Mick!' Raising her clenched fist, she was about to knock on the door when Peter Williams sprang out of the darkness and sent her flying. 'If you know what's good for you, you'll keep well out of my way!' he warned, as she lay, hurt and shaken, on the ground. Then, standing back, Peter sent his two henchmen in to kick down the door.

In the parlour, Mick was already yelling out instructions. 'Take the women out the back,' he told his father. 'Get as far away as possible. I'll keep the buggers busy as long as I can.'

Peter and his men burst into the room before Ernie could take Ruth and Freda to safety. Mick stood his ground, ready for the fight of his life. The two thugs made straight for him, and there followed a long, brutal exchange of blows. Mick gave as good as he got, and for a moment it seemed he might even come through the victor. But when one of the men hit him hard across the back of the head with a chair, he went down like a felled ox. Peter Williams stood back, his eyes on Ruth who, with Freda and Ernie, had kept their distance. Now, seeing his son bloodied and broken on the floor, Ernie gave a blood-curdling scream and launched himself at the two men. But he was no match for them and soon he too had buckled beneath their fists.

When Freda ran to help him the two thugs grabbed her by the arms and dragged her away; not even the sound of her sobbing could touch their miserable souls.

Coldhearted and merciless, Peter took Ruth by the throat. 'I had a mind to have you back,' he murmured sweetly in her ear. 'Now though, seeing the company you've been keeping, I don't think I could ever take you to my bed again.'

Convinced he was about to kill them all, Ruth pleaded with him. 'Don't hurt them any more,' she said softly. 'I'll do whatever you say.'

Laughing in her face, he growled, 'You don't understand, do you? *You've humiliated me. I don't want you!*' His two hands closed around her throat, and he leered at her as she began to lose consciousness. In the background Freda began to scream, then stopped abruptly as she was smacked hard in the mouth.

Suddenly the sound of Ellie's voice rang in Ruth's head. 'LEAVE HER ALONE! GET OFF HER!' There was a scuffle, but Ellie continued to shout and threaten; she was not so easily silenced.

In his dazed mind, Mick heard Ellie's cries. He opened his eyes to see one brute tearing at her blouse while the other held her skirt high, showing her underclothes. 'Seems a shame to waste a pretty young thing like this,' he was saying.

Enraged, Mick found the strength to shake off his pain and confusion. Scrambling to his feet, he leapt across the room, astonishing the two men who instantly threw Ellie aside. But they had not reckoned on the wrath of a man who had seen his father lying beaten on the floor, and the woman he adored being manhandled by filth not worth naming. With the cry of a madman, Mick flung himself through the air at them, startling Peter, who relaxed his grip on Ruth's neck, giving her the chance to run from him. Mick's first blow knocked down one of the thugs and, driven by rage and hatred, he was like a giant, pinning Peter to the wall with his fists while the second brute flailed helplessly at his back. Ellie grabbed the poker from the fireplace and was about to strike Mick's attacker from behind when suddenly she was embraced by Larry, and the room filled with policemen.

When the three men had been handcuffed, Ruth told the police she believed Peter Williams was responsible for the deaths of Ellie's parents. At that moment, Ellie relived the full horror of that Christmas night, and she knew that Ruth's words rang true.

Larry looked at the smug grin on the face of Peter Williams, and read his guilt. It took three officers to keep Larry off the monster who had murdered his parents and nearly destroyed his life.

PART FOUR

NEW YEAR'S DAY
1936
FULL CIRCLE

Chapter Eighteen

T HE OLD YEAR was over and now, with the dawning of a new year, the bad things seemed a long way off.

Gathered round the big table in Jonas Carter's office, Ellie and her sister, together with their grandad and Larry, were about to hear the Last Will and Testament of their grandmother, Ada Williams.

Before he went any further, Jonas told them how he had been summoned to the hospital, and there found Ada sinking fast. 'She was determined to talk to us,' he said. 'Between the three of us, myself, the doctor, and Ada, she managed to communicate everything, little by little. It took a long time, but we managed it.' He pointed to the will set out in front of him. 'Your grandmother was a very special lady,' he said. 'There was never anything wrong with her mind, as you will see when I read out her last wishes.'

He then proceeded to read the following message:

. . . I have never been happy with what I did all those years ago. Leaving my baby daughter Sylvia has haunted me throughout my later life, and when I set about putting things right, a terrible tragedy took her from me.

At first I imagined it was a fitting punishment for my sins; then after a time I began to suspect that my son had killed her, so he would not lose the inheritance he believed was his.

Sadly, therefore, my beloved daughter is not able to enjoy the money I am leaving behind.

I, Ada Hermione Williams, leave all my worldly belongings to my two granddaughters Betsy and Ellie Bolton, and to my grandson Larry Bolton who I now know was hurt badly in trying to save his parents. I pray they will be happy and content in a more secure future.

I ask that they will spend the money wisely, and try not to think of me too harshly . . .

Ada's hand, he told them all, was held by him while she signed this last document.

Afterwards, with two nurses and a second lawyer present, the letter was signed, dated and witnessed by both the solicitor and two doctors, who certified that the patient was of sound mind.

Betsy was so excited she could hardly sit still. 'All that money!' she gloated. 'Whatever will I do with it?'

Larry and his grandfather sat quietly, thinking.

Ellie was stunned. She had never known her grandmother, and now she was gone, so she would never get the chance. 'Why didn't you tell us?' she asked her grandfather, and when he began to cry, she was mortified. 'It's all right.' She put her arms round him. 'I know you did what you thought was right.' *Let the past go now, she thought.* There was nothing to be gained by raking it up.

Mr Carter offered any help they might need once the money had come through. 'There will be a lot of red tape,' he warned. 'It may take some time.'

Bertie shook his hand and thanked him for being such a good friend to Ada. 'And for being there at the end, when none of us could be.' There were tears of sorrow in his eyes; relief too, in a strange way. Ada had haunted him for so many years, and now she was gone.

'In a way, it's a blessing in disguise that her son Peter was not there,' the solicitor said compassionately. 'Otherwise, who knows what might have happened?'

Larry stood up on his own two legs and walked across the room to shake Mr Carter's hand. 'Thank God that monster is away behind bars, where he belongs. To think he can claim kinship to us as our uncle – ugh! I hope they string him up from the highest tree for what he's done.'

Thankfully, with the recovery of his strength, the all-consuming hatred had finally gone away. But the memory of the night he had finally run the bastard to ground would stay with Larry Bolton for ever.

When the business was concluded, Mr Carter showed them out. 'I'll be in touch,' he said, and they went away, deeply thoughtful and a little saddened.

All but Betsy, who kept on about how she would make sure Peggy and Ted had everything they had ever wanted, and how she would pack in her job at the factory the very next day. Ellie laughed sadly, despite herself. Some things never changed! And one of them was her incorrigible twin sister!

⟫◦⟪

THREE DAYS BEFORE the twins' sixteenth birthday, the legacy from their grandmother came through.

On the day of the actual party, everyone was there. John, who still had one arm in plaster, had recovered really well after the terrible beating. On his good arm was Ruth, as bonny as ever, cuddling her three-month-old son, Nathan John. Freda and Ernie were there, full of smiles, Grandad with his Tilly, Betsy and Peggy and Ted, hugging each other and exuding a happiness at their new closeness.

Ellie kissed her twin and wished her a very happy birthday, and now, with Mick beside her, as the wonderful party came to an end, they had an announcement to make.

Tapping his spoon against his glass, Mick called them all to attention. 'We're engaged proper,' he said, and Ellie proudly showed her ring – a simple sapphire that matched her eyes and meant all the world to her.

Everyone congratulated them, and Tilly took the opportunity to whisper in Bertie's ear: 'We'd best get wed now, luv. We can't have the young 'uns showing us how.' And to everyone's absolute delight, he took her in his arms and kissed her soundly on the mouth, complaining when his false teeth clattered together. 'I allus meant to mek an honest woman of you,' he chuckled, and the laughter started up again.

———⇒•⇐———

R UTH AND JOHN kept the news of their own impending wedding to themselves, at least for now. Since hearing of how Peter Williams had caused John to be beaten to within an inch of his life, Ruth had suffered many complications with the bairn. It had been a worrying time.

Freda was aware of the situation, and as she told her daughter, 'If you ask me, and I'm not being cruel, happen it might be for the best if the poor thing doesn't get born at all . . . not with that man's blood running through its veins.'

Happily, though, Ruth had been destined to keep the baby.

Nathan was a fine, plump and contented child, with a full head of downy red hair, adored by Ruth *and* John, who never bore the tiny infant an ounce of ill-will for his sorry start in the world.

Afterwards, Ruth and John would wed, and have three more fine sons of their own.

With his share of the bequest, Larry bought two vans and established a successful delivery business, during which time he met his wife-to-be – a dark-haired lass by the name of Mary.

Now that he was reunited with his son, Ernie Fellowes found a new lease of life. He never married Freda, but they stayed together and were content into great old age.

Betsy took Sunshine off with her to a small cottage in the country, and there she bred Labradors, kept her own chickens and ducks, and ended up doing Bed and Breakfast for commercial travellers.

As for Ellie, she and Mick got married two years later, when she was eighteen. With her share of her grandmother's money, the couple bought a house down Preston New Road. They also invested in a shoe-shop in the centre of Blackburn town, and were pleased to stock a fine array of Brindle's best footwear! When she was twenty years old, Ellie gave birth to the first of their four children, a boy christened James Ernest Fellowes, followed by three lasses.

Life was good.

———◆———

O N THIS BRIGHT summer's day, some many years later, after the long shadow of war had finally retreated, Ellie and Mick were in the garden, where he was mending one of the younger children's bicycles. She watched him for a long time, before he caught her looking at him. Embarrassed, she turned away.

Scrambling off the bench, he took hold of her by the shoulder. 'No, sweetheart, don't turn away,' he murmured.

She smiled. 'Why not?'

'Because just now, when I looked up and saw you there, I spotted the most wonderful thing.'

'Did you?' She was puzzled.

'In the sunlight I saw the love shining in your eyes.'

His profound words touched her deeply. 'It will always shine for you, Mick,' she whispered.

He placed his finger under her chin and raised her face to his. 'Let me see it again,' he coaxed. 'Let it shine for me now.'

And when she looked up again, there it was, her love for him, shining out of those pretty sapphire-blue eyes.

When they kissed, they couldn't know all their children were watching. Until they heard the laughter.

And their hearts were full.